PRAISE FOR KERI ARTHUR

Nominated for *Romantic Times* 2007
Reviewers' Choice Awards for
Career Achievement in Urban Fantasy

Winner of the *Romantic Times* 2008
Reviewers' Choice Awards for
Career Achievement in Urban Fantasy

"Keri Arthur's imagination and energy infuse
everything she writes with zest."
—CHARLAINE HARRIS

Praise for *Full Moon Rising*

"Keri Arthur skillfully mixes her suspenseful plot with
heady romance in her thoroughly enjoyable alternate
reality Melbourne. Sexy vampires, randy werewolves,
and unabashed, unapologetic, joyful sex—you've gotta
love it. Smart, sexy, and well-conceived."
—KIM HARRISON

"*Full Moon Rising* is unabashedly and joyfully sexual in
its portrayal of werewolves in heat . . . Arthur never
fails to deliver, keeping the fires stoked, the cliffs high,
and the emotions dancing on a razor's edge in this
edgy, hormone-filled mystery . . . A shocking and
sensual read, so keep the ice handy."
—*TheCelebrityCafe.com*

"Keri Arthur is one of the best supernatural romance
writers in the world."
—HARRIET KLAUSNER

"Strong, smart and capable, Riley will remind many of Anita Blake, Laurell K. Hamilton's kick-ass vampire hunter . . . Fans of Anita Blake and Charlaine Harris' Sookie Stackhouse vampire series will be rewarded."
—*Publishers Weekly*

"Unbridled lust and kick-ass action are the hallmarks of this first novel in a brand-new paranormal series . . . 'Sizzling' is the only word to describe this heated, action-filled, suspenseful romantic drama."
—*Curled Up with a Good Book*

"Desert island keeper . . . Grade: A . . . I wanted to read this book in one sitting, and was terribly offended that the real world intruded on my reading time! . . . Inevitable comparisons can be made to Anita Blake, Kim Harrison, and Kelley Armstrong's books, but I think Ms. Arthur has a clear voice of her own and her characters speak for themselves. . . . I am hooked!"
—*All About Romance*

Praise for *Kissing Sin*

"The second book in this paranormal guardian series is just as phenomenal as the first . . . I am addicted!!"
—*Fresh Fiction*

"Arthur's world building skills are absolutely superb and I recommend this story to any reader who enjoys tales of the paranormal."
—*Coffee Time Romance and More*

"Fast paced and filled with deliciously sexy characters . . . readers will find *Kissing Sin* a fantastic urban fantasy with a hot serving of romance that continues to sizzle long after the last page is read."
—*Darque Reviews*

"Keri Arthur's unique characters and the imaginative world she's created will make this series one that readers won't want to miss."
—*A Romance Review*

Praise for *Tempting Evil*

"Riley Jenson is kick-ass . . . genuinely tough and strong, but still vulnerable enough to make her interesting. . . . Arthur is not derivative of early [Laurell K.] Hamilton—far from it—but the intensity of her writing and the complexity of her heroine and her stories is reminiscent."
—*All About Romance*

"This paranormal romance series gets better and better with each new book. . . . An exciting adventure that delivers all you need for a fabulous read—sexy shapeshifters, hot vampires, wild uncontrollable sex and the slightest hint of a love that's meant to be forever."
—*Fresh Fiction*

"Pure sexy action adventure . . . I found the world vividly realized and fascinating. . . . So, if you like your erotic scenes hot, fast, and frequent, your heroine sassy, sexy, and tough, and your stories packed with hard-hitting action in a vividly realized fantasy world, then *Tempting Evil* and its companion novels could be just what you're looking for."
—*SFRevu*

"Keri Arthur's Riley Jenson series just keeps getting better and better and is sure to call to fans of other authors with kick-ass heroines such as Christine Feehan and Laurell K. Hamilton. I have become a steadfast fan of this marvelous series and I am greatly looking forward to finding out what is next in store for this fascinating and strong character."
—*A Romance Review*

Praise for *Dangerous Games*

"One of the best books I have ever read. . . . The storyline is so exciting I did not realize I was literally sitting on the edge of my chair. . . . Arthur has a real winner on her hands. Five cups."
—*Coffee Time Romance and More*

"The depths of emotion, the tense plot, and the conflict of powerful driving forces inside the heroine made for [an] absorbing read."
—*SFRevu*

"This series is phenomenal! *Dangerous Games* is an incredibly original and devastatingly sexy story. It keeps you spellbound and mesmerized on every page. Absolutely perfect!!"
—*Fresh Fiction*

Praise for *Embraced by Darkness*

"Arthur is positively one of the best urban fantasy authors in print today. The characters have been well-drawn from the start and the mysteries just keep getting better. A creative, sexy and adventure filled world that readers will just love escaping to."
—*Darque Reviews*

"Arthur's storytelling is getting better and better with each book. *Embraced by Darkness* has suspense, interesting concepts, terrific main and secondary characters, well developed story arcs, and the world-building is highly entertaining. . . . I think this series is worth the time and emotional investment to read."
—Reuters.com

"Once again, Keri Arthur has created a perfect, exciting and thrilling read with intensity that kept me vigilantly turning each page, hoping it would never end."
—*Fresh Fiction*

"Reminiscent of Laurell K. Hamilton back when her books had mysteries to solve, Arthur's characters inhabit a dark sexy world of the paranormal."
—*The Parkersburg News and Sentinel*

"I love this series."
—*All About Romance*

Praise for *The Darkest Kiss*

"The paranormal Australia that Arthur concocts works perfectly, and the plot speeds along at a breakneck pace. Riley fans won't be disappointed."
—*Publishers Weekly*

Praise for *Bound to Shadows*

"The Riley Jenson Guardian series ROCKS! Riley is one bad-ass heroine with a heart of gold. Keri Arthur never disappoints and always leaves me eagerly anticipating the next book. A classic, fabulous read!"
—*Fresh Fiction*

By Keri Arthur

PENUMBRA

KERI ARTHUR

DELL
NEW YORK

2014 Dell Mass Market Edition

Copyright © 2005, 2014 by Keri Arthur

All rights reserved.

Published in the United States by Dell, an imprint of The Random House Publishing Group, a division of Random House LLC, a Penguin Random House Company, New York.

Dell and the House colophon are registered trademarks of Random House LLC.

Originally published in different form in paperback in the United States by ImaJinn Books, Hickory Corners, MI, in 2005.

ISBN 978-0-440-24660-2
eBook ISBN 978-0-8041-7954-6

Cover design: Lynn Andreozzi
Cover illustration: © Juliana Kolesova

Printed in the United States of America

www.bantamdell.com

9 8 7 6 5 4 3 2 1

Dell mass market edition: October 2014

PENUMBRA

ONE

SAMANTHA RYAN PLACED HER HANDS on the front of her boss's desk and said, "I want a transfer, not more of your damn excuses."

She knew that speaking to Stephan in such a manner wasn't the best idea, especially when he was the man in charge of both the Special Investigations Unit and the more secretive Federation—a man who'd ruthlessly do whatever it took to get the answers he needed or the job done. She knew *that* from firsthand experience; she'd suffered through his interrogation without the medical help she'd required after she'd been shot while trying to stop the shapeshifter imitating her partner—a man who also happened to be his brother.

Not that she thought he intended her any sort of harm right now. He had as much interest in finding out who and what she was as she did. But he certainly *could* make her life hell—though how much worse it would be than her current hell was debatable.

She leaned across the desk and added, *"Sir,"* a touch sarcastically.

Stephan Stern raised one blond eyebrow, as if mildly surprised by her outburst. An outburst he'd *known* was coming for months. "You know I don't want to do that."

"I don't honestly care what you want. This is about what *I* want." She pushed away from the desk, unable to stand still any longer. Damn it, she'd spent more than half her life with her head in the sand, cruising through life rather than participating, and she'd had more than enough. The time had come to get greedy—to think about *her* wants, *her* desires, for a change. And what she wanted right now was not only a more active personal life, but a working life that involved something better than a broom closet. "Transfer me back to State, let me resign or find me another partner. As I said, I don't care. Just get me out of my current situation."

Her angry strides carried her the length of the beige-colored office in no time and she turned to face Stephan. His expression was as remote as ever, but she'd learned very early on that Stephan was a master at hiding his emotions—and that his dead face was just as likely to mean fury as calm.

"I prefer to leave you with Gabriel, as I still believe you two will make a formidable team."

Sam snorted softly. "That has never been an option, and I think we both realize that now."

It wasn't as if she hadn't tried, for God's sake. But her partner was still going out of his way to exclude her from everything from investigations to chitchat. Access to the SIU's vast computer system just wasn't worth this frustration and unhappiness.

Especially since she was getting jack shit in the way of information about the past she couldn't remember.

Hell, her dreams were providing more information than the SIU's system. The only trouble was, how much could she actually trust the dreams?

And how much could she trust the man who constantly walked through them?

She didn't know, nor did she have anyone she could talk to about it—and that was perhaps the most frustrating thing about this entire situation. She *needed* to get a life. Friends. People she could trust and talk to. Hell, even a pet would be better than going home alone to a soulless hotel room every night.

"I prefer to give the situation more time." Stephan crossed his arms and leaned forward. "However, I do have another option that might suit us both."

Sam met his gaze. His blue eyes were sharp, full of cunning and intelligence. Stephan was a shark by nature—and this was the reason he, rather than his twin, Gabriel, ruled the SIU and the Federation.

Of course, that also meant she was beating her head against a brick wall where Gabriel was concerned, because Stephan was always going to look after his twin's interests first. Even if said twin didn't appreciate his efforts any more than Sam did.

She came to a stop in front of his desk and couldn't help feeling like a fish about to be hooked. "What might that be?"

"You remember Dan Wetherton?"

She nodded. "Last I heard, no one was sure if the body Gabriel found was the real Wetherton or a clone."

"Well, as it happens, it was the original."

Sam snagged the nearest chair and sat down, interested despite her wariness. "Gabriel and I theorized about the possibility of whole brain transplants making clones a viable replacement option, but officially—as far as I'm aware—it's still considered impossible to create a clone that exactly duplicates the mannerisms and thoughts of the original person. They may be genetically identical, but they are nevertheless different." She hesitated, frowning. "Besides, I read the in-house reports and tests done on the living Wetherton. He was declared human in all scientific results."

"And a clone isn't?"

She grimaced. Clones were human, no doubt about that. But whether that actually granted them *humanity* was a point of contention between the scientists and the theologians. "Having only met one clone, who was trying to kill me at the time, I don't feel qualified to answer that particular question."

Amusement touched the corners of Stephan's thin lips. "As it happens, the test results were altered by a party or parties unknown long before we got them." He picked up a folder from his desk and offered it to her. "These are the originals. Have a look."

From past experience she knew that it was pointless to ask how he'd gotten hold of the original papers. Stephan worked on a need-to-know basis—and generally, that meant the less everyone knew, the better. She doubted even Gabriel was privy to all his secrets.

Not that Gabriel himself was particularly open. Not with *her*, anyway.

She leafed through the information inside the folder. It included the genetic tests on both Wetherton and the clone, the coroner's report and Wetherton's medical history.

"Wetherton had cancer," she said, looking up. "Incurable."

"Which the current version no longer has."

She threw the folder back on the desk. "If you know he's not the original, why not simply kill him?"

"Because we wanted to know why he was cloned. And where."

"But not who had cloned him?" Did that mean they suspected the mysterious Sethanon was behind it all?

"As I said, we don't know the where and the why. But there is only one suspect for the who."

"But the military is experimenting with genetics. There's no reason why Wetherton can't be their boy."

"No, there's not."

His tone seemed to dismiss her speculation, and yet she had a vague notion that she'd hit upon the very issue that was troubling Stephan. Only, for some weird reason, he didn't want to acknowledge it. "And what about the replacement parts industry? Have you checked to see if they have started developing fully formed beings, or is that just too obvious?"

His expression became briefly annoyed. "We never overlook the obvious."

Of course not. She smiled slightly. Irritating Stephan might be akin to prodding a lion with a very short stick, but when she got even the slightest reaction, it was oddly satisfying.

"The black-market trade in cloned parts is booming," she said. Of course, it was fueled mainly by humanity's desperation to cheat death. An incredible number of people seemed willing to pay exorbitant prices to grow new body parts, so why not take it a step further, and attempt a cloning miracle? Not just a replacement heart or liver or whatever other part had failed, but a whole new body?

But humanity was more than just a brain; it was also a heart and soul. Medical science might be able to transfer flesh and brain matter, but how could anyone transfer a soul? Even if they could pin down what a soul actually was?

Not that rules ever stopped anyone—especially when there was huge money to be made.

And somewhere along the line, someone had succeeded in achieving at least part of the impossible—fully fleshed, viable clones who looked and acted like the original. Wetherton, and her ex-partner, Jack Kazdan, were proof of that. Although something *had* gone wrong with Jack's clone; it might have looked like him, but it had had serious problems speaking. But then, it had been given a shitload of growth accelerant, so it wasn't truly a surprise that it couldn't speak well. It had never really had the time to learn.

"His source is not black market. We're sure of that."

She studied him for a moment, then changed tactics. "Wetherton's just been made Minister for Science and Technology, hasn't he?"

Stephan nodded. "Two years ago he was trying to shut down many of the science programs, stating that the money could be better spent on the health care system. Now he's in charge of the lot."

"Why hasn't anyone questioned this sudden change of heart? Surely the press has noted it?"

"Noted a political backflip?" Amusement touched his lips again. "You're kidding, right?"

Point made. Flip-flopping politicians were such a fact of life that even the press had gotten tired of them. And the public at large simply ignored them, except when the flops directly affected their bottom line.

"What advantage would having a clone in such a position be for someone like Sethanon?"

"Sadly, we don't know the answer to that one yet."

Not until they caught Sethanon, anyway. And *he* had proven as elusive as a ghost.

"So you've had Wetherton watched?"

"We've had an agent in his office for the last two months, but she can't get close enough. Wetherton plays his cards very close to his chest."

If the man was a clone, he'd have to. One mistake and the truth would be out.

"What does all this have to do with my wanting a transfer?"

He smiled—all teeth and no sincerity. "The minister has recently received several death threats. He was given police protection, but the would-be killer has slipped past them on a number of occasions and left notes. The minister has now requested the SIU's help."

She regarded him steadily. "So who did you use to drop the notes? A vampire or a shapeshifter?"

Amusement flickered briefly through his eyes. "The original threats were real enough."

Yeah, right. There was just a little too much sincerity in his voice for her to believe that. "Am I the only agent being sent in?"

"No. You'll handle the night shift—it suits your growing abilities better. Jenna Morwood will do the days."

Morwood wasn't someone she'd met. "What's her specialty?"

"Morwood's an empath and telekinetic."

So she'd be able to see an attack coming by simply reading the emotions swirling around her—a good choice for this sort of work. "Are we the only two going in?"

"Yes." He hesitated. "Wetherton has requested that the night watch stay at his apartment when he's there at night. Since the first two threats were hand-delivered, I've agreed to his request. I want you to observe everyone he meets. Become his shadow and learn his secrets."

A huge task. "And the reason you're sending two female agents?"

Once again, that insincere smile flashed. "Wetherton appears less guarded around females."

"Meaning what? That he's likely to hit on us?"

"It's a distinct possibility. And before it's mentioned, no, I do not expect or want you to sleep with the man."

"Good, because I wouldn't." She hesitated, frowning. "Wetherton's made much of his caring, family-man image over the last few years. That doesn't quite jell with him hitting on anything with breasts."

"He and his wife separated not long after the original's death. Since then, he's bought a nice apartment on Collins Street and now spends most of his nights there. He's also been seen with an endless stream of beauties on his arms."

She frowned. Wetherton wasn't exactly a looker—though that in itself didn't mean anything. Some of the ugliest spuds in the world had immense success with the ladies simply because of the wealth they controlled, or their sheer magnetic power. But from what she remembered of Wetherton, neither of these was a factor.

"I'm surprised the press haven't had more of a field day."

"They did initially, but a politician behaving badly isn't exactly news these days."

That was certainly true. "I doubt whether I'll learn all that much doing night shift. Surely most of his business will be conducted during the day, no?"

Stephan smiled grimly. "Wetherton has a surprising number of business meetings at night—and usually at nightclubs, where it's harder to get a bug in."

"He'll be suspicious of me. He's not likely to trust me with anything vital."

"Not for a while. It may take months."

Months out of her life and her need to find her past. But also months away from Gabriel. Would absence make his heart grow fonder? A smile touched her lips. Unlikely. "What about time off? You can't expect either of us to work seven days a week."

He nodded. "You'll each get two days—though which two will depend on Wetherton's schedule. Generally, it will be the days he spends at home with his children. We have other arrangements in place there."

"Will the press buy our sudden appearance in his life? This sort of protection is usually handled by the feds, not the SIU."

"They won't question our appearance after tonight, believe me."

The dry coldness in his voice sent chills down her spine. "Why? What are you planning for tonight?"

"A spectacular but ineffectual murder attempt.

Wetherton may be injured, and will, of course, demand our help."

"So who's the patsy?"

Stephan shrugged. "A young vampire we captured several weeks ago. He'd been something of a political dissident in life, and his afterlife has only sharpened his beliefs."

And Stephan had no doubt been feeding his madness, aiming it toward Wetherton. Meaning this plan had been in motion for some time, and that this assignment was part of a bigger picture than he was currently admitting to.

Goose bumps ran up Sam's arms and she rubbed them lightly. Perhaps the vampire wasn't the only patsy in this situation.

"I gather the vamp will die?"

"He murdered seven people before we captured him. His death is merely a delayed sentence."

"What if he escapes?"

"He won't."

Sam shifted in her chair. "If Wetherton is up to anything nefarious, it's doubtful I'll be privy to it."

"No. There will be certain times you'll be sent from the room; this is unavoidable. To counter it, you'll bug the room."

"Most federal buildings have monitors. The minute a bug is activated, an alarm will sound."

"They won't detect the ones we'll give you. Our labs have specifically developed bugs that will function in just this sort of situation."

And no doubt developed a means of detecting them, too. "How long do you think I'll be guarding Wetherton?"

Stephan shrugged. "I can't honestly say. It could be

a month; it could be a year. Parliament doesn't convene again until the middle of next month. By then, you will be such a fixture in his life that no one will comment."

By then, she hoped Wetherton would have revealed all his secrets and she could get on with her life. Spending months in Canberra, yawning her way through endless cabinet sessions, was not something to look forward to.

She crossed her arms and stared at Stephan. He returned her gaze calmly. The uneasy feeling that he wasn't telling her everything grew.

"You're doing this to get back at Gabriel, aren't you? You want him to care."

"I'm doing this because no other agents have your particular range of talents. Your ability to detect evil could be vital in this case."

No lies, but not the exact truth, either. She sat back, feeling more frustrated than when she'd first entered Stephan's office. Guarding Wetherton was not the job she really wanted, but what other choice did she have? It was either this or put up with endless hours of mind-numbing paperwork in her shoe-box office in the Vault.

"How do I keep in contact?"

"You'll be wearing a transmitter that will be monitored twenty-four hours a day." Stephan reached into his desk and pulled out what looked like a gold ear stud. "This is the current model. It records sound and pictures. You turn it on and off by simply touching the surface."

"I don't have to get my ears pierced, do I?" She'd rather face a dozen vampires than one doctor armed with a body-piercing implement.

Stephan's smile held the first real hint of warmth she'd seen since she walked into his office. "No. The studs are designed to cling to human flesh. You actually won't be able to get them off without the help of the labs."

Just as well she could turn them off, then. She needed some privacy in her life, even if it was only to go to the bathroom. "When do I start?"

"Tomorrow night." Stephan picked up another folder and passed it across the desk. "In here you'll find detailed backgrounds on Wetherton's friends, family and business acquaintances."

She dropped the folder onto her lap. There was plenty of time to look at it later. "You were pretty certain I'd take this job, weren't you?"

"Yes. What other choice have you actually got?"

Indeed. "And Gabriel?"

"Will be told you've been reassigned."

Which would no doubt please him. He'd finally gotten what he wanted—her out of his life. "And will I be? After this assignment is over, that is?"

Stephan considered her for several seconds. "That depends."

"On what?"

"On whether or not he has come to his senses by then."

A statement she didn't like one little bit. "You owe me, Stephan," she said softly. For ordering his agents to shoot when she'd been trying to stop the shifter who'd taken Gabriel's form. For the hour of questioning she'd faced afterward when she should have been in the med center. For saving his twin's life. "All I want is permanent reassignment."

His gaze met hers, assessing, calculating. "All right,"

he said slowly. "As I said, this assignment could take more than a year to complete. If you still wish a new partner at the end, I will comply."

She stared at him. He had agreed to her demands far too easily. She didn't trust him—and didn't trust that he meant what he said. But for the moment, there was little she could do about it.

"What happens if I need access to files or information?"

"You'll have a portable com-unit with you, coded to respond only to your voice and retinal scan. You'll also have priority access to all files, though a copy of all requests and search results will be sent to me."

She raised an eyebrow. Priority access? Whatever it was Stephan thought Wetherton was involved in had to be huge.

The intercom buzzed into the silence and Stephan leaned across and pressed the button. "Yes?"

"Assistant Director Stern to see you, as requested, sir."

"Send him in." He gave her a toothy smile that held absolutely no sincerity. "I thought you might like to say goodbye."

Gabriel was the last person she wanted to see. She could barely control her temper around him these days, and hitting a superior officer would only get her into more trouble than Gabriel was worth. And Stephan damn well knew it. She thrust upright. "You're a bastard, you know that?"

"No, I'm a man faced with two people who won't acknowledge that they are meant to be partners."

The door opened, giving her no time to reply. She clenched the folder tightly but found her gaze drawn to the tall man entering the room. His hazel eyes narrowed when he saw her.

But just for an instant, something passed between them—an emotion she couldn't define and he would never verbally acknowledge. And that made her even angrier.

"Sam," Gabriel said, his voice as polite as the nod he gave her.

"Gabriel," she bit back, and glanced at Stephan. "Will that be all, sir?"

A smile quirked the corner of Stephan's mouth. He hadn't missed her reaction. "Yes. For now."

Gabriel stepped to one side as she approached. It was probably meant to be nothing more than a polite gesture—he was simply making way for her to get past—but it fanned the fires of her fury even higher. One way or another, this man was always avoiding her.

She met his gaze and saw only wariness in the green-flecked hazel depths of his eyes. Ever since the factory shootout with Rose and Orrin nearly two weeks ago, he'd treated her this way. She wasn't entirely sure why. And in all honesty, it was time she stopped worrying about it. She had more important concerns these days.

Like finding out who she really was. *What* she really was. Like getting a life beyond the force.

She stopped in front of him and his scent stirred around her, spicy and masculine, making her want things she could never have. Not with this man.

"You win, Gabriel. You have your wish. I'm out of your life." She held out her hand. "I wish I could say it's been pleasant, but you sure as hell made certain it wasn't."

His fingers closed round hers, his touch sending warmth through her soul. A promise that could never be.

"You've been reassigned, then?" Relief edged his deep voice.

"Yeah."

He released her hand and her fingers tingled with the memory of his touch. Part of her was tempted to clench her hand in an effort to retain that warmth just a bit longer. But what was the point of holding on to something that was little more than an illusion? A desire that probably came from loneliness more than any real connection?

"Who's the new partner?"

There was something a little more than polite interest in the question. Were he anyone else, she might have thought he cared. With Gabriel, who knew?

Sam shrugged. "It's really none of your business now, is it?" She glanced back at Stephan. "I'll talk to you later."

He nodded and she met Gabriel's eyes one final time, her gaze searching his—though what she was looking for, she couldn't honestly say. After a few seconds, she turned and walked out, her fury a clenched knot inside her chest.

GABRIEL WATCHED HER GO AND the anger so visible in every step seared his mind, reaching into places he'd thought well shielded and far out of reach. Whatever this connection was between them, it was breaking down barriers not even his twin had been able to traverse, and raising emotions he'd long thought dead.

Which was just another reason to get her out of his working life. Whether or not she should then appear in his social life was a point of contention between the two parts of his soul. The hawk half—the half that had already lost its soul mate—wanted no strings, no ties, nothing beyond those that already existed, but the human half wanted to pursue what might lie between them. Wanted to discover if, given the chance, it could develop into something more than friendship.

Not that there ever *would* be a chance, if her anger was anything to go by. Which was precisely what he'd wanted, what he'd been aiming for over the nine months they'd been partners. So why did his victory feel so hollow?

He shut the door and walked across the room to the chair. "So," he said as he sat down. "Where has she been reassigned?"

Stephan leaned back in his chair, his blue eyes assessing. "She's right. It really *is* none of your business now."

"Don't give me that crap. Just tell me."

Stephan smiled, though no warmth touched his expression. It was that, more than anything, which raised Gabriel's hackles. Stephan was up to something, something *he* wouldn't like.

"She's on special assignment as of tomorrow."

Gabriel regarded him steadily. His brother was enjoying this. He could almost feel his twin's satisfaction. "Give, brother. What the hell have you done?"

Stephan steepled his fingers and studied them with sudden interest. "I've assigned her to the Wetherton case."

The Wetherton case? The *one* case she should have

been kept well away from, if only because of its possible links to both Sethanon *and* Hopeworth? "Get her off it, Stephan. Get her off it *now*."

His twin's gaze finally met his, filled with nothing more than a steely determination. "She *is* the best person for the job, whatever the risks."

"You haven't even warned her, have you?" Gabriel scrubbed a hand across his jaw. *Christ*, she could be walking straight into a goddamn trap, and there was nothing he could do to save her.

"She knows we believe Sethanon is involved," Stephan commented.

"Which is the *least* of our worries. Wetherton's and Kazdan's clones can have only one source, and we both know it. Neither the government labs nor the black marketeers have succeeded with personality and memory transfers. Hopeworth has."

"Or so our spy tells us. It's not something we've been able to confirm."

The Federation had attempted to place spies in Hopeworth on several occasions, but it was only in the last few months that one of their operatives had leaked this information—though so far it was only his word backing it up.

"I think Hopeworth basically confirmed their involvement when they maneuvered to get Wetherton's clone in charge of their budget."

"If they wanted their clone in charge of their budget, they should have got him assigned to Defense."

Gabriel crossed his arms. Hopeworth had fingers in both pies, and Stephan knew it. "Did you even mention Hopeworth to Sam?"

"It was mentioned. But we don't know for sure if Hopeworth is involved."

"Then did you at least tell her Sethanon is more than likely involved with Hopeworth?"

"No, because we have nothing more than a suspicion to back this up. We have no photographs of him. We don't even know if he truly exists. He is currently nothing more than a name."

"A name that has over thirty SIU and Federation deaths attributed to it. And I don't particularly want Sam's name added to that list." His voice was tight with the anger coursing through him. True, he'd wanted to lose her as a partner, but he certainly hadn't wanted to throw her to the lions, and that's basically what his brother had done. She would have been safer remaining his partner than taking this mission.

Stephan grimaced. "Nor do I, brother. Believe me. But we need to uncover the source of these clones. We need to draw Sethanon out, and we need to uncover whether or not he is involved as deeply with Hopeworth as we suspect. And the truth is, she's the best bait we have to achieve those aims."

"What about our source in Hopeworth? Has he heard any whispers about Sethanon?"

Stephan shook his head. "It's not a code name the military uses."

"Kazdan knew who he was, so others must. It's just a matter of uncovering the various layers of his organization."

"Which is why Samantha has been assigned to Wetherton. We know he's a clone. We know his name was on that list she got from Kazdan. We need to know what that list was, and what Wetherton had promised to do in return for life eternal. And why the original was deemed expendable enough to kill and clone and not directly exploit."

"But that still puts her too close to Hopeworth. That could be extremely dangerous."

Stephan leaned back in his chair and regarded his brother steadily. "Only if, as you presume, she is a product of Hopeworth itself."

"You've seen the initial reports from O'Hearn. You've seen the coding. Whatever Sam is, she's definitely not a product of natural selection."

"Yet it was Sethanon who assigned Kazdan to monitor her every move. Sethanon who appears to know just who and what Samantha is. You noted that yourself. Couldn't that mean he's responsible for her creation?"

Possible, but not likely. Gabriel didn't doubt that Sethanon wanted to use her, but if the man had been responsible for her creation, why would he take the risk of releasing her?

"Sam had a military microchip in her side," Gabriel pointed out. "The same sort of chip that we found in both the Generation 18 rejects and in Allars." She was also afraid of Hopeworth. Though she had never said anything, he could feel her fear as clearly as if it were his own.

"And yet our source in Hopeworth can find no record of her, though he can find records on every other reject."

"Maybe because her project was destroyed by a fire years ago."

"A fire would never destroy every scrap of information. Nor could it erase every memory."

"And yet everyone says that Penumbra *was* destroyed that completely."

"People still remember the project, Gabriel. They just don't remember her."

Mary Elliot, the nurse who'd worked on the project, apparently did, but she was just one of many, and a woman with a faulty memory at that. Partially thanks to Alzheimer's, and partially thanks to the military's habit of "readjusting" memories. Gabriel shifted restlessly in the seat. "What if she isn't a reject? What if she's something else entirely?"

Stephan raised an eyebrow. "What do you mean?"

He didn't really know. It was just a feeling. The extent of Sam's memory loss, the depth to which the truth appeared to be buried and the fact that someone was willing to bomb the SIU in order to destroy her test results—it all spoke of intent. It suggested that someone, somewhere, was protecting her from her past, whatever that might be.

He actually doubted that it was Hopeworth trying to conceal who she was, even if they were her creators. The military wasn't that subtle. Besides, if Sam *was* one of their creations, they would never have let her go—especially not with the potential she was now showing.

"Look," Gabriel said, somewhat impatiently. "All I'm saying is that if Sethanon feared her enough to place a watch on her, we should not risk using her as bait in an attempt to catch the man."

"We don't even know if, in fact, it is a man we are after."

Gabriel leaned forward and glared at his twin's altered features. It was in moments like this—moments when he almost wanted to punch the cold smile from his brother's face—that Stephan's ability to shapeshift into the form of any male he touched became a problem. It was harder to restrain the urge to hit him when he wasn't wearing his own face. "Damn it, Stephan, don't play word games with me!"

Something flickered through his twin's blue eyes. Anger perhaps. Or regret. "Do you, or do you not, agree that we must learn more about Sethanon?"

"Yeah, but—"

"And do you, or do you not," Stephan continued, his voice soft but relentless, "agree that Sethanon's interest in Sam might be the lever we need to draw him out of the shadows?"

Gabriel rubbed his forehead. This was one battle he wasn't going to win—not that he ever won many against Stephan. "At the first hint of danger, I'm going in."

"Samantha can take care of herself. She's proven that time and time again."

But this was different. This was leaving her roped, tied and blindfolded in front of an express train. "I won't see her harmed."

Stephan smiled. "And here I thought you didn't care for her."

"I've never said that. All I've ever said is that I don't want her as a partner. That I don't want to see her dead."

"Have you ever considered the fact that this fear of losing partners is irrational, and that maybe you should seek psychiatric help for it?"

"Considered it? Yes. Acknowledge it? Yes. Am I going to seek psychiatric help? No." He met his brother's stony gaze with one of his own. "If I wanted to talk to anyone, I'd talk to our father."

"Because, of course, you couldn't talk to your brother." Stephan's voice was almost bitter.

Almost.

"My brother has a tendency to put the needs of the Federation and the SIU above the needs of everyone else—including his brother."

Stephan didn't immediately comment, just leaned forward and picked up a folder from the desk. "Here's the file on your new partner."

Gabriel ignored the offered folder and stared at his twin through narrowed eyes. "What do you mean, new partner?"

"I've told you before. All field agents, whether SIU or Federation, now work in pairs. There have been too many murder attempts of late to risk solo missions."

"How many times do I have to say it? *I don't want a partner!*" What was his brother trying to prove?

"Then you'll remain at your desk and leave the field work to the agents in your charge."

He was tempted, very tempted, to do just that. But both he and Stephan knew that being confined for any length of time would make him stir-crazy.

Besides, he was more valuable to the SIU and the Federation in the field.

"Who have you assigned me?"

Stephan dropped the folder on the desk and leaned back in his chair. Though there was no emotion on his face, Gabriel could feel his twin's amusement.

"James Illie."

Who was the State Police officer they'd recruited after he'd made a series of spectacular arrests—arrests that involved one of the biggest vampire crime gangs in the city. He was good, no doubt about it.

The only trouble was, the man was a womanizer who was always on the lookout for his next conquest.

"It won't work." And Stephan knew it.

"Then make it work. And don't try dumping Illie in the dungeons. He'll bring in the unions the minute you try."

Wonderful. "Is this all you called me in here for?"

Stephan smiled. "No. There's been a break-in at the Pegasus Foundation that we've been asked to investigate."

"The Pegasus Foundation?" Gabriel frowned, trying to recall what he knew of the organization. "They won a military contract recently, didn't they?"

"To develop a stealth device for military vehicles, yes. But whoever broke in wasn't concerned about stealth devices."

"Then what were they after?"

"That's something you'll have to find out. All I've been told is that the person or persons involved managed to get past several security stations, three laser alarms and numerous cameras. It was only due to the fact that the intruder set a lab on fire that they were even aware someone had slipped their net."

"So we're saying that the person who started the fire is someone who can become both invisible and insubstantial? Is such a thing even possible?"

"We've never seen it before," Stephan answered. "But then, we've never seen a lot of the things we are now encountering, so who knows?"

"Was it just the lab that was destroyed?"

"That I don't know. They're not giving much away—not over the phone, anyway."

No real surprise there, given how easily phone conversations could be hacked these days. "So why were we called in? The Pegasus Foundation has more military ties than we have agents. Why not ask them to investigate?"

"It was the military that asked *us* to investigate." Stephan hesitated. "They asked specifically for you and your partner."

"So they want Sam." But if the military didn't know anything about her, why had they specifically asked for her to be included in the investigation?

"Who signed the request?"

"A General Frank Lloyd."

As Alice would say, curiouser and curiouser. "Sam met Lloyd at Han's." She'd been wary of the general and convinced they'd meet again. "You have to warn her about the military's interest."

"No, I won't." Stephan hesitated. "And neither will you."

Like hell he wouldn't. It was one thing to let her go; it was another to leave her blind. He crossed his arms. "What time is the Pegasus Foundation expecting us?"

Stephan glanced at his watch. "You're to meet with the director—Kathryn Douglass—at four thirty."

It was nearly four now. Then Gabriel frowned. "Kathryn Douglass? Why does that name sound familiar?"

"Because her name is on that list Kazdan gave to Sam."

A list that had marked potential clones and vampires, as well as assassination possibilities. "So which one is she? Clone, vampire or potential dead meat?"

"That we can't say, as there's no note beside her name," Stephan said. "Illie's requisitioned a car and is waiting out front."

Gabriel met his twin's gaze. "Thought I'd skip without him, huh?"

Stephan's smile touched his eyes for the first time.

"I know you, brother. I know the way your mind works. Don't ever forget that."

Then he'd know Illie wasn't going to be a fixture in Gabriel's life for very long. If he'd wanted a partner, he'd have kept Sam.

"Then you'll know precisely what I'm thinking now."

Stephan's smile widened. "Yeah, and it's not polite to abuse a family member like that."

Although it was when your brother was being such a bastard.

Stephan's smile faded. "Keep away from her, Gabriel. She has a job to do, and I don't want you getting in the way."

"What I do in my own time is my business, not yours," Gabriel said, voice flat. "I'm warning you, don't ever try to control my personal life."

Stephan raised an eyebrow. "You have an obligation to both the SIU and the Federation, just as I have."

"Yeah, right." Gabriel turned and headed for the door. The Federation and the SIU could go hang if it meant letting Sam walk into a trap out of no more than ignorance.

He may have succeeded in getting rid of her as a partner, but that didn't mean he wanted her dead.

"Gabriel, I'm warning you. Leave her alone."

Gabriel stopped with his hand on the doorknob and glanced over his shoulder, meeting his brother's gaze. "Or you'll what? Censure me? Bust me down to field agent again? Do it. I don't really give a damn."

"This could be our one chance to draw Sethanon out!"

"That doesn't justify sending her in *blind*."

"Gabriel, I'm giving you a direct order. Do not go near her. Do not warn her."

"Then you'd better get my file out and add the black mark to it now, because that's one order I have no intention of obeying."

And he slammed the door open and stalked from the room.

TWO

SAM GLANCED AT HER WATCH as she entered her office. It was just after four. She had an hour before she was due at the labs to have the studs attached and be shown how they worked.

All she really wanted was to go home—not that she currently had a home to go *to*. Her Brighton apartment had sold almost as soon as she'd placed it on the market. The new owners had gushed over its size and closeness to the beach. That it had been bombed twice in recent months was a fact she and the real estate agents had failed to mention.

She slapped the folder on the desk and sat down. "Computer on."

A pink fluff ball with chicken legs appeared onscreen. "Afternoon, sweetness."

"Afternoon, Iz. Any messages from that useless real estate agent of mine?"

"Not one."

Typical. Two days ago he'd promised to get right back to her with the latest housing list. The man was either extremely forgetful or was tired of her nagging and trying to get rid of her.

Probably the latter, she thought ruefully. She leaned back in her chair and wearily rubbed her eyes. Maybe it would have been wiser to wait until she'd found somewhere else to live before she'd sold the apartment—as Gabriel had informed her the one time this week that he'd deigned to grace her broom closet with his presence.

And yet she didn't really regret her actions, even if staying at hotels was costing a fortune. The apartment had never truly felt like hers—maybe because it was something she had been given rather than earned. Or maybe because the reasons for the gift had never really been clear.

Or perhaps it was the cop in her that couldn't get past the idea that, in the end, such gifts usually proved costly.

She reached forward and picked up the folder Stephan had given her. Inside she found a series of photos—Wetherton's friends, family and immediate associates.

She shuffled through them until she found one of Wetherton. He was small, round and balding. Spud material, definitely. And yet, there was something in his brown eyes that was not quite right—an odd sort of blankness that chilled her.

She threw the photo back down onto the desk. At least this assignment would save her some money, if nothing else. And she could still use the days to continue her search for a home.

Although, as her real estate agent had said—and more than once—if she weren't so particular, she'd have something by now.

Someone knocked on the door. It opened before she could answer, revealing Gabriel.

"AD Stern. Fancy seeing you again so soon." She couldn't help the sarcastic note in her voice. The only time he'd ever bothered crowding into her closet was when he had some inane task for her to complete. But he wasn't her partner now, wasn't her boss, so why was he here?

He crossed his arms, leaning a shoulder against the door frame. His presence filled her small office in much the same manner as his frame did the doorway. With any other man, it might have felt threatening. With Gabriel, it felt cautious, almost aloof.

"Stephan told me about your new assignment."

There was a touch of concern in his rich voice. She raised an eyebrow. "And?"

"And he hasn't told you everything."

Like *that* was a surprise. "That's because he works on a need-to-know basis. Like someone else I know."

Annoyance flickered through Gabriel's warm hazel eyes. "I've never let you walk into an assignment blind."

She snorted softly. "Yeah, because you've never *given* me an assignment. Only desk work."

He at least had the grace to look guilty, if only for a second or two. "Look, I just came down here to warn you, not to argue."

"Then warn me and leave." Before she asked him to stay, simply to warm the empty coldness in her office. In her life.

"Fair enough." He hesitated for a moment, studying her with a slight frown. "He omitted two major facts. One, we believe that Hopeworth is the source of the Wetherton clone, and two, we think Sethanon may be linked to both Wetherton and Hopeworth."

And Stephan was using her as bait to draw them out. She'd been right. The vampire set to attack Wetherton wasn't the only patsy in this situation. "Why does he think my presence will affect Sethanon's actions?"

"Because Sethanon placed Kazdan in your life to keep watch over you both personally and professionally. And because Sethanon had to have been the source for the birth certificate Kazdan gave you. He seems to know more about your history than anyone else. And that it implies a long-term interest."

Or long-term responsibility. She rubbed her arms uneasily. Though she didn't want to mention it to Gabriel, the mysterious, hirsute stranger she knew only as Joe had admitted to giving the birth certificate to her—yet had never explained how it had come to be in Jack's possession. And when she asked him, point blank, if he was Sethanon, he had said that Sethanon was not a name he'd ever given himself. But what did that mean? That other people had called him that? Was Sethanon her secret ally or not? But all she said now was, "Sethanon is little more than a name. How the hell am I supposed to draw him out when no one even knows what he looks like?"

"Stephan's hoping he might try to snatch you."

Yet if he'd intended that, why not do so before now? He'd had ample opportunities, especially when Jack was her partner. Few people would have missed her back then save Jack, and he'd been Sethanon's right-hand man.

"I doubt the man would be fool enough to try it himself."

"No, but the transmitter you're getting also acts as a tracking signal. Stephan hopes to trace you to Sethanon's headquarters, at the very least."

And then what? A quick raid in the hope of flushing out the upper echelons of his organization? Stephan was a fool if he thought it would be so easy. They were talking about someone who had successfully covered his tracks for years.

"How deep are Wetherton's ties to Hopeworth?"

"Very, if Hopeworth is in fact responsible for his cloning."

"It doesn't make sense, you know. Why clone someone like Wetherton? From what I've read of the man, he's never been considered prime ministerial material."

"But David Flint was. And remember, Sethanon has already tried to replace him with a clone."

Which suggested that if the clones *were* coming from Hopeworth, then Sethanon was in control of the base. And yet, if that were true, why would Hopeworth be showing interest in her if Sethanon already knew what she was and was monitoring her? And what of Joe, who seemed to be actively protecting her from Hopeworth? If he were Sethanon and in charge of Hopeworth, why protect her from them? There was too much conflicting information to make heads or tails of it. "So this whole assignment is simply a setup to discover who is pulling Wetherton's strings?"

"Setup? No." Gabriel hesitated slightly. "But is that one of its goals? Yes. We need to uncover who is behind Wetherton, and stop this whole clone replacement business before it goes any further up the government ladder."

"Meaning Wetherton's bait, and so am I. So what?

No matter what the dangers, it's sure as hell better than spending the rest of my life in this broom closet." She watched the impact of her words hit him, watched the regret and annoyance flit through his expression, then added, "And I'll be careful. Anything else, Assistant Director?"

He hesitated again, then shook his head. "Keep in touch," he said softly.

A hint of regret was in his eyes and she steeled herself against it. She'd tried hard enough. Now it was his turn. "Why? I thought it was your life's ambition to get rid of me."

"I never said I wanted you out of my life."

But he'd never said he wanted her in it, either. He had never truly thrust out the hand of friendship. Everything she knew about him she'd learned during the course of their work. And he'd never attempted to extend the boundaries of their working relationship, despite the fact that there was obviously some sort of attraction between them.

Whether that attraction would have led to anything more than a night or two in the sack was anyone's guess. If she were the betting type, she would have said yes. But it takes two to tango, and Gabriel was having no part of it.

"Why do you think it's safer to have me as a friend than as a partner?" she asked. "I know you've lost partners, but you've also lost a sister and, I believe, a brother. *Not* being your partner is no protection from death. Not when you, the SIU and the Federation pursue the type of characters for whom dispensing death comes as easily as breathing."

He stared at her. His face held no emotion, and yet she could sense his unease as clearly as if it were her own. He didn't want to examine his reasoning, didn't want to look closely at his feelings. If he had shut himself off from his twin brother, what made her think she had a hope of cracking his reserve?

She waved a hand before he could answer her question. "Forget it, Gabriel. Call me sometime and we'll go out for coffee or something."

"I will." He stared at her a moment longer, his gaze searching her face, as if memorizing her features. Then he turned and walked away.

She picked up the folder and shoved it into her bag. Then she opened her desk drawer, grabbing the few personal items she'd left in there: perfume, the pin Joe had given her, a hairbrush and several scrunchies.

Then she stood and grabbed the coat from the back of her chair. But on the verge of leaving, she hesitated. As much as she'd hated what the broom closet had represented, at least it had been hers—somewhere she could escape to and be safe. A place few people knew existed or could be bothered finding. Whatever happened after the Wetherton assignment, she knew she wouldn't be coming back here. One way or another, her life was about to change.

Whether it was for the good or the bad, she wasn't entirely sure. And right at this moment, she didn't really care. Any sort of change had to be better than stagnating—which was precisely what she'd spent the last few years doing. She'd let Jack take over her life to the extent that she had no life beyond the force. And, in some ways, she'd started to make the same mistake again with the SIU and with Gabriel.

"No more," she vowed to the emptiness. From now on, she would try to follow her own course, no matter what.

Grabbing her bag, she turned and headed down to the labs.

GABRIEL CLIMBED OUT OF THE car and slammed the door shut. The headquarters of the Pegasus Foundation was on a huge strip of barren land out in the middle of goddamn nowhere. The main building was square-shaped, draped in black glass that seemed to suck in the light and cast thick shadows over the parking lot and the nearby limp-looking garden.

He took off his sunglasses and looked upward, squinting slightly against the bright sunlight. The building was six stories high, and even from where he stood he could see the radar dishes, antennas and various other bits of apparatus bristling from the roof. But he also caught sight of something else—security, armed with guns. And the uniforms those men were wearing looked a hell of a lot like military uniforms.

Once again, the same question arose. If the military was this involved with Pegasus, then why bring in the SIU? It didn't make sense.

They were clearly being played—but to what ends? Well, he'd never find out by standing here. He rubbed the back of his neck and headed across the parking lot toward two black-glass front doors.

Behind him, the passenger door slammed and footsteps echoed, and Gabriel found himself clenching his fists. He slowly flexed them in an effort to relax. An hour in Illie's company and he was ready to punch the man. Not the best of beginnings.

The glass doors opened. He headed across to security and flashed his badge. "We've an appointment with Director Douglass."

The security officer nodded. "Take the second elevator down to level five. Someone will meet you in the foyer and take you to the director's office."

"Thanks." Gabriel continued on. His new partner followed quietly. Maybe he'd finally caught on to the fact that silence got him more than an endless stream of chatter did.

As Gabriel punched the elevator call button, Illie stopped and cleared his throat. "Have you seen the recent photos of the director? She's quite the babe."

Then again, maybe Illie was silent only because he'd temporarily run out of inane things to say. "We're not here to assess the director's hotness rating."

Illie's responding grin was pure cheese. "Hell, man, it doesn't hurt to look, does it?"

"I'd prefer it if you concentrated on the matter at hand, not on adding another notch to your belt," Gabriel said severely. He stepped into the elevator and pressed the button for sublevel five.

Illie's gray eyes narrowed slightly. "That would be easier if I knew why the hell we were here."

Gabriel shrugged. "If you've read the file, you know as much as I do."

"Nothing like sending agents out blind," Illie muttered. "Though it's no wonder this place got robbed. Security didn't even bother checking us for weapons."

Gabriel smiled. Despite his years in the State Police, Illie had a lot to learn. "They didn't have to. Did you notice the black globe in the ceiling?"

Illie frowned. "Yeah. Camera, wasn't it?"

"No, it's a device that renders energy weapons inef-

fective. There were also metal detectors on either side
of the entrance, so if we'd been carrying standard
weapons, the guard would have known."

"I didn't see any metal detectors."

"You wouldn't; they're built into the frame. The
only giveaway is a faint red beam." Something human
sight rarely picked up.

"Damn," Illie commented. "Must have missed that
session of training."

According to his file, Illie hadn't missed any—but
that didn't mean he was actually paying attention.
"O'Donnell was your instructor, wasn't she?"

A slow smile stretched Illie's mouth. "Yeah."

Which accounted for the lack of memory. O'Donnell
was a pretty blonde in her mid-thirties, and decid-
edly single.

The elevator doors slid open and the waiting guard
led them down a sterile white corridor.

They passed through two more security stations
before the whiteness began to bleed away, replaced
by muted greens and blues.

Kathryn Douglass turned from the window when
they were ushered into her office. She was a tall, slender woman with silver-flecked brown hair and ala-
baster skin. Her age was hard to guess. Gabriel
thought mid-fifties, but he wouldn't have been surprised if she was older. Either way, she was striking.

"Assistant Director Stern," she said, offering her
hand. "Thank you for being so prompt."

Gabriel clasped her hand. Her touch was firm, almost challenging, more like a man's than a woman's.
"This is my partner, James Illie."

She ignored Illie's outstretched hand and waved
them toward two well-padded armchairs before sit-

ting down herself. Her gaze was assessing, almost critical.

"I was under the impression that your partner was a woman," she said.

The back of Gabriel's neck began to itch. The director's manner wasn't what he'd expected from a woman whose company had just suffered a major robbery. No concern, no tension, just an odd sort of watchfulness.

He met her cool, gray gaze. "Then your informant was wrong. Tell us about the break-in."

The director leaned back in her chair, a slight frown marring her almost perfect features. "One of our research wings was breached last night around two. The destruction was localized to one section of our secure file rooms that houses our more recent project notes and findings."

"Was all the research in the secure room destroyed?"

"No, because the fire was very localized, and only lasted a few minutes. Fortunately, that project happened to be one I have a keen interest in, and I'd taken a copy of the notes home with me to study the night before."

"Meaning you don't use computer filing? You use *paper*?" Illie said, almost in disbelief.

The director's smile edged toward condescending. "Computers can be hacked too easily. Most of our top projects are paper-only. This is a high-security center. Until last night, we'd thought it perfectly safe."

No building or security system was ever impervious. There was always a weak spot somewhere. All you had to do was find it. "So you had no idea this building had been breached until the culprit set fire to your files?"

"None at all. It's most vexing."

She didn't sound particularly vexed. "What was destroyed?"

She hesitated. "The lab is involved in the development of a light-and-matter shield for the military."

"Then why call us in? Wouldn't it have been more appropriate to call in the military?"

"We did. But whoever broke into the lab first managed to get past five security stations and three laser alarms, and they were never picked up by the cameras. Clearly they were in some nonhuman form—and maybe in no form at all—and *that* is more SIU territory than the military's."

But not if what they'd learned about Hopeworth over the last month was true. "Who recommended that you call me?"

Illie gave him a sharp glance. Obviously he hadn't known they'd been requested.

"General Frank Lloyd. He said he'd had some dealings with your partner." She hesitated, her gaze shifting to Illie. "I'm sure he said your partner was female."

"Does it really matter what sex my partner is?" Gabriel said, unable to keep the slight edge of annoyance from his tone. This was looking more and more like a setup. But why?

The director raised an eyebrow. "No, I suppose it doesn't. Do you wish to see the lab?"

"If you want us to actually solve the crime, then yes, that would be a good idea."

A small smile stretched her too-perfect lips, but there was little amusement in her cold gray eyes. She

reached to her left and pressed a button on the intercom. "Security will escort you there. Please feel free
to come back if you have any further questions."

Gabriel rose. "We will need to see the security
tapes from last night."

"Of course. They'll be available by the time you
finish in the lab."

"And we will need to question the guards who were
on last night."

She nodded. "They're off duty, but a list of names
and addresses will be provided."

This whole situation just wasn't sitting right. This
was a top-secret facility, one with tight military ties.
No matter how seriously they wanted the crime
solved, the director was being entirely too helpful.

No, whatever they wanted, it had something to do
with Sam, not with solving this crime. But why was
Sam so important to them?

"We'll see you afterward, then," Gabriel said, and
followed Illie from the room.

As promised, a second security guard waited for
them beyond the office doors. He led them back into
the antiseptic white corridors and down a series of
ramps.

Gabriel glanced at the ceiling. Cameras tracked
their movements, but as far as he could tell, there
were no voice recorders attached.

"Opinion?" he said softly. As an empath, Illie was
able to read and define emotions to such a degree that
he could practically tell what a person was thinking.

Illie cast a wary look at the security officer in front
of them, then met Gabriel's gaze. "That woman was
lying through her back teeth," he muttered. "She has
another agenda entirely."

That much he'd already guessed. "Did any particular statement stand out?"

Illie frowned. "Yeah. The bit about it not being important whether your partner was male or female."

Because they wanted Sam, not Illie. But why? What had they intended to do once they'd gotten her here? Not even the military could think they could kidnap an SIU agent and get away with it.

"Who was your partner before me?" Illie asked.

"She's not important right now." But even as he said the words, he knew it for a lie. Sam *was* important.

But he'd been through hell once with the death of Andrea, who'd been not only his childhood sweetheart but both his lover *and* his partner, and that, more than anything, strengthened his resolve to remain alone whenever it started slipping.

He blew out a breath and added, "Did you detect any lies when Douglass spoke about the break-in?"

"No, that much was true." Illie studied him thoughtfully. "You have unresolved issues with your former partner, haven't you?"

"I told you, it's not important." And certainly it wasn't anything he intended to discuss with a man who'd been his partner for precisely an hour and a half.

Illie raised a skeptical eyebrow, but amusement danced in his eyes. "Maybe I'll have to get a second opinion on that."

Gabriel found himself clenching his fist again. "Let sleeping dogs lie, Illie."

The younger man studied him a minute longer, then smiled slightly. Surprisingly, he made no further comment. Though, as an empath, he would know when to push—and when to stop.

They continued on. The white corridor seemed to stretch on without end. The itch at the back of Gabriel's neck grew.

He tapped the security officer on the shoulder. "Where the hell is this lab? Siberia?"

The man shrugged. "It's one of the outer labs. We're accessing it through the underground tunnel system."

They finally approached another doorway. The guard swept his pass card through the slot and the metal door slid aside to reveal a pale green corridor. Several doors led off it, though they were all currently closed. Windows lined one wall, and through them they could see several white-coated technicians going about their business.

The guard continued on, but Illie nudged Gabriel's arm and pointed toward the lab. "They seem okay to you?"

Gabriel watched a scientist measure some clear liquid into a vial. "I suppose so. Why?"

Illie's frown deepened. "Because I'm not getting any readings from them. It's as if they're emotionally nonexistent."

"Might distance be a factor? The walls look fairly thick here in the labs."

Illie shook his head. "It shouldn't matter when I'm this close."

"Maybe the labs are psi nullified?"

"Then I wouldn't be able to read you, would I? Or the guard."

True. So what was going on? "Can you feel anything else about them? Anything odd?"

Illie hesitated, his expression thoughtful. "No, but look at them. It's almost like they're on automatic—as if they're doing nothing more than following a set list of instructions."

"Which they could well be if they're performing a specific experiment." Even so, as Gabriel stared at the five men, he couldn't help noticing that they all seemed to be doing the exact *same* thing.

"I know," Illie muttered. "But it just doesn't feel right. *They* don't feel right."

The guard stopped and punched several numbers on a keypad to the right of a doorway. The door slid open.

"This is the lab, gentlemen. I'll be out here if you need anything."

Illie stepped past the guard and Gabriel followed. The lab was narrow but long, all white walls and gleaming metal benches. The far end was lined with a map and upright cabinets, and nearby were several tables strewn with papers and folders—none of which had been so much as scorched. The only things that *had* been burned were two cabinets to the far right of the tables, and these were little more than melted blobs. A fire fierce enough to do *that* should have destroyed the rest of the lab, let alone the nearby cabinets and scattered paperwork. But they weren't even scorched.

"None of this makes sense." Illie walked down the aisle between the rows of tables, his footsteps echoing in the cold silence. "If our thieves could get into this lab unseen, why just destroy only a couple of cabinets? Why not destroy the lot?"

"Maybe they wanted to destroy something very specific."

"Maybe." Illie stopped beside one of the tables. "Yet the alarms went off the minute the fire was set, so how the hell did they escape? I get the feeling there's only one entrance to this place."

"One entrance, but perhaps more than one exit." Gabriel bent to study the melted remains of what looked like a lock—probably from one of the cabinets. It appeared to have been made of tungsten metal, which was yet another pointer as to how hot the fire had been. And that had to mean it was no ordinary fire.

"I'll tell you one thing—some of these projects weren't new, if these plans are anything to go by."

Gabriel glanced up. Illie leaned against the table, studying the papers strewn there. "Why do you say that?"

"Simple; they're dated. These plans are over two years old."

"Check the other cabinets." Gabriel rose and walked over to the second melted cabinet. There wasn't even anything that *looked* like a lock on this one; it was just one huge congealed mass of different metals. He glanced at the untouched cabinets; the gauge of steel used in them and the thickness of the doors suggested they were fireproofed, and he had no doubt these ones would have been as well. But what type of fire could so utterly destroy fireproofed cabinets in a matter of minutes? As far as he knew, not even firestarters were capable of creating a burn so fierce and hot in such a short space of time.

"The end cabinet has more recent projects," Illie said into the silence.

The end cabinet was one of the few that hadn't been ransacked. "Maybe our thief was working his way through the plans. Maybe he wanted the complete set of plans, past and present."

"Good theory, except there are no plans for light or matter transmitters in this lot."

"Then the thieves might have taken them."

"If theft *had* been their goal, they could have gotten in and out without anyone being aware. So why set the fire? It makes no sense."

"It does if they specifically wanted the destruction to be noted. Maybe it was some kind of message." But what was it about the light-and-matter project they'd destroyed that they'd wanted to make such a point about? It was a question only Douglass could answer—and one he suspected she wouldn't. "Anything else of interest in the cabinets?"

"A lot of projects marked unviable." Illie slammed the cabinet door shut. "I'm getting a bad feeling about this."

Gabriel had passed the bad feeling point a while ago. Now it was more of a sick certainty that something bad was about to happen. "Let's head back upstairs and view the tapes. Then we'll go interview the security personnel from last night."

"I don't think we'll find much on the—"

A strident siren cut off the rest of Illie's sentence. A muffled explosion rumbled in the distance, then the floor began to shake. Slowly at first, but with increasing intensity.

"Quake," Illie said, calmly studying the ceiling as if searching for any sign of collapse.

Gabriel did likewise. Spider-like lines began to splinter across the concrete. Too quickly, he thought, and frowned. "I don't think so."

Another explosion vibrated the air around them.

The siren cut off abruptly and the ensuing silence was almost eerie.

"I think we'd better get out of here, Stern."

Gabriel didn't reply. Wind stirred his hair, as if some unseen force was moving toward them. The back of his neck burned. Something was very, *very* wrong.

He lunged forward, grabbed Illie by the scruff of the neck and thrust him toward the nearest cabinet.

"Get in there, close the door and do not come out until I say it's safe!"

"Have you gone mad?"

"The cabinets are fireproof." The concrete bucked underneath him and Gabriel stumbled several steps backward before he regained his balance.

"Holy shit." Illie's mutter was etched with fear. "The back wall is melting."

Gabriel glanced over his shoulder. Rivulets of concrete rushed toward them. A good third of the wall had melted, revealing a maelstrom of fire.

"Shut the door, damn you!"

Another explosion ripped through the air, followed quickly by a sharp crack. He glanced up and saw the cracks on the ceiling widening and joining.

Chunks of ceiling began to rain down as Gabriel dove for the nearest cabinet, hoping like hell it would hold against the approaching firestorm.

THREE

THE LOCKER SHUDDERED AS THE force of the storm
hit. The walls began to burn, becoming too hot, too
quickly. The air seethed with heat, and every intake
of breath burned Gabriel's throat and lungs.

He hunched in the middle of the locker and prayed
that the thing would hold up long enough to ride out
the storm. Sweat skated across his body, drying as
fast as it appeared in the soul-sucking heat. He shifted
his arm and licked several droplets before they could
evaporate. It might not be much, but his mouth felt
drier than the Sahara, and he knew he had to keep
some moisture in his body or he wouldn't survive.

His wristcom vibrated. It might have rung, too,
only he couldn't hear it against the whirlwind of fury
battering the cabinet. He didn't answer it. Couldn't.
He didn't dare move, lest he touch the sides of the
locker. They glowed with heat, and one touch could
be deadly.

Two heartbeats later, the noise began to bleed
away. Silence reigned for several more heartbeats,
and then a hissing began—softly at first, but then

gaining in momentum. Water began to seep into the locker.

The sprinklers. Some of them must still be active, despite half the ceiling coming down. He waited several more minutes, then cautiously touched the door. Hot, but not unbearable.

He turned the handle, but the door didn't budge. He shoved harder. A crack of light appeared along one edge. Through it, he could see chunks of concrete, scattered about like some giant's abandoned toys.

He shifted around until he could get his feet against the door, then pushed with all his might. The door buckled under the force he applied, but eventually the slabs of concrete moved enough that he could climb out.

Water misted the air, quickly soaking through his clothes. He lifted his face and closed his eyes, allowing the moisture to cool his skin.

Then he remembered his new partner. He quickly picked his way across the rubble to the locker that held Illie. The door moved slightly and relief swept through him. At least he hadn't managed to kill yet *another* partner—though a tiny, callous part of his soul suggested that if death came in threes, then Illie's might have freed him to partner with Sam.

But it was *not* the way he wanted to break the curse on his partners.

"Hang on," he said. "There are several concrete blocks piled up against the door."

He threw them to one side and forced open the locker.

Illie scrambled out, his face red and his suit stained

black with sweat. "Now *that* was an experience I don't care to relive!"

"Yeah, pretty awesome," Gabriel muttered.

His wristcom rang into the silence—a shrill sound that made him jump. He tapped the screen and said, "Stern," as he studied the mess that had once been a lab. What had probably saved them was the far wall; only a third of it had melted under the intense heat of the maelstrom. The rest had held, offering some form of protection.

Sam's features appeared on the vid-screen, her blue eyes clouded with worry. "Gabriel? Are you okay?"

Gabriel swore softly and rubbed a hand across his eyes. He'd hoped that by shattering their working relationship, he'd break the psi bond that was growing between them. That obviously wasn't going to happen—or maybe it was just too soon to have any real effect.

"Yeah, I'm fine, but I can't talk now."

It came out sharper than he'd intended, and the warm concern left her face, replaced by an iciness he'd seen all too often of late.

"Sure. Talk to you later."

She signed off before he could say anything else. *Way to go*, he thought sourly. *Continue speaking to her like that and she'll definitely remain a part of your life.*

"You know," Illie said casually, "you really have fuck-all idea how to talk to a woman."

"Shove it up your ass," Gabriel muttered, then turned at the sound of footsteps.

Half a dozen men came into the lab, some carrying hoses and others medical equipment. Prepared for the worst, Gabriel thought.

"They're surprised," Illie muttered. "They didn't expect to see us alive."

"Relieved surprised, or annoyed surprised?"

Illie hesitated, studying the approaching white suits. "Relieved."

So if this *was* a setup, these men didn't know about it.

One man separated from the pack, pulling off his breathing mask as he approached. "Assistant Director Stern? I'm glad to see you alive, sir!"

Gabriel glanced at the man's name tag. "What the hell happened here, Rogers?"

"Near as we can figure, a chemical spill in the lab next door resulted in an explosion. You're lucky to be alive, sir."

Wasn't that the truth. Though he had to wonder, if this *was* a trap, what had the military hoped to achieve? "Were there many casualties?"

Rogers nodded, his face bleak. "The security officer who escorted you down here, and the five scientists working in the lab."

"Those were the scientists I couldn't get a reading on," Illie murmured. "The ones who felt wrong."

"Indeed," Gabriel said. And it would be worth ordering extra tests done on their remains, just to discover what was going on with them. And what they were.

"If you don't mind," Rogers continued, "I'll have one of my men escort you down to the medical center, just to make sure that you're both okay."

Gabriel nodded. "And we'll need to talk to the director again."

"Once the doc's given us clearance."

"Let's get it over with, then."

Rogers motioned to one of his men and moved away. Gabriel glanced at Illie, noting his frown. "What's wrong?"

"This is what they got us down here for," he muttered. "So they can do tests—on you and your partner."

Undoubtedly meaning his former partner, not his current one. "Who are you getting this from?"

"The small gent at the back. He was surprised when he first came in, then excited." Illie met Gabriel's gaze. "What's so special about your former partner that this mob is willing to kill six people just to run some tests on her?"

The bigger question was, why did they continue with the tests when it was obvious his partner *wasn't* Sam? What did they hope to achieve? Was it merely a means of getting rid of him and Illie? Though why would they do that, when it would only bring down closer scrutiny of their activities by the SIU?

"We don't know." And that was becoming more and more of a problem.

Rogers's assistant approached. "If you'd like to follow me, gentlemen, we'll get this over with as quickly as possible."

No doubt they would. Without Sam, though, it was pretty much a pointless exercise—thankfully.

"They still want to test you, you know." Illie muttered. "Something you did during the firestorm has excited that scientist."

Gabriel frowned. "But I didn't do anything."

"Yeah, you did," Illie said. "You sensed what was happening early enough to save our lives."

"Are you sure you're reading him right?"

"Yeah. Positive."

They approached a set of doors marked with a red

cross. Their escort swiped a card and the doors slid open. How many med centers needed a security clearance to get into? Gabriel wondered. Why bother, unless the med center did more than simply patch up accident victims?

Whatever the military was up to, he'd just have to let it play out—for now. But the Pegasus Foundation and its director certainly needed closer scrutiny.

Their escort motioned them toward two well-padded chairs. Gabriel sat down and watched the man disappear through a second set of doors. "When we get back to HQ, I want you to do a complete background check on Kathryn Douglass."

Illie nodded. "Including home security tapes?"

"If you can get them." It would keep Illie off his back for a while, at least. In the meantime, he'd do a check of his own—on one General Frank Lloyd. There had to be information about the man somewhere.

His first priority, though, was Sam. Illie was right. If the military was willing to kill six men just to get the chance to examine her, it could only mean they had a fair idea about who and what she might be.

And that, in turn, made her current assignment even more dangerous.

If Hopeworth *was* behind this bombing attempt, they wouldn't leave it at that. There would be more.

But he couldn't watch Sam's back twenty-four hours a day. Not without help. It was, Gabriel thought, time to arrange a meeting with his sister.

THE SHRILL RINGING OF THE telephone jerked Sam awake. She rubbed her eyes and glanced at the clock.

It was just past eight in the evening. She must have dozed off while reading the riveting account of Wetherton's life.

She blindly groped the coffee table behind the sofa arm and finally picked up her wristcom. "Yeah?"

"Samantha? Doctor O'Hearn here."

O'Hearn was the nonhuman and rare species specialist she'd been sent to by Gabriel and Stephan. Apparently, if anyone could sort out precisely what she was, it would be this woman. A sliver of tension ran through her. Surely it was too soon to have reliable results back? She'd been told it could take months of checking and cross-checking. "Hi, Doc. What can I do for you?"

"I want your permission to discuss your case with Karl Morgan."

Karl? Gabriel's friend? "Sure, but why? Karl's an herbalist healer. How would he be able to help?"

"He also happens to be the Federation's resident expert when it comes to extinct races. I think he might be able to help make sense of some of these results."

Obviously, O'Hearn had been unable to match the gene coding in the test samples with any known races if she was now considering extinct ones. Walkers were, apparently, a very rare race who were vaguely related to the vampires, without possessing their need for blood to survive. A race who could completely disappear into shadows. *Become* shadows, in fact. They also apparently had eyes just like hers—eyes that wavered between blue and gray. "Karl did say he suspected there might be walker blood in me, but he never got around to doing the tests."

Mainly because he'd been blackmailed into handing her over to Jack, who'd wanted to use her emerging abilities to overthrow Sethanon.

"Yes," O'Hearn said. "Gabriel mentioned Karl's suspicions, which is why I want your permission to talk to him."

"If it helps uncover what I might be, then sure, go ahead." Sam hesitated. "Was there any match to what's supposedly on my birth certificate?"

"Oh, yes. There are traces of shifter and changer, as I mentioned earlier. We've also pinpointed the partial code of the were-people. But there's something else, something I've never seen before."

If she *had* come from Hopeworth, that wasn't altogether surprising. "I want to know the minute you come up with anything."

"Of course."

Sam hung up and yawned. What she needed was an early night. She shoved the folders to one side and got ready for bed.

Sleep came. So, too, did the dreams.

She was in a large, white room. Lights glared above her, their brightness as warm as the sun and almost as blinding. Sweat trickled down her face and her back. She was standing alone in that room, but she was being watched. Down at the far end was another room. Men in white stared at her from behind the safety of shatterproof glass.

Joshua was with them, his small form dwarfed by the doctors. Silent but not afraid. Josh was never truly afraid.

"Feel the heat. Draw it in," the man with the dead gray eyes commanded.

Just hearing him speak made her shudder. Not because of the threat in his tone—though she knew from experience that threat all too often became reality—but because of what lay underneath his voice and his words. Evil soaked his very essence. Just being near him sickened her.

She looked at the fire, but she saw only flames, dancing brightly. She couldn't do what he wanted. He was asking the wrong person.

"I *can't*."

The lights grew brighter, burning her skin as fiercely as the flames. She couldn't back away, couldn't move. They'd chained her down this time.

"Become one with the fire. Feel its power. *Use* its power," Gray Eyes said.

The urge to scream ran through her, but it wouldn't matter to them if she did. It never mattered. Her gaze met Joshua's.

You have to do something, or they'll kill you, his voice whispered into her mind, calm despite the anger she could almost taste.

Fire is not my element.

No. They are fools who do not look beyond the obvious. But you have other abilities. Use those instead.

They'll know. They'll see the difference.

They know nothing about us, despite all their tests. Trust me, Samantha.

She briefly closed her eyes and took a deep breath. Then she stared at the fire burning fiercely in the pit three feet away. The flames shivered, as if dancing away from an unseen wind. Sweat tracked down her face, stinging her eyes. She ignored it, concentrating, drawing power up from the depths of her soul. From the ground itself.

The fiery mass rose from the pit and hovered in

midair for several seconds. She glanced at the control
room and saw Joshua step back, well out of harm's
way.

She smiled—a cold smile. A hateful smile. Aimed
not at him, but at the men with him. The men who
wouldn't let them be, wouldn't let them go.

The burning mass leapt across the arena and
smashed through the control box's glass. White coats
scattered like confetti. Then the lights went out and
the screaming began.

Laughter filled the air, mingling with the screams.
Her laughter; Joshua's laughter. Both of them old
beyond their years and full of hate. The fire leapt
from the men to the computers, and she realized he
was feeding it, making it destroy the sensor readouts.
Once again they would have no record of what had
happened here today. Nothing more than the words
of those who survived.

Josh, I'm chipped. They'll kill me.

The flames died suddenly, sucked back into the
void that had fed them. *I know. It is not our time to
escape yet. But when it is, they will taste the fires
more fully.*

The malevolence in his voice made her shiver . . .
and she woke, a chill encasing her body. She ran a
hand through her sweaty hair and stared at the ceiling for several seconds. Were the dreams memories
trying to break free? Or simply the imaginings of a
fertile mind?

There was no way to be certain. But if *this* dream
were to be believed, then she had not only killed, but
she'd enjoyed it. Nor was it the first or the last time it
had happened.

And she'd been no more than seven years old at the time.

"Lights on," she murmured, wanting to banish the shadows and the last remnants of the dream.

Brightness flooded through the hotel room. She sat up, drew her knees close to her chest and hugged them tightly. If Joshua was in fact her brother, as the dreams insisted, why did he call her Samantha? According to Mary Elliot, the woman who'd supposedly looked after the two of them in Hopeworth, Joshua's sister had been called Josephine.

And why was she dreaming of a scientist with gray eyes when all the scientists who had dealt with the Penumbra project were dead?

Or were they?

They'd had only Allars's word on that, and Allars was an old man whose memories might well have been altered by the military. No matter how reliable his information had seemed, no matter how much it had jelled with other sources, they had to take everything he said with a grain of salt.

She rubbed her arms and looked at the time. It was nearly eleven. Wetherton would be leaving the theater soon and heading home. According to the file, the vampire would attack just before Wetherton climbed into the car.

The theater was only four blocks down from her hotel. If she hurried, she just might make it there in time to see what happened. She had a horrible suspicion that things would not go as Stephan had planned.

And investigating was certainly better than sitting here in this hotel room, trying to stay awake in an effort to avoid the dreams that made no sense, and yet terrified her.

* * *

GABRIEL SWIPED HIS CREDIT CARD through the cab's slot and climbed out. Illie had offered to drive him home, or even here, to his sister's, but he'd had more than enough of his new partner. At least Sam had been able to appreciate moments of silence—not to mention being a whole lot easier on the eyes.

Not that he'd ever admit either to her.

He scrubbed a hand through his hair and wished he could just stop thinking about her. Damn it, he'd gotten what he wanted—and what was best for both of them.

So why did he feel so damn depressed about it?

Maybe it was just exhaustion. He and Illie had spent an hour in the med center at Pegasus being poked and prodded. Then they'd wasted another three hours viewing the security tapes and talking to the evasive Kathryn Douglass. Whatever secrets the woman hid, she wasn't giving them away easily. Even Illie had trouble reading her.

Right now, he wanted nothing more than to go home, have a drink and go to bed. But he couldn't— not until he'd looked after the woman he couldn't stop thinking about.

He climbed the front steps and reached out to press the doorbell, but the door opened before he could. His sister stood before him, green eyes concerned despite her welcoming smile.

"A visit from my little brother at this hour of the night? Things *must* be bad." Her voice was soft as she rose on her toes to kiss his cheek.

Gabriel smiled and kissed her back. "I need help."

"I gathered that. Head on through to the kitchen. Alain's making coffee."

He made his way down the shadowed hall, his boots echoing loudly on the wooden floors. Alain, Jessie's brown-haired, large-limbed husband of six months, stood near the sink, pouring hot coffee into three mugs.

He glanced around as Gabriel entered, giving him a quick look over before his lips split into a wide grin. "Man, you look like shit."

Gabriel smiled and dragged out a chair. "That's a pretty accurate description of how I feel."

Alain placed a mug in front of him and sat opposite. The scent of coffee wafted up, teasing him.

"Things not going well?"

Though there was a sympathetic edge in Alain's voice, amusement crinkled the corners of his brown eyes. Gabriel had an odd feeling he wasn't actually referring to work. What had Jessie been telling him?

"Yeah, you could say that. I almost got blown up this afternoon."

"Tough days at the office are the pits."

"But you're not here for sympathy, are you?" Jessie said, as she sat down and leaned her shoulder against Alain's.

Loneliness swirled through Gabriel. If only briefly, he found himself wanting what most of his siblings had—someone to lean on. Someone to come home to. He rubbed a hand across his eyes. God, he *definitely* needed some sleep if he was thinking that. Besides, his chance at such a life had slipped away when Andrea died. "No, I want you to help me guard Sam's back."

Jessie shared a look with her husband, concern evident. Alain leaned forward, interlacing his long fingers. "Stephan's not going to like that."

"Stephan doesn't have to know."

Jessie smiled slightly. "You can't keep secrets from Stephan. None of us can. He has a nose for secrets."

Well, this was one secret he'd better keep his nose well out of or there would be hell to pay. "Look, Stephan's assigned Sam to the Wetherton case. He's hoping her presence will draw Sethanon out. But I think it's more likely to draw out Hopeworth."

Alain's frown deepened. "Why would Hopeworth be interested in her?"

"Hopeworth's been playing in the genetic sandbox for years, and Sam is more than likely one of their creations. And even if she's not, she's caught their interest."

Jessie picked up her mug and regarded him steadily over the rim. "Why didn't you just keep her as a partner? You wouldn't have had this problem then."

"My partners have a bad habit of dying." He hesitated and rubbed his eyes again. Andrea might have died by an assassin's bullet, but Mike's death had been *his* responsibility. He'd fired the killing shot. "I prefer to work alone. You know that."

A small smile touched her lips. "What I know, brother dearest, is that you're using your fear as an excuse."

He raised an eyebrow. "An excuse for what?"

"I remember a man holding the woman who was both his girlfriend and his partner in his arms and vowing to never let another woman come so close to his heart. A promise he has kept, until now." She hesitated, green eyes regarding him steadily. "Sam threatens that vow because you know, deep down, that she is the one for you. *That's* why you got rid of her."

Though an empath, his sister could sometimes be surprisingly off base. He frowned and sipped his coffee. There was *some* truth in her words, though. He *did* have a connection with Sam, and he was definitely attracted to her. But as much as he might occasionally hunger for it, he really didn't want emotional complications of *any* kind in his life. That was part of the reason he continued to block Stephan's thoughts. Why he was so comfortable with Sandy, another SIU officer and his sometime lover. She wanted no commitment, no emotion, beyond friendship.

As for Sam being the one . . . He put down his mug and tried to ignore the ache in his heart.

"Andrea was my destiny, my life mate. Not Sam. Whatever I feel for Sam, it could never evolve into something that lasts. My heart died with Andrea."

"Are you so sure, lad?" Alain said, his deep voice holding a touch of compassion.

"Yes." At least Alain understood. Jess, and the rest of his family, probably never would. They weren't shapechangers, and weren't cursed with the knowledge that there could be only one permanent mate for them—ever.

Jessie sniffed. "Andrea was your first love, Gabriel. Don't be so certain that what you felt then was life-altering."

"Look, I came here to ask for help, not to be emotionally dissected."

Jessie placed a hand on his, squeezing gently. "I'm sorry." She hesitated, her face losing animation, her green eyes suddenly clouded, distant. "Sam is one half of a force—light to his shade. You are her anchor, her

reality. Push her away and you force her into his circle
of influence."

"Whose circle?" Gabriel said softly.

Jessie blinked. Warmth returned to her face and
her eyes. She rubbed her arms and smiled ruefully.
"I'm sorry. The vision's gone."

Gabriel cursed silently. Perhaps he shouldn't have
spoken. Her visions were fragile at the best of times.
"Will you help me?"

She glanced at Alain and nodded. "But I wouldn't
hold much hope of keeping this from Stephan for too
long."

"Let me worry about Stephan." Gabriel gulped
down the rest of his coffee and rose. "I'll head to the
office now and grab a copy of Wetherton's schedule.
I'll email the roster once I work it out. Hopefully,
between the three of us, we can keep her out of Hopeworth's hands."

SAM SHOVED HER HANDS IN the pockets of her
jacket and leaned a shoulder against the bus shelter
wall. Across the width of Exhibition Street, people
were beginning to file out of Her Majesty's Theatre,
and reporters jostled with spectators for the best position to view the exiting celebrities. Limos lined the
curb, waiting for their passengers.

It was the perfect place to attempt an assassination.
With the noise and the milling crowd, it was unlikely
anyone would notice anything until it was too late. As
yet, though, there was no sign of anything untoward.

The latest teen sensation came into sight, his blond
head promptly disappearing amongst the crowd of
waiting paparazzi and fans. Two seconds later, Wether-

ton came into view and was greeted by resounding indifference.

He wasn't happy about it, either, if the look on his face was anything to go by. He hovered near the doors for several minutes, then roughly grabbed the woman by his side and guided her away. Three others followed in their wake—two men and another woman—as Sam pushed away from the bus shelter wall. Wetherton's chauffeur hadn't been quick enough to grab a good position, so he was waiting half a block away.

Sam ran across Exhibition Street and fell into step several yards behind them. Though she kept an eye on the shadows surrounding the nearby buildings and shop fronts and listened to the sigh of the wind, there didn't seem to be anything out of place. No sign of the vampire, no sensation of evil haunting the night.

And yet, something *was* here—a presence that itched at the back of her mind. A memory waiting to surface.

She frowned and eyed Wetherton's group uneasily. The sensation was coming from their direction for sure—but what it implied was anyone's guess.

Frown deepening, Sam tore her gaze from them and checked the night again. They were now distant enough from the theater and the crowd. So why hadn't the vampire attacked? If they went much farther, there would be no witnesses, no press. No point.

A chauffeur climbed out of a white limousine when Wetherton's group approached it. As the chauffeur walked around to open the passenger door, Wetherton stopped and looked around. His gaze fell on Sam before she could avoid it, but quickly moved on. *Eas-*

ily dismissed, she thought wryly, but stepped into the shadows of a nearby shop entrance anyway. She wasn't supposed to be here, so it was better if she kept out of sight as much as possible.

Once the chauffeur had opened the car door, Wetherton climbed in, followed quickly by the two women and one of the men. The last man hesitated, one hand on the roof, his gray hair gleaming silver under the wash of the streetlights as he turned to study the night in much the same manner as Wetherton had.

His blunt-nosed profile sent shock crashing through her.

He was the man from her dream.

The evil man with the dead gray eyes.

FOUR

SAM PRESSED THE EAR STUD, quickly activating it.
"I want a search done on the man with the gray hair,"
she murmured. "All details, ASAP."

The man in question hesitated a bit longer, then
climbed into the car. The chauffeur walked back to
the driver's side and, within seconds, the car purred
to life and was jockeying for position in the jam of
other cars attempting to leave the theater district.

So much for Stephan's spectacular attack. What
the hell was going to happen now? Without the attack, there was no reason for her to become one of
Wetherton's bodyguards. No reason that wouldn't
look suspicious, anyway.

And that, in turn, meant a return to the broom
closet.

"There's never a vampire around when you bloody
need one," she muttered, as she stepped from the
shadows, eyeing the car that now had its nose out
into the street. "Someone had better contact me and
tell me if this assignment is still a go."

She touched the transmitter and switched it off.

Then she resolutely turned away. A return to her hotel was her only option now.

She'd barely taken three steps when an explosion ripped through the night. As her heart leapt to the vicinity of her throat, a wave of heat hit, sending her staggering. She swore loudly, but the words were lost under the sound of screaming. She caught her balance and swung around.

What lay before her seemed more like a scene out of an action movie than something that could happen on a Melbourne street.

Wetherton's car was up on two wheels, skidding through the line of cars under the force of the explosion. It spun the two closest away, then crashed into a car parked on the right side of the road and thumped back down, the back wheels on fire and the flames spreading fast.

People were scattering—some running back inside the theater and others running down the street through the line of now-halted cars—most of them screaming and obviously terrified. The paparazzi were in a frenzy, cameras flashing as they jostled for the best position. Wetherton had finally gotten the attention he'd missed earlier.

Had he lived to bask in it?

The chauffeur scrambled from the car, blood pouring down his face from a cut above his eye. Then a line of blue light bit through the night and hit him in the chest, and he dropped like a stone out of her sight.

Laser fire.

He'd been hit with laser fire.

That certainly wasn't a part of Stephan's plans. Sam drew her weapon and ran forward, using the cars as cover as her gaze swept the surrounding rooftops.

The laser shot had come from the top of a building to the right of the theater, but the light glaring from the many signs prevented her from seeing if the shooter was still up there.

Only there was no reason to believe he wasn't.

She glanced at the limo. There were no movements from inside. Maybe the occupants had seen what had happened to the driver and were staying put, despite the dangerous fire. Or maybe they were unconscious.

Or dead.

The answers to those questions were something she had to find out—fast. But the closer she got to the car, the more the heat lashed at her skin. Oddly enough, the heat seemed to concentrate on one side of her face—it almost felt as if *she'd* been burned. The smell of burning rubber damn near choked her, and thick smoke spun through the night. If Wetherton and his people *were* alive and didn't get out soon, the fumes and the heat would kill them. Not to mention the growing danger of the gas tank exploding.

From across the road, a familiar voice yelled at people to get back, that everything was under control. She smiled grimly. Briggs—someone she'd worked with and trusted.

But she hoped like hell that Briggs wasn't the only one Stephan had sent in, because right now she had a feeling they were going to need every agent they could get.

Sam hesitated at the nose of the last car before the burning limo. A few feet of free space now separated her from the wreck. She blew out a breath, glanced up at the rooftop, then sprinted forward.

Blue light nipped at her heels, melting the asphalt before a secondary wave of kinetic energy sent jagged asphalt pieces exploding upward. Not a laser, but rather a plasma weapon, which ionized matter and projected it with sufficient force to cause secondary impact damage in addition to the initial high thermal damage. She swore and dove behind the burning car, ripping her jeans down to her skin. She swore again and rose on one knee, squinting against the smoke and the heat as she scanned the rooftops. She could see little through the thick, soupy haze.

Coughing as the smoke began to catch in her throat, she edged forward and knelt down by the chauffeur, feeling for a pulse. Nothing. Though with a hole the size of her fist burned through his chest, that wasn't too surprising.

She closed his eyes, then shifted position. Flames were beginning to lick at the underbelly of the limo, and, this close, the heat was intense, almost suffocating. Every breath burned and the sweat sliding down her forehead seemed to sizzle. She had to get out of here—had to get Wetherton and his people out—before they were either fried or suffocated or the gas tank exploded.

Sounds whispered through the crackling of flames—quick footsteps, approaching from the front of the limo. She swung and sighted her laser, only to recognize the blonde who approached. She lowered her weapon hastily and said, "What the hell is going on, Briggs?"

Briggs stepped over the chauffeur's body and squatted near her. "I don't know. The vamp was supposed to attack as Wetherton was coming out of the theater. This wasn't part of the plan, believe me."

"Were you the only agent assigned?"

"Yeah. We're only talking about one vamp, and

he's little more than a kid, at that." Briggs hesitated, a grim smile touching her lips. "Dead easy. Or it should have been."

Should being the operative word. "Our first priority's getting Wetherton out."

"You check, and I'll cover."

Sam nodded. Smoke and flames enveloped almost every part of the car now. The paint had begun to peel, tearing away like sunburned skin. She pulled the sleeve of her jacket over her hand and opened the back door. Smoke boiled out, pungent and black. Inside the car, someone coughed. At least one of them was alive, though how, she had no idea.

Another blue beam bit through the night and the rear window of the car shattered, spraying bright shards of glass everywhere. Briggs rose and fired several shots at the rooftop of a café to the left of the theater.

Heat itched across Sam's skin—heat that whispered secrets and had nothing to do with the flames. It wasn't a vampire up there firing at them, but a shifter. Obviously, the vamp had done a runner, and others were in control here tonight. But who? Still, if there was one thing she'd learned over her years as a cop, it was that things rarely went the way they were planned. Mainly because all the various players were usually following a different script.

"SIU," she said, in between coughs. "Is anyone seriously hurt in there?"

"Wetherton's unconscious. His girlfriend has serious facial lacerations. The rest of us have minor cuts and scrapes."

The voice was cold, efficient. Familiar. She knew

without looking that it belonged to the man with the dead eyes.

"We're going to lay covering fire so everyone can get out. One of you will have to drag Wetherton clear." She hesitated, coughing again as the thick smoke and heat caught in her throat. "Make for the foyer of the theater."

At least there, Wetherton and his companions should be relatively safe from the laser fire. Unless, of course, the shooter moved.

Or there was more than one shooter.

"Say when," Gray Eyes said.

Sam checked the charge on the laser, then glanced at Briggs and nodded. As one, they rose and began firing.

"Go!" she screamed.

The twin lasers seared through the night, spraying the darkness with bright beams of light that danced across the metal rooftop with deadly force.

The car lurched. A woman scrambled out, followed quickly by a man who turned, reached back and hauled Wetherton out of the vehicle. Gray Eyes appeared, blood pouring down the left side of his face as he wedged a shoulder under the minister and hoisted him up, then quickly moved away from the limo with Wetherton on his back. The other man and two women followed, the second looking dazed and with blood flowing freely down her face.

"Go with them, Briggs," Sam ordered, and she continued firing until Briggs and the others had reached the theater doorway, even though the shadow on the roof had disappeared as soon as they'd returned fire.

If he moved too far, they'd lose him. And with him would go any chance of understanding what the hell

was going on. Sam pressed the transmitter as she rose
and ran back across the road.

"The attacker is a shifter, not a vampire. I'm in
pursuit. Cleanup team and ambulance required."

Sirens were already screaming in the distance and
people milled on the sidewalk, drawn like moths to
the flame. Though the paparazzi feasted on it all, several of them ran in her wake, as if in anticipation of a
scoop. She dug out her badge and flashed it in their
direction.

"SIU, gentlemen. Get the hell back!"

With reluctance, they complied. At least initially.
She had no doubt they'd follow—just a lot less obviously. That was another thing she'd learned over the
years—the press and a good story weren't easily separated.

And there was a hell of a good story here—one she
wanted uncovered as much as they did.

She ran onto Little Bourke Street, heading for the
alley behind the cafés. The nearby streetlight flickered off and on, briefly illuminating the broken asphalt and grimy puddles of water that littered the
alley's mouth. She slowed. The perfume of rotting
rubbish, urine and water long gone stale rose to greet
her, and she wrinkled her nose. So much for the hope
that she'd left places like this behind when she'd become a spook.

The alley ran behind half a dozen shops, and rubbish bins lined the rear fences, most of them either
overflowing or overturned. At the far end, huddled in
the rear entrance of a building, was a sticklike mass
of gray hair and stained clothing. He whispered ob-
scenities to the wind, his voice harsh, strained, as he
gestured wildly at the night.

A drunk, not the shifter who'd attacked Wetherton.

She holstered the laser and climbed the old wooden fence. Once on the other side, she hesitated, listening. Lights glowed from the back windows of the café. People talked, a distant sound of confusion and concern that meshed perfectly with her emotions.

She looked up. The shifter was still up on the roof. His evil rode the air as easily as the wind stirred her hair.

Why hadn't he run? What was he waiting for?
Her.

A chill raced down her spine. It was ludicrous, it truly was, and yet the thought—or rather, the certainty—that it was true was absolute.

And yet, she was here by chance, by whim. How could anyone be so certain of her actions that he would know where she'd be at any given moment? It was impossible.

Though not, perhaps, for the man who shared her dreams and her thoughts.

And perhaps it wasn't even beyond the capacity of her makers, whoever they might be. Who really knew? Not her, that was for sure.

She rubbed her arms, but it did little to erase the cold sensation of dread running through her.

One problem at a time, she thought, and headed resolutely for the fire escape. Her footsteps echoed on the old metal stairs as she began to climb—a loud warning of her approach. Yet no sound greeted her appearance on the roof. No movement. She frowned, not liking the feel of it.

A billboard dominated the concrete expanse. Spotlights lined its base, their brightness aimed upward, leaving the rest of the rooftop a wasteland of shadows. A big old air-con unit rattled to her left. The awareness trembling across her skin suggested that the shifter hid behind it.

She raised her laser. "SIU. Drop your weapon and then come out with your hands up."

The man hiding in the shadows didn't respond. On the street below, the wailing sirens abruptly stopped. Flashes of red and blue light ran across the darkness, splashing color across the glass-walled office building opposite. Almost normal sights and sounds in a night that felt anything but normal.

She forced her attention back to the air-con unit and the man who hid behind it. "I repeat, this is the SIU. I know you're there. Drop your weapon and come out."

Still no response. She stepped onto the rooftop and edged forward. Underneath the sigh of the wind, she could hear the shifter. If the easy rhythm of his breathing was anything to go by, he wasn't worried by her presence.

She fired a warning shot. The blue beam flew across the darkness and hit the edge of the air-con unit. Metal sheared away in a jagged cut whose edges glowed with heat.

Still nothing. He didn't move. Didn't twitch. She frowned and moved closer. She'd almost reached the right edge of the unit when he exploded forward, his body little more than a shadowed blur as he sprinted across the roof.

He was too fast for a shifter; his speed was more like a vampire's.

She was nowhere near *that* fast—a tortoise compared to the hare. But she ran after him anyway. If nothing else, she could track him with her senses until someone from the SIU got here to help her.

Speaking of which, where the fuck were they? This was Stephan's baby, his master plan, so why the hell didn't he have backup here already?

Or was this all part of a wider scheme—a scheme she knew nothing about?

No. Whatever was going on here, with this shifter, it had nothing to do with Stephan or the SIU. She was sure of that, if nothing else. But right now, she had no time to worry about it. The shifter leapt across to the next rooftop and ran on. His body faded in and out of existence as he moved, almost as if he were an image viewed through some badly focused lens. *Weird.*

She jumped the small dividing wall, then went down on one knee and sighted the laser. "Last warning. Stop or I'll shoot."

His only response was a fresh burst of speed. As he became little more than a shadowed blur, she fired.

The blue beam arced across the night and hit him in the left shoulder. He flung his arms wide and went down with a thump. She waited, laser still raised and at the ready, for several seconds. When he didn't move, she rose and cautiously approached. Her shot might have caught him in the shoulder, might have torn through flesh as easily as it had his clothes, but that didn't mean he was down for the count. Far from it.

Her gaze went briefly to the wound. At least with lasers there was no bleeding and little chance of infection. The laser beam cauterized the wound in an instant—not that it made it any less painful.

The shifter himself was hooded and dressed in

black from head to toe, his body solid but smudged around the edges, as if he were a drawing that wasn't quite complete. Odd, to say the least. There was still no movement, no sign of breathing. Warily, she nudged his foot. No response. She tried a little harder and got the same result. Maybe he was unconscious, because he couldn't be dead. Not from a shoulder wound.

Cautiously, she knelt and reached for his wrist to feel for a pulse. In that instant, he came to life, twisting around to throw a punch. She dodged, but not fast enough. His fist hit her cheek, the force of the blow reverberating through her skull and throwing her backward. Her head smacked back against the rooftop, sending a shock wave of pain through the rest of her body. For a moment, stars crowded her vision.

Air stirred, accompanied by sound. The scrape of a heel against the roof. A grunt of effort.

She blinked back tears and tried to concentrate. She felt a force of air coming from her left and rolled right. A booted foot landed inches away, the sheer power behind the kick seeming to shudder through the entire roof. If that blow had landed, he would have crushed her face.

He laughed. *Laughed.*

Then he tried stomping her with the other foot.

"Bastard," she muttered, firing the laser even as she dodged.

The bright beam of light speared into his chest. Skin and bone were seared into blackened bits that scattered on the wind even as his body dropped lifelessly to the ground. The smell of burned flesh was fiercer than before because of her proximity.

She closed her eyes and took several deep breaths.

She hadn't meant to kill him, but her instincts had taken over. Yet worse than the knowledge that she'd killed was the sensation that something felt *very* wrong.

With the speed that shifter had, he should have been able to dodge the laser. He didn't even try. Why not?

Did he want to die?

She sniffed, then winced as pain slithered across her face. A light probe with her fingers revealed a rapidly swelling cheek as well as a warm stickiness that could only be blood oozing toward her chin. The cut was a good inch long. The creep must have been wearing a ring of some kind when he'd hit her. The inside of her mouth was just as tender, and at least two teeth seemed horribly loose.

She spat out a mouthful of blood and slowly climbed to her feet. For an instant, the night swam and her stomach rose. Then she swallowed and rubbed the back of her head where an egg the size of a football was forming.

Great. Showing up looking like a boxer who'd taken one too many punches was just what she needed to impress Wetherton.

Sam grimaced and walked across to the body. Tendrils of smoke were rising from the wound. Maybe it was steam from his still-warm body.

Or maybe it was something else entirely.

What that something else could be she didn't *want* to know—though her imagination was certainly firing up some fantastical ideas, such as maybe it was his soul rising.

As if *anyone* could see something like that.

Ignoring the goose bumps running rampant across

her skin, she picked up his hand and studied the ring on his finger. It was a thick gold band with a square front. The symbol carved into it looked like a flame wrapped in barbed wire. *Odd.*

She let his hand drop, then leaned forward and pulled off the mask covering his face. He had red-gold hair and gray-green eyes that were wide with shock. So this wasn't any ordinary assassin, but a product of Hopeworth.

But if Hopeworth was the birthplace of the Wetherton clone, why would it send an assassin after him?

And why send one after *her*, if they wanted to find out more about her?

It didn't make any sense.

But then, when had anything in her life ever made sense? It was frustrating, to say the least.

She rose to her feet and walked across to the edge of the building. The fire had been controlled and SIU officers were headed her way. She crossed her arms and waited for them. Right now, there was nothing else she could do.

THE PHONE RANG LOUDLY. GABRIEL reached out, making several empty grabs before he hit the vid-phone's receive button.

"This had better be good." He opened an eye and glared blearily at the time. Six in the morning. Couldn't he have even one day off without someone contacting him?

"You should try getting an early night for a change." Stephan's voice sounded altogether too cheerful.

Something *must* have happened. Gabriel rose on his elbows and looked at the vid-screen. His own

image stared back at him. Stephan had to be at the
Stern compound, and not at his home or at the office.
It was the only place he ever used his true form.

"You should try calling at a decent time." Gabriel
yawned and dropped back down to the pillow.
"What's up?"

"Hopeworth tried to assassinate Wetherton last
night."

The last vestiges of sleep skittered away and Gabriel jerked upright again. "Is Sam okay?" Even as he
asked the question, he knew the answer. Given their
growing bond, he'd have known if she weren't.

"Yeah, though she shouldn't have even been there.
According to her report, the assassin was one of
Hopeworth's creations. We can't ID him. Hopeworth
is currently denying all knowledge, but I tend to agree
with her."

Why would Hopeworth risk the life of one of their
specialist killers on a man who was supposedly one
of their own? It didn't make any sense.

Gabriel rubbed a hand across his eyes. "What
about your vampire? Did he come through?"

Stephan frowned. "There was no sign of him. It
looks like he may have taken the opportunity to run."

"You knew it was a possibility."

"A ten percent chance. And worth the risk, given
what's at stake."

To draw out a man who was little more than a
name, they'd let a killer back on the streets. *Was* it
worth the risk? They wouldn't really know until
Sethanon took the bait—*if* he took the bait.

"A warrant been issued?"

"Yeah. Thornhill and Edmonds are turning over
his known haunts."

If the kid had any sense, he'd avoid known haunts like the plague. But then, young vampires were inclined to think they were invincible, which tended to be their downfall. "Anything else? Or did you call at this ungodly hour just to piss me off?"

Stephan grinned, and Gabriel wondered if his brother had been drinking. The last time he'd seen him like this was when they'd gone on a weeklong twenty-first birthday bender. And *that* was years and years ago.

"Lyssa's gone into labor."

"Hey, congrats." At least that explained why he was at the compound. He must have taken Lys there so she'd have someone close while he was at work. It also explained why he was grinning like a drunken fool. "How's she doing?"

"Fine. I called O'Hearn down, just to check things out. She reckons it'll be a good five or six hours before anything major happens."

Changer births tended to be a lot longer than human births. He hoped Lyssa was strong enough. "You want me down there?"

"No point until something actually happens. Come down when he's born, and we'll get drunk together."

"Are Mom and Dad hovering?"

Stephan snorted. "Half the bloody clan is hovering. The rest are on their way."

"Well, your son *is* the first male grandchild." Gabriel grinned. The Sterns didn't get together that often, but when they did, they made the most of it. There'd be a hell of a party at the compound tonight. "Give me a call the minute anything happens."

"Will do."

The vid-screen went black and Gabriel scrubbed a

hand across his eyes again. Though he couldn't have been happier for Stephan, this birth came at an awkward time. As much as he wanted to be with his brother, he also needed to ensure that Sam was safe. Hopeworth was after her, of that he had no doubt—even though, as yet, there was no real evidence to back that up. He stared out the window for several seconds, listening to the starlings in the trees outside his window squabble, then reached for the vid-phone and quickly dialed Karl's number.

His friend answered on the second ring, looking as if he'd been up for several hours. His wild brown hair was tied back in its customary bandana, and dirt caked his weather-lined face.

Gabriel raised an eyebrow. "You eating mud for breakfast these days?"

Karl grinned. "You'd think so. It's been pissing down out here. I went out to check the greenhouses and lost my footing."

"You busy tonight?"

Karl hesitated. "Yeah. David's got the lead in a play at school. They're performing tonight. Why?"

David was Karl's youngest and Gabriel's godson. "Thought I'd ask you to do me a favor, but it really doesn't matter."

"I'm free after about eleven, if that's any help."

Gabriel hesitated. "No, it's okay." If Hopeworth *had* orchestrated the attack on Wetherton, surely they'd lay low for a day or two before moving again. He was probably worrying over nothing.

Karl scratched his chin, smearing the mud further. "Are you aware that I'm seeing that pretty partner of yours today?"

Gabriel smiled. He obviously didn't mean Illie. "Why? Is something wrong?"

"Nah. O'Hearn called me in. She wants some help decoding the gene patterns."

"So you've had a chance to look at the test results I gave you?"

"Yeah." Karl hesitated. "Look, why don't you come down to the clinic today? I think we may need to talk to you both."

And no doubt Sam would be utterly delighted to see him there. He smiled grimly. He had only himself to blame. If he hadn't been such a bastard over the last few weeks, maybe she'd be a tad happier about seeing him outside of work.

"Why would I need to be there?"

Karl frowned. "I've been doing some research on shadow walkers. If O'Hearn's samples match the test results from Finley, Sam's definitely got walker in her."

"That still doesn't explain why you need me there."

"Her appointment's at five. Be there and I'll explain."

Obviously, Karl had no intention of explaining *anything* over the unsecured vid-phone. Gabriel blew out a breath. "Fine. I'll see you there, then."

The vid-screen went black again, and Gabriel stared up at the ceiling, part of him wanting to get up and hit the gym and the other half desperate to go back to sleep. The phone rang before he could decide between them. Didn't *anyone* sleep in these days?

Frowning, he shifted and checked out the caller ID. It was Sandy. He reached out to answer the call, then hesitated and pressed the auto-answer button instead.

"Morning, Gabe. Seeing we've both got the day off, I thought we might get together."

Her voice was mellow, sultry, but for once it had little effect on him. Maybe he was more tired than he'd thought. Maybe he was simply getting old.

"Give me a call when you wake up," she continued. "Lunch is my treat."

Her words invoked memories of the last time she'd treated him to lunch. Eating hadn't exactly come into it, and damn if it hadn't been fun. Again he reached out. Again he hesitated.

If he went and saw Sandy, he'd have a hard time breaking away anytime before dinner. He couldn't go there simply for sex and then walk away. It wasn't fair to her, no matter how casual either of them was about their relationship.

Better for them both if he simply didn't respond. He rubbed a hand across his eyes and climbed out of bed. Seeing as he had nothing else planned for today, he might as well grab the chance to exercise, then head down to Federation headquarters.

Surely, somewhere in the vast archives there, he'd find something about shadow walkers.

SAM TUCKED A LEG BENEATH her as she sat on the sofa. After placing her coffee on the table, she grabbed the portable com-unit and pressed her thumb into the lock.

"Voice identification required," the unit stated.

"Sam Ryan, SIU officer, badge number 1934."

Talking still hurt, but nowhere near as much as it had only hours before. Though her mouth still felt tender, at least the swelling had gone down, her teeth seemed to have reanchored, and the bruise that stretched from her lip to her eye was already beginning to get that faded, yellow look. Even the cut had begun to heal.

At least she looked less like a boxer that had taken too many hits and more like something a cat had dragged in and toyed with for several hours. It was a definite improvement.

"Voice scan correct. Eye confirmation required."

She looked into the small scanner fitted into the left-hand side of the unit. A red beam swept over her eye.

"Eye scan correct." The unit clicked open.

Izzy appeared onscreen. "Morning, sweetness. Being portable is a new experience, I must say."

Sam grinned. Having her cyber character on the unit was an unexpected bonus. She'd thought Stephan would place voice-only response software on the portable unit, as both he and Gabriel seemed to prefer it. But maybe he wasn't as insensitive as she'd thought.

"Morning, Iz. Listen, I asked for a trace to be done on a gray-haired man last night. Are the results back yet?"

Izzy twirled her purple boa for several seconds. "Yep. Got it right here. No ID match so far."

Sam frowned. How could there be no match? The man had to exist on a computer *somewhere*. "Have they checked the Motor Registration records?"

"Yup. There is no car registration, no driver's license and no Medicare card match."

Every adult in Australia had a Medicare card. You couldn't go to the doctor without one these days. She picked up her coffee and sipped at it for several seconds.

"What about the shooter?"

"Again, no ID match. A formal request for ID has been sent to Hopeworth, though."

Sam raised her eyebrows. That could cause a few waves. "Any response from Hopeworth?"

"Not a fig, sweetie."

Not surprising. What *was* surprising, however, was the fact that the SIU still had the body. She'd have thought Hopeworth would have tried a clandestine retrieval by now.

"Are they doing tests on the body?"

"Agent Finley is currently examining it."

Then she'd have to remember to ask him what he discovered when she saw him at the meeting O'Hearn had arranged for later today.

"Do I have any mail from that real-estate cretin yet?"

The boa twirled; the response time was slightly slower on the portable unit. "Yep. One came through last night."

"Put it onscreen, and thanks, Iz."

Izzy disappeared, replaced by a three-page list. Sam smiled slightly as she scanned it. He was obviously sending her everything in the State of Victoria that had a sea view, not just those apartments within the metropolitan area. Some of them were as far away as Warrnambool, while others were over on Western Port Bay.

It wasn't until the very last page that one caught her interest. It was an old A-frame house, surrounded by trees and close to the top of a hill, so that it overlooked the bay.

Kingston, she thought with a frown. It was a hell of a distance to travel to work every day, even with the recently completed Western Port tollway. Still, she had nearly a whole day ahead of her and nothing to lose by looking. Leaning sideways, she grabbed the phone and quickly dialed the real-estate agent's number.

"YOU COULD FIT SIX TO eight villa units on a block this size, easy. It's a great investment for the future."

Sam ignored the agent's ramblings and stared out the ceiling-high windows. Though listed as a part of Kingston, the house was actually several kilometers outside the resort township. Built on the side of a steep hill, the house had an almost unhindered view of Western Port Bay. Just across the dirt road, the cliffs plunged toward the ocean. With the wind blowing hard, as it was today, the waves reared high, as if trying to escape the bay's grasp, and foam sizzled across the black rocks lining the cliff top. The bay looked stormy—dangerous—and yet it called to something deep within her. At night, she could lie in bed and watch the sea. Watch all the brightly lit tankers glide by or the storms roll in.

She opened the sliding door and walked out onto the deck. The wind carried the rich tang of the ocean, and gum trees tossed and shivered. She leaned on the railing and looked at the ground.

The whole place was a run-down mess. Half the fence line had either fallen over or was in the process of doing so. The garden had long since turned to weeds, and the driveway had ruts deep enough to lose a football in. The house itself was in little better shape. The kitchen was decorated in orange and green, and it didn't even have an autocook. Appar-

ently, the old couple who'd owned the house had preferred to do their own cooking and had installed an
old-fashioned stove. Most of the walls were in desperate need of paint, the carpet covering the stairs
leading to the upper floor was threadbare and the
banister wobbled worse than a drunk after a ten-hour
binge. Sections of both this deck and the one on the
side above the garage were half-rotten and would
need replacing.

It would cost a fortune to fix it up—a fortune she
didn't really have. The money she'd gotten from the
sale of her apartment would pay for this outright and
leave enough to buy a car. But that was it. There'd be
nothing left for repairs. It would be madness to even
consider buying it.

She raised her gaze and stared at the sea for several
minutes, watching the foamy fingers of ocean creep
across the damp black rocks. She felt the power of the
waves shiver through her until her entire body seemed
to tingle with its energy.

Common sense could go hang. There was something about the run-down, out-of-date old house that
she just loved. And there was something about the
raw closeness of the ocean that she needed.

She walked back into the bedroom. "I'll take it."

The agent's face lit up—no doubt from the prospect
of finally having her off his client list.

"I'll just run downstairs and get my com-unit. We'll
get all the paperwork signed now, if you like."

He disappeared in a cloud of dust, probably afraid
that she'd change her mind. Smiling slightly, she
turned back to the window with its amazing view.

And noted the white Toyota parked down the road.
Under normal circumstances, she might not have

taken notice. But the road was private and clearly marked as such, and it didn't lead anywhere beyond the last house. The real-estate agent had already told her that the owners of the other nine properties were summer residents.

It might simply be someone enjoying the view, or it might be someone casing his next hit.

The question was, would the car remain here at the property, or would it follow her when she left? She'd just have to wait and see. Then she would know if this was a job for the SIU or just the local police.

Having made her decision, she turned and walked downstairs. The agent bustled back inside and motioned her toward the dilapidated kitchen counter. She'd contacted her solicitor earlier, getting him to do a quick check on the property. Everything was legit. Still, just to be safe, she scanned the countless forms with her wristcom and sent them on, refusing to sign anything until he'd given the all clear. Only then did she key in her bank details and transfer the funds. The house was hers.

"It'll take a day or so for this paperwork to go through and be fully registered," the agent said, holding out the keys. "I'll pass everything on to your solicitor to be double-checked, of course."

She took the keys, an odd feeling of elation bubbling through her. "Thanks."

He nodded. "You going to hang around for a while?"

She glanced at her watch and regretfully shook her head. "I can't. I'm working tonight."

He nodded again and held out his hand. "It's been a pleasure doing business with you."

The relief in his voice made her grin. "They make you say that, don't they?"

His startled smile showed a hint of true warmth. "First lesson," he said cheerfully.

She checked the doors, ensuring everything was locked, then followed him out. At her rental car, she stopped and breathed in the heady aroma of eucalyptus and the salty hint of sea. Excitement pulsed through her. The scent of *home*. God, how she wished she didn't have to go back to the city and Wetherton.

Before the call to stay overwhelmed her common sense, she climbed into the car and headed back to the city. She hadn't yet reached the tollway when she spotted the Toyota again.

Okay, so it wasn't a thief and it wasn't a tourist. It was someone *tailing* her. That meant the SIU. She watched the car in the rearview mirror for several minutes, then tapped her wristcom.

"Christine," she said, when the SIU's electronic receptionist came online, "Agent Ryan here. Patch me through to someone in operations."

"One moment, please."

The screen flickered and a thin-looking black man replaced Christine. "Agent Donner here. What can I do for you, Agent Ryan?"

"I think I've picked up a tail. Four cars back from my current location. White Toyota."

"Hang on while I do a trace."

He turned away and she glanced at the rearview mirror. Whoever was driving the Toyota was damn good. She could barely see the driver behind the green four-wheel drive.

"Okay, got you. Fourth car back, you said?"

"Yep. I'd like a license plate and registration search done, if possible."

"I've gotta zoom in the satellite. That could take a few minutes."

"I'll wait."

Donner whistled tunelessly for a good five minutes, then gave a satisfied grunt. "Got him. Or her, as the case may be."

"Who's the registered owner?"

"One Jessie McMahon, from Eltham."

Sam swore softly. Jessie McMahon. Gabriel's sister. The bastard was having her followed.

FIVE

"YOU WANT ME TO ARRANGE an intercept?" Agent Donner asked.

Sam flexed her fingers in an effort to relax her grip on the steering wheel. "No, I think I'll handle it. Thanks, Donner."

He nodded. "Give me a call if you need help."

"Thanks. I will." She flicked off the wristcom and stared at the white Toyota through the rearview mirror.

Why was Gabriel having her tailed? And why have his sister do it when he practically had the entire SIU at his beck and call?

She doubted that he'd provide any answers if she confronted him, but Jessie might. The few times she'd met his sister, she'd seemed more upfront, more accessible, than her brother.

A green-and-gold sign came into view, indicating there was a side road half a kilometer ahead, on her left. *Perfect.*

She leaned forward, switched the computer from auto-drive to manual and moved into the left-hand lane. Leaving the indicator on, she slowed and glanced in the rearview mirror. The Toyota had also switched lanes and was sitting behind a red Commodore.

Sam turned left. Not far ahead, the road did a sharp turn right and disappeared behind some trees. She put her foot down, accelerating around the corner. Once around it, she braked hard, the car shuddering as the tires struggled for purchase on the dirt road. As dust puffed around the car, she threw open the door and climbed out. A quick glance confirmed that the beginning of the road was hidden by the trees. Jessie wouldn't know Sam had stopped until she rounded the corner, though she'd left plenty of room for the Toyota to stop. She wanted to question Jessie, not hurt her.

Sam walked across the road to the gum trees and waited. Two minutes later the Toyota came around the corner, making an unintentional beeline straight for her car. She had a brief glimpse of Jessie's surprised expression. Then Jessie braked and the Toyota slewed to a stop. Sam hurried over and opened the door.

"You okay?"

"Yeah. Just chagrined." Jessie glanced up, a wry smile touching her lips. "Gabriel's going to kill me for being caught."

"If he's still alive after I get through with him." Sam hesitated, trying to control the swift jab of anger. "You want to explain why he's got you tailing me?"

Jessie ran a hand through her dark curls. "There's a roadside diner about a kilometer up the road. Why don't we talk there? I need some coffee anyway."

"I'll follow you there."

Sam slammed the door shut, walked over to the Ford and climbed in. After starting up the car, she followed Jessie back onto the main road.

Once they reached the diner and had their order taken by the gum-chewing waitress, Sam crossed her arms on the table and leaned forward. "So, why is your brother having me tailed?"

Jessie sighed. "He's worried about your safety."

"Yeah, so worried he wanted me dumped as a partner." Sam snorted softly. "Be honest, at least."

"I am." Jessie hesitated, her gaze suddenly intent. "And you know why he didn't want you as a partner, don't you?"

"He thinks he's jinxed."

Jessie nodded. "His standard excuse for wanting to work alone."

Sam raised an eyebrow. "Do I detect a hint of sarcasm in that statement?"

"More than a hint." Jessie hesitated, glancing up with a smile as the waitress placed their coffee on the table. "Personally, I think he was desperate to get rid of you simply because you forced him to *feel*."

"Well, if I had that effect on him, I sure as hell couldn't tell it." He'd shown more emotion with Sandy, in the brief ten minutes she'd seen them together, than he ever had with her over the nine months they'd been partners.

Jessie's smile was a touch wry. "Gabriel's become very adept at controlling his emotions. But I think the fact that he's gone against Stephan's direct orders here proves he does indeed care."

"Or it could simply mean he wants to ensure my safety until you've all discovered just how useful I might be to the Federation, his first and greatest love."

"The Federation is not his greatest love. It's Stephan's." Jessie tilted her head. There was a sharpness in her green eyes that made Sam uncomfortable. It almost felt like this woman was capable of seeing far more than most. "How do you feel about Gabriel?"

"He pisses me off more than any man I have ever known."

"You're not alone there." Amusement ran through her voice. "But other than that, I mean."

Sam raised her eyebrows. "Why do you want to know? And what does it matter anyway?"

"I want to know because I'm a busybody with the best interests of my brother at heart. And it matters because I think he's acting like a goddamn fool."

"Because he's having me followed?"

"No, because he's ignoring the blindingly obvious."

"Which is?"

Jessie smiled. "Answer the question first."

Sam sighed. "Okay, I'm attracted to him. Whether it's just a physical thing, or whether it could be more, I'll probably never find out."

"Why not? There's no law stating a woman can't ask a man out. In fact, in this day and age, a woman is a fool if she doesn't go after what she wants."

"I asked him out for coffee and he refused. I dressed sexily and he didn't bat an eyelid. If he's attracted, he obviously has no intention of acting on it."

Jessie chuckled softly. "Yeah, well, it's going to take a little more effort than that to land this particular fish."

Sam picked up her coffee, blowing lightly on the steaming liquid as she studied Jessie over the rim. "And what makes you so sure that I want to land him? That's his choice. It's his life."

"In our family, no one flies solo." Jessie smiled, but Sam had a feeling she was deadly serious. That it was a statement of fact and, perhaps, a warning. "And believe me, he is worth landing under all that prickly armor. But if you want him, you must take the lead. Be the hunter, even if it isn't in your nature."

"Are you telling me to go after your brother?"

"Yes. Until you nail him." Jessie grinned. "And whether that be sexually, emotionally or both, I don't care."

"Why?"

"Because he is going to end up a very lonely and bitter old man if someone doesn't crack his reserve, and I don't want to see that happen." Her grin grew. "Besides, he's crazy about you, even if he's not willing to admit it, even to himself."

Something Sam found *very* hard to believe. "So, why me, specifically? Especially when he apparently has a sexual relationship with another agent?"

Jessie waved a hand. "That's just a mutual relieving of tension. You're the first person in a long time that he has shown any sort of emotion toward. Therefore, you're the logical choice."

"I can't believe you're discussing something as intimate as your brother's love life with someone you don't even know!" And actually, she couldn't believe *she* was doing the same. But there was something very comforting *and* comfortable about this woman's presence.

"Ah, but I do know you. And we are going to be very good friends."

Sam raised her eyebrows. "So, basically, you're the crazy one in the family?"

"No. The clairvoyant. The future is my playground."

"I'm betting it isn't always a pleasant one."

Jessie's bright eyes briefly shadowed. "No."

Sam sipped her coffee. Then, in an effort to get onto a safer topic, she said, "So, Gabriel's actually having me tailed because . . . ?"

"Because he believes Hopeworth is after you."

If last night was any indication, they were. And they didn't particularly care if they found her dead or alive. Goose bumps skated beneath the small hairs along her arms.

"What makes him think that?"

Jessie shrugged. "I don't think he's got anything substantial. It's just a feeling."

And feelings were often more reliable than hard evidence—she'd learned that during her years as a cop. "And as the clairvoyant, what are your feelings?"

"That he could be right."

"Then he should have talked to me, not arranged this all behind my back."

"Would you have allowed him to arrange it?"

"No."

"Which is probably why he didn't bother asking."

True enough. Sam smiled wryly and glanced at her watch. If she didn't get moving soon, she'd be horribly late for her appointment with O'Hearn. She sipped more of her coffee and said, "If I admit that

I'm on to you, he'll simply replace you with someone I don't know, right?"

Jessie smiled, tucking several dark curls behind her ear. "Very likely."

"Who else has he coerced into this?"

"My husband, Alain."

Sam raised her eyebrows. "Just the three of you? Doesn't he intend to sleep?"

"Obviously not. As I said, you mean more to him than he's willing to admit."

She'd try to remember that the next time he was giving her hell over something stupid. "Next time you're on watch, why not give me a call? If I'm off-duty, we might as well be bored together."

Jessie nodded. "Are you going to tell him you know?"

"Maybe. Maybe not." If Gabriel had the feeling Hopeworth was after her, she wasn't about to refuse any protection he offered, however covertly. And yet all roads seemed to be leading to that place, and if she wanted answers, then maybe her only real choice was, in the end, to allow herself to be taken by Hopeworth. It wasn't something she wanted to even contemplate, but it was nevertheless a reality.

"Good." Jessie paused, green eyes suddenly intense. "Give me your hand."

Sam frowned and didn't move. "Why?"

"Because I have an urge to do a reading." She arched a dark eyebrow. "It doesn't hurt—unless, of course, you're afraid of what I might find."

Which, of course, Sam was. What rational person wouldn't be? God, she had no past to speak of. Why on earth would she take the chance on knowing that there was no future, either?

How depressing would *that* be?

Though if she knew the future, then maybe she could change it. Surely such things weren't set in concrete but fluid, shifting according to the decisions she made?

She gulped down more coffee, then, after a slight hesitation, held out her hand. Jessie's fingers wrapped around hers, her touch warm.

Almost too warm.

Sam resisted the temptation to pull away and watched the other woman carefully. Though she'd often seen clairvoyants work the Brighton market near her old apartment, she'd never been tempted to get a reading done herself.

Jessie's face lost its animation, and her eyes were suddenly distant. "Do not trust the dream man. He tells no lies and yet speaks no truths."

Dream man? Did she mean Joshua, or Joe? Both haunted her nights and her thoughts. But Sam held the question back, knowing that if she spoke, she might break Jessie's concentration.

"Do not fight the storm bond. It will save you when nothing else can."

Again, a statement that only raised more questions. Jessie knew about her ability to siphon the power of the storms; she'd been at the warehouse when the storm's energy had helped her defeat Orrin and Rose, and save Gabriel's life. And yet, she had an odd feeling it was not *that* storm bond that Jessie was referring to.

"When Hopeworth tests, remember the dreams. Channel, as you did back then."

Not *if*, but *when*. Gabriel's feeling about Hopeworth would obviously reach fruition, and trepidation danced a chill across her skin.

"Watch the man with the dead gray eyes. He is more than his makers believe. He beds the devil and walks the path of treason. He is our enemy, but not yours."

And yet he'd seemed very much her enemy in all of her dreams. So who was right? The dreams, or Jessie's sight?

Jessie suddenly shuddered, and she squeezed Sam's fingers lightly before releasing them.

"Not what I'd expected, to say the least," Jessie said, wiping a hand across her brow.

Sam smiled at the wry edge in her voice. "You were trying to get a reading on me and Gabriel, weren't you?"

"Yes." Worry clouded the amusement in her eyes. "My visions merely show a possible outcome. They don't always come true, you know. Life has a way of taking its own path."

But Sam had a bad feeling that this was one set of visions that would come true.

"Then I'll try not to panic just yet." Sam glanced at her watch again. "Look, I really have to go, or I'll be late for my appointment with O'Hearn."

Jessie smiled again. "At least if I lose you on the way back, I'll know where you're going."

Sam grabbed the bill and stood up. "You won't tell Gabriel about the house, will you?"

Jessie raised her eyebrows. "Did you buy it?"

"Yes." And no doubt he'd tell her she was a fool to spend so much money on a run-down pile on the edge of nowhere.

"I won't if you don't want me to. But be warned: Gabriel's almost as adept as Stephan when it comes to sniffing out secrets."

"He doesn't see me enough to know whether or not I'm keeping secrets." He barely saw her enough to say hello.

"That will change, believe me."

"Oh yeah? Saw that in your visions, did you?"

Jessie's sudden smile was almost blinding. "No, just a sister's instinct. You'd better get moving. My next shift to watch you is Monday. I'll give you a call then, okay?"

Sam nodded. As she paid the bill and headed for her car, she couldn't help feeling oddly buoyed. Maybe she'd not only gained a house today, but the beginnings of a lasting friendship.

GABRIEL DRUMMED HIS FINGERS AGAINST the steering wheel. If the traffic didn't start moving soon, he was going to abandon the car right here and take to the sky. It was four forty already. Twenty minutes to get through the center of the city to O'Hearn's office was cutting it fine.

Why the doctor had decided to move her practice out to Southbank was beyond him. It wasn't as if she'd gained any space, and he knew for a fact that the rent wasn't any cheaper because the Federation was still picking up half the bill.

Of course, he *should* have left the archives earlier. But if he had, he wouldn't have found the journal. It had been written by a Vietnam vet back in the mid-twentieth century, at a time when the human race was still in semi-denial about the existence of "nonhuman" races. Amongst its catalog of death and destruction, there was a brief description of a man who had walked from the shadows and saved the soldier's life.

From the brief description given, it might have been easy to think the soldier had encountered a vampire, except for two facts: it happened at midday, and the stranger had walked into the flames surrounding the soldier and consumed them.

Vampires might not be killed by fire, but they certainly *were* killed by sunlight. Particularly midday sunlight.

So was the journal nothing more than the ramblings of a crazy man? Maybe. But Gabriel had heard more than once that walkers *had* been used in the Race Wars. The fact that he could find no hard evidence of it didn't mean it wasn't true. And if the government had used them in those wars, then why not in earlier wars? Or later wars?

And what did the ability to consume fire say about the walkers? Firestarters were one thing, but fire-eaters?

The sharp ring of the wristcom broke the silence and made him jump slightly. Which, he thought irritably, was just plain stupid. He pressed the receive button.

Illie's cheery features came online. "Hey boss, how's the day off going?"

"Great." He'd choose a day spent hunched over a com-screen over several hours of hot sex anytime . . . *not*. Still, he could hardly complain when the decision had been his own. "What do you want, Illie?"

"I ran a background check on Kathryn Douglass. There was nothing out of the ordinary, though it struck me as odd that a woman with her salary has so damn little in the bank."

"How little is little?"

"Just over fifty thou. Not much, when you consider what she makes in a year, which is over a million, if we include bonuses and perks."

Gabriel frowned. "What about other assets? Stocks and such?"

"According to her broker, she's been selling steadily over the past year, though always at huge profits. The money's obviously going somewhere other than the bank."

"Boyfriend? Husband?"

"Currently, neither. Several of each in the past, but no alimony is being paid."

So what the hell was she doing with all her money? "I'll put a request through for her full banking records. Did you get her home security tapes?"

"Yeah, and she had one visitor last week who was not on the list of known associates—a bloke by the name of Les Mohern. A small-time criminal—petty theft, arson, that sort of stuff."

"So why is he associating with the likes of Douglass?"

"A question I thought I'd ask when I caught up with him."

"Good. Have you had any luck with the security guards who were on duty last night?"

"I've contacted one so far. He wouldn't let us see him till tomorrow."

Until after he'd been briefed, perhaps? "What time?"

"Nine."

Great. As if he needed an early start after standing

watch all damn night. "Have our labs gotten back with the autopsy reports on those scientists?"

"Not as yet."

"Follow that up this afternoon, then, and I'll see you tomorrow."

Illie's grin was almost cheesy. "You sure will, boss."

Gabriel punched the off button and stared at the traffic ahead. Les Mohern? He'd heard that name before. But where?

"Computer on," he said.

"ID required," the metallic voice intoned.

"AD Stern. Badge number 5019."

"Voice patterns correct. Please proceed."

"I want a search done on Les Mohern. All details, including immediate family."

"Search proceeding."

He glanced at his watch, then resumed his steering-wheel tapping. He was going to be late, no doubt about it.

"Details onscreen," the computer intoned after several minutes.

He studied the rap sheet. As Illie had said, Mohern had a long history of minor crimes. But it wasn't *him*, specifically, that he'd remembered, but his brother Frank. Like Les, Frank was a small-time crim, but he'd also been listed as a source for Jack Kazdan, Sam's former partner.

That's where he'd seen the name before. Sam had purloined Jack's phone records and diary the day she'd been suspended from State under the suspicion of murdering him. Of course, it had been a clone she'd killed—a clone sent to test her—and it had been deemed self-defense in the end. Yet Jack had still ended up dead at her hands—killed in the process of trying to kidnap the Prime Minister and replace him with a clone.

Frank Mohern was one of two phone calls Jack had made just before he'd disappeared, but now he, too, was dead—he'd been killed in a drive-by shooting, according to the report.

But why would someone like Les visit someone like Kathryn Douglass? Hell, she was more likely to be his target than his friend or even business associate.

He'd have to have a closer look at both the diary and the transcripts to find out not only why the Mohern brothers had been involved with Kazdan, but why Les might be involved with Douglass. He had an itchy feeling it just might provide some much needed clues as to what Douglass was *really* involved with at the Pegasus Foundation.

As O'Hearn's green-glass office building came into sight, Gabriel took the car off auto-drive, sped into a side street and parked illegally. Then he flipped his ID onto the dash, just to ensure the car wasn't towed away, and ran the rest of the way to O'Hearn's office.

Karl was already seated on one of the waiting-room sofas when Gabriel arrived, his bearlike frame dwarfing the seat. His blue Hawaiian shirt and the red-and-gold bandana restraining his brown hair looked totally out of place in the muted, soothing colors of the waiting room.

Sam wasn't in the room, but Finley, the SIU's resident research doctor, was.

"I didn't realize you were involved in this, Finley," Gabriel said as he sat next to Karl.

"O'Hearn called me in." The young doctor pushed his thick glasses up the bridge of his nose. "She thought I might be able to sort out some of the test results."

"And did you?"

"Some." Finley cleared his throat. "Karl here proved of more use than me."

Gabriel raised an eyebrow and glanced at his friend, but Karl merely smiled and patted Gabriel's knee.

"Wait until your partner comes; then I will explain all."

"You'd better." Gabriel stretched out his legs. "And she's not my partner anymore."

"More the fool you, then," Karl said. And when Gabriel glanced at him, he grinned and added, "Well, she's pretty and she's single, and you haven't exactly got a social life."

A mix of amusement and annoyance ran through him. He got this sort of lecture from his brother, his mom and his sister. He didn't need it from his friends as well. "And this is important to you because?"

"Because you're my friend, and I care about your emotional well-being."

"I'd almost believe that if it weren't for the insincerity in your voice."

Karl chuckled. "Well, let's just say that a man your age needs a good woman to look after him."

Gabriel raised his eyebrows. "A man my age? You make it sound like I'm old."

"Well, you *are* rolling rapidly toward the big four-o . . ."

"Which is barely a baby in shapechanger terms, and you know it."

"I know it, but *you* try explaining it to my good wife."

Gabriel groaned. "Don't tell me she's plotting another matchmaking session?"

"Well, it seems she has this second cousin who
would be perfect—"

"Tell her I have a girlfriend I'm perfectly happy
with."

Karl raised his eyebrows. "Really? You with a girlfriend? I'm just not seeing that."

"Depends on how you define the term 'girlfriend.'"

"Ah. A bed buddy." Karl nodded. "Not as good as
the real thing, but a suitable decoy for determined
matchmakers. She won't be put off for long, though.
You know that, don't you?"

Gabriel opened his mouth to reply, but it was lost
to a sudden buzz of awareness. Though perhaps *buzz*
was the wrong word to use—it was more a flash fire
that ran across his senses and then slid deep inside,
seeming to warm his very soul. He glanced at the
door as it opened and Sam stepped in, nodding a
brief acknowledgment Finley's way before her gaze
met his.

The awareness that burned his mind was more
than one-way now. He could see the flame of it in her
eyes.

She stopped in the doorway and said, "What the
hell are *you* doing here?"

He shrugged. "Karl asked me to come."

Her angry gaze switched to Karl. "Why?"

"Because you both need to hear what I have to
say." Karl hesitated. "And I don't think either of you
are going to like it."

Gabriel met Karl's eyes again and saw the compassion mingled with excitement in their brown depths.

Something clenched in his gut. Whatever Karl had to say, it boded no good for *his* future.

"Fine, but that doesn't mean he comes into that room with me." She thrust a finger in the direction of O'Hearn's office. "My business is *not* his business."

"I'm afraid," Karl said heavily, "that in this case, it is."

Karl's comment left her looking more disgruntled than before, if that were possible.

Not that Gabriel could really blame her. Hell, the last few months hadn't exactly been easy for her, and here he was, the creator of many of those problems, sitting in on her medical briefing.

It was a wonder she wasn't ranting and raving about the injustice of it all. He would be, in her place.

Then the door to the office opened and O'Hearn's matronly figure appeared. "Is everyone here? Good. Why don't you all come in and get yourselves something to drink?"

Sam walked straight to the autobar and ordered a double scotch. Gabriel did likewise. She raised her glass in a brief salute, then downed half its contents before sitting on the chair nearest the window. Her hair gleamed like fire against the darkness gathering outside, but the rest of her seemed cloaked in shadows.

He sat on a chair opposite her—not that he really needed to see her reaction to anything said here this evening; he could feel it all. The link that had sprung to life the minute she walked in the door had become a freeway of emotion. If it weren't for the fact that he was so used to blocking his brother, the assault might have overloaded him.

Karl and Finley helped themselves to coffee and sat

down to either side of him. O'Hearn leaned against the edge of her desk.

"Okay, I'll start this off," O'Hearn said. "I've managed to isolate coding sequences from four different races—shifter, changer, vampire and were. But there was one I couldn't identify. I called in Finley, but he's been unable to define the sequences either. Then there was the problem of the unknown chromosome."

"How can there be an extra chromosome?" Sam asked, her voice terse. "From what I understand of genetics, humans have forty-six chromosomes, and they work in pairs. So how can there be just one unknown chromosome?"

O'Hearn raised an eyebrow, as if surprised by the question. "Humans do have forty-six. Vampires who were once human have forty-eight. Shifters have fifty, changers and weres fifty-two. If any of those becomes a vamp, then they gain an extra pair of chromosomes. You, my dear, have fifty-five."

"Meaning what?" Sam crossed her arms. The gray ring around the blue of her eyes gleamed ice-bright in the fading light. "You said you detected partial shifter coding, but even with the extra chromosome that still only gives me a max of fifty-three."

Finley cleared his throat. "The two extra come from the vamp coding we found."

Gabriel frowned. "I thought you had to undergo the change to gain the extra chromosomes."

"So did I." O'Hearn's voice was dry.

"Normally, yes," Finley said. "But in recent government tests, vamp chromosomes have been successfully introduced into both pig and rat embryos."

Sam's face echoed the horror Gabriel felt. Govern-

ment meddling with the very beginnings of life could
never be a good thing.

"What the hell is the government doing that for?"

Finley shrugged. "Vampires have what humanity
has long searched for—life everlasting."

Sam snorted. "Yeah, but at what cost?"

"To some, the cost doesn't matter." Finley hesitated,
frowning slightly. "Anyway, while we were trying to
decode the unknown strands, I remembered my father
once saying he worked with a man who could melt
into shadows. Handy, when you were a member of
covert operations. At the time, I thought my father
meant a vampire, but since AD Stern here questioned
me about the existence of shadow walkers, I began to
wonder."

"So you questioned him?" Gabriel interrupted
tersely. Finley had a tendency to ramble if left un-
checked.

The young doctor nodded. "He confirmed the man
was a walker. One of six the Australian military had
on the payroll."

If they were on the payroll, why was there no record of them now? "What happened to them?"

Finley shrugged. "Dad wasn't sure. It seemed they
disappeared after the Race Wars."

Sent to Hopeworth, perhaps? It was certainly a
possibility—especially if Sam proved to have walker
blood in her.

"Could he point you to anyone who might know
more?"

"He did—to two men, actually. Robin Deleware
and Frank Lloyd. Deleware died some three years
ago, and Lloyd—"

"—is a general stationed at Hopeworth," Sam muttered. Her gaze met Gabriel's. "That man keeps reappearing."

And the reason behind Lloyd's interest in Sam was becoming clearer. "Lloyd's not likely to help us."

"No," Finley agreed, "but Deleware still might. It appears he was Karl's uncle."

"On my mother's side," Karl explained with a grin. "I inherited all his books when he died, you see. Among them were his journals."

Gabriel raised an eyebrow. "I thought personal journals were banned in covert operations?"

Karl's grin widened. "Rules are made to be broken, as you should know."

Ignoring the jibe, Gabriel asked, "So what did the books reveal?"

"The answers, at least to some extent. It appears that both Lloyd and my uncle were involved in the research side of operations. Walkers are mentioned extensively in three of his journals, and then they disappear abruptly."

Because the walkers themselves disappeared? Or was there a more sinister reason?

Sam shifted slightly on her chair, and her tension was a darkness that crawled through his mind. Her thoughts flashed like fire behind that darkness. He only had to reach out and he could be there, sharing them. But he didn't reach out. He didn't dare. He had a feeling that if he breached them one more time—as he had when he'd used their bond to find her at the condemned hospital—he would never again be able to raise the barriers that had protected him for so long against the psychic bond of his twin, and the more recent one he'd developed with Sam. "What did the journals say?"

"For a start, they noted that the walkers had an extra chromosome, one that resembled an S. While it had no pair, it seemed able to fuse itself onto the X and Y pairings. To what purpose, we have no idea, but it's exactly what we've seen in Samantha."

"All of which means squat to me." She hesitated, drinking the remainder of her scotch in one quick gulp. "Nor does it really tell us what the hell walkers were."

Karl smiled. "I suppose it's hard to get excited if you're not a scientist. From what the journals say, walkers were not, in fact, human—not even in the sense that changers and shifters are human. They are, in fact, an entirely new species rather than a human offshoot."

Other than a slight leeching of color from her face, there was no immediate reaction from Sam. But her shock clubbed at Gabriel's mind, almost numbing in its intensity.

"Not human in what way?" she said, her voice soft and tightly controlled.

"They were elementals—the essence of nature itself. There were apparently four types—sun, earth, wind and water."

"Then a sun elemental could, say, control a fire, or even appear to swallow it?" Gabriel said, remembering the story he'd read in the archives. And a water elemental could control a storm, using the lightning as a weapon, as Sam had done.

Karl nodded. "Each walker was the master of his element. Their ability to disappear into shadows came from the fact that they were more energy beings rather than flesh. Vampires disappear into shadows by exerting psychic pressure on the human sense of sight, making it appear as if the shadows have wrapped around them. A walker merely loses his human shape, reverting to an energy form."

Sam scrubbed a hand across her eyes. "So basically, what you're saying here is that *I'm* not human? That I never was?" She hesitated, swallowing heavily. "How is that even possible? I'm not made of energy, for Christ's sake. I'm flesh and blood."

"Sam, you have human elements in your coding, the same as a changer, a shifter or even a were." O'Hearn's voice was gentle, almost soothing. "But the dominant coding in your DNA seems to be what we presume is walker coding."

"If the walkers were all-powerful, why even bother patching in changer or were coding? It's not as if I can shift or change." Sam ran a hand through her hair, eyes a little wild.

She didn't want to be anything more than human, Gabriel realized. She might want to discover her past, but in many respects she feared it, too. Or, rather, feared discovering just what she might be— and what she could do. And while that fear was totally understandable, if what O'Hearn was suggesting was true—and he had no doubt that it was— then it was more important than ever that they press forward on the quest to discover who had made her, and why.

Because not only was the military now interested in her, but someone far worse also held an interest. Sethanon.

"But you *can* channel the power of the storms," O'Hearn continued softly. "Which suggests, perhaps, that the walker strands *are* dominant."

"Meaning I'm likely to dissolve into darkness at any given minute?"

The silence seemed filled with sudden tension, and Gabriel wondered why.

Finley cleared his throat. "As a matter of fact, you have already begun to fade."

"What the hell are you on, Finley?" Gabriel snapped. Sam was sitting there, as plain as day, despite the darkness that had gathered in the office. He could see the fear in her blue-gray eyes, the whiteness of her knuckles as she clasped her hands in her lap.

O'Hearn and Karl shared a look. Karl waved a hand in Sam's direction. "You can see her?"

Stupid question—wasn't it? "Yeah." He frowned. "You honestly can't?"

"No," Karl said, and glanced at O'Hearn again. "It's as we thought."

"Yes." O'Hearn sighed.

Gabriel took a deep breath to calm a surge of anger. "Would you three kindly explain what the hell is going on?"

"Sorry, my friend, but we just had to be sure." Karl held up a hand as Gabriel opened his mouth to make a retort. "My uncle's journals had one very interesting side note about walkers. They come as a pair. They have to, apparently. If a walker does not have a base—someone to call them back, if you like—there is a huge risk of them becoming lost in the powers they seek to control."

Something cold washed through him. *You are her anchor, her reality,* Jess had warned. "I'm not a walker."

"No," O'Hearn agreed. "But I've talked to your father, and I checked your genetic background. It's highly possible that there is walker blood in your line."

"Meaning what?" The question came out harsh and was, in some ways, inane. He understood the implications clearly enough. He just didn't want to face them.

"Meaning," Karl said softly, "that it's possible that you and Sam are destined to be a pair, and there's not one damn thing either of you can do about it."

SIX

SAM MET GABRIEL'S GAZE. THOUGH there was absolutely no emotion on his face or in his hazel eyes, his horror washed through her mind like lava.

He'd spent half his life fighting a similar bond with his twin, and he was not likely to accept it with her.

Not that *she* wanted to be tied to anyone right now, either. Her social life might suck, but being alone was far better than being forced into the company of a man who didn't want to be there.

Damn it, why was *nothing* ever simple in her life?

Right now, she wasn't sure whether she should laugh or cry or rant at the heavens and fate itself for throwing so many wrenches her way . . .

She glanced back to Karl. "What exactly did your uncle say about the walker pairing?"

Karl sipped his coffee, as if considering the question. Though it was more likely he was considering how to phrase his reply without upsetting anyone, she decided.

"He said it was destiny. That, in much the same manner as a shapechanger, they pair for life. They share thoughts, and to a lesser extent, powers—and even when apart, they know what the other is feeling or doing."

"Two halves of a whole," Gabriel murmured. But he wasn't looking at her, wasn't looking at anyone. His gaze was withdrawn, internal. He was seeing—remembering—things to which none of them were privy.

And yet his words sent a chill through her. Joe had said that exact same thing more than once. And he certainly *hadn't* been referring to Gabriel and her.

"So simply because Gabriel can see me when I fade into shadow, you're presuming he's my . . . what did you call it? Base?"

Karl nodded. "That, plus the fact that you've formed a connection, despite Gabriel's efforts to stop it."

"A connection that is entirely one-sided, I assure you." Which was not exactly true, but, damn it, she couldn't help fighting the finality of Karl's words. Life had thrown some pretty shitty things at her lately, but being stuck with a man who really didn't want her in his life had to be one of the worst.

And it didn't matter a damn just how much she was attracted to him. Being forced together would destroy any chance she had of changing his mind.

"Since your abilities are still in their growth stage, perhaps that is to be expected," O'Hearn said.

But her abilities *weren't* in their growth stage—not if what she was now seeing in the dreams were to be believed. "Or it could be taken as a sign that you are way off course."

"Maybe. But when you add the fact that Gabriel shares your pain when you've been injured, I think it's pretty conclusive." O'Hearn hesitated, her gray gaze eagle sharp. "You might be interested to know that, now that we've noted your fading, you've become solid."

"A subconscious reaction rather than conscious," Finley murmured. "Interesting."

Sam glanced down—not that the lower half of her body looked any different now than it had a few minutes ago, when she'd apparently become one with the darkness. She met O'Hearn's gaze again. "If I do have walker genes that are beginning to assert themselves, then there's another possibility. Base-wise, I mean."

O'Hearn frowned. "What?"

Sam glanced at Gabriel. There was a sudden stillness about him that spoke of . . . not shock, not anger, but a weird mix that was both. Suddenly she wished she'd never spoken. Hell, she didn't even *know* who Joe was. He could be a mortal enemy of everyone in this room. *She* could be, for all she knew. She swallowed to ease the sudden dryness in her throat.

"I mean that I'm in telepathic contact with another man. I have been for months." *Years.* "He seems to know an awful lot about me, and he's said more than once that we're two halves of a whole."

Gabriel didn't move, didn't physically react. But his gaze burned into hers, and his tension washed through her mind. Tension, and something else— something she couldn't define.

"Who is this man?" His voice was soft, as devoid of emotion as his face.

It was a shame she couldn't say the same about the link they seemed to have developed. She rubbed her arms. "I don't know. He tells me his name is Joe

Black, but it's an alias. There's no information on record for a Joe Black matching his description."

"Then you've met him?"

She hesitated. "I had coffee with him. He's a shapechanger. His other form is a crow."

"I see."

She had a horrible feeling that crows had just made his hit list, which made no sense. Surely he should be happy that there was a possibility that he wasn't her base. That there was someone else who might fill that role. He didn't want ties of any kind—not with his twin and certainly not with her.

O'Hearn cleared her throat softly. "You've never mentioned this before."

She shrugged. "I never thought it was important before."

The doctor glanced at Karl. "This puts an interesting spin on things. Did the journals mention anything else about the pairings?"

Karl shook his head. "Regretfully, no. As I said, the mention of the pairing was little more than a side note."

"Well, we certainly need to find out more about Mr. Black."

"Leave that to me," Gabriel said, his voice a monotone.

O'Hearn raised an eyebrow but didn't comment. "I'd also like to perform some tests with you both. See just how strong the connection is between you."

"We also need to perform tests," Finley added, "to define your psychic talents and strengths."

Sam frowned as his words brought back memories of the dream. Memories of being chained to a chair while the flames licked her face and the trauma and anger it had caused. The deaths *she'd* caused as a result.

If the dream was to be believed, that is.

But even if it wasn't, there'd been too many tests in her life already. She really didn't want to do any more. Yet if she wanted answers, what other choice did she have? Still, that didn't mean she had to be an overly willing guinea pig, either.

"That might be difficult, given my current assignment."

Especially since whatever spare time she *did* have she wanted to spend down in Kingston fixing up her house, not hanging around either SIU's or O'Hearn's labs. As much as she wanted to discover who and what she was, she also longed to get on with her life. She'd already been in a holding pattern for far too long. For the first time, she actually had something she was *excited* about.

Besides, what was the point of discovering how strong the connection between her and Gabriel was when he had every intention of fighting it?

"Surely you can spare an hour or so a day." Finley's tone suggested she was a fool if she didn't. But then, he was the scientist, not the lab rat.

"Maybe." She glanced at her watch. She was due to meet Wetherton at his office by six thirty. If she left now, she'd not only make it there with time to spare, but she'd beat the storm brewing outside. And how she knew *that* without even turning around to look was something she didn't want to think about right now. "Look, can we wrap this up soon? I really have to get going."

O'Hearn nodded. "Shall we book you both in for Friday, then? After lunch, perhaps?"

Sam sighed. "Try three. That'll give me time to catch up on sleep after my shift."

The doctor nodded, her gaze on Sam's. Not meeting it, just *looking* at it. Sam raised an eyebrow and said, "What?"

"The blue in your eyes is receding as the night falls. The silver is growing brighter."

"There's a storm gathering outside," Karl commented. "If storms are her element, then that could be an indicator of power."

"Or maybe just a sign that it's easier to see the silver in my eyes at night." And yet, even though her back was to the window, the electricity of the oncoming storm danced across her skin, filling her with power, energy.

And *that* was terrifying.

Sam rose. "Let's continue this Friday, then."

"Gabriel, perhaps you'd better escort—"

She held up her hand, halting Karl before he could finish. "I'm a big girl now. I don't need a nanny."

"But the storm—"

"Is just a storm, like a thousand other storms I've walked through before without harm." Something clunked at her feet, and she looked down to see her phone had somehow fallen out of her pocket. As she reached down to pick it up, she noted the tiny sparks leaping from finger to finger. As if the storm's energy had filled her to overflowing.

She wrapped her hand around the phone, hiding her fingertips in the process. Maybe it was a stupid reaction since she was here to discover answers, but right now, she just wanted out. Wanted time to contemplate everything she'd been told—the worst of which was not the fact that she was something other than human, but rather that she could be eternally tied to a man who—no matter what his sister might think—wanted nothing to do with her.

She straightened and gave the watching scientists a tight smile. "I'll see you all Friday."

"Be careful," Karl said. "If you *are* a walker and the storm is your element, you could find yourself lost in its power without even realizing it was happening."

"The walker gene might appear dominant, Karl, but it is only one part," O'Hearn said. "Don't you think the nonhuman mix might mute its force?"

Karl shrugged. "Until we do more tests, we don't know."

"So, I'll be careful." Sam glanced at Gabriel. He didn't say anything, just looked at her with an annoyed light in his eyes. Yeah, he was *really* pleased with the turn of events—and Jessie, for all her clairvoyance, had to have been mistaken. She turned and walked out the door.

It wasn't until she stood outside the building that she remembered she hadn't asked Finley about the tests on Wetherton's would-be assassin. She half-turned to go back inside, then stopped and took a long, shuddering breath. She couldn't do it. She couldn't face them all again. Not yet. She could ring Finley later, or send him an email or something. Right now, she desperately needed time alone to absorb everything she'd been told.

God, that was *so* not the result she'd been expecting.

It was finally confirmed. She *wasn't* human. She

was something else. Something created in a lab somewhere and brought up in clinical surroundings. But to what end? That was the question she had to seek an answer to, though her last dream was perhaps an indicator. Hopeworth had been playing in the genetic and psychic sandbox for some time, trying to create the perfect soldier, the perfect weapon. And her dreams indicated that she'd begun training to control her abilities at a very young age.

But if her walker genes were the strongest, did that mean she wasn't a product of Hopeworth? Her birth certificate—her *real* one, not the fake one that had been placed into the system the day she'd appeared on the steps of the State Care center for orphaned kids—gave the names of the eight people who were her "parents." None of them were walkers, but shifters and psychics.

So if she was a product of the Penumbra project, as they were all presuming, where in hell did the walker strain come from?

The "real" certificate could be a fake, of course. But she had confirmation of both the project and the people involved from a man and a woman who were at Hopeworth at the time of Penumbra. She even had confirmation, albeit from a woman with memory problems, about her presence there. But that same project had been totally—and perhaps a little conveniently—destroyed by fire, so there were no records available to confirm anything they were told.

The one person who might be able to shed some light on her confusion was the mysterious Joe. Every discussion she'd ever had with him had taken her just a little bit further along her path of remembering. But how much could she really trust him? She knew even less about him than she did about herself.

As she stood there, contemplating whether she should try and contact him, the heavens opened up. Big, fat, heavy drops of rain began to splatter across the pavement, quickly darkening the concrete inches away from her feet. Thunder rumbled, the sound so loud it seemed to rattle the air itself. Two seconds later, lightning split the sky, briefly turning the night as bright as day. The energy of that flash burned across her senses, as warm as the sun and as sharp as glass.

A tremor ran through her, but it wasn't fear. It was something far worse.

Excitement.

Pleasure.

As if part of her soul rejoiced in the storm's energy.

She rubbed her arms and warily stared at the skies. Maybe Karl was right. Maybe she should have an escort to Wetherton's . . .

Damn it, no. She'd been touched by the power of the storms before and had drawn it deep into her body. This storm was no fiercer than the one she'd used to help find Gabriel, and she'd walked away from that with nothing more than a brief bout of shakiness and exhaustion. If it hadn't affected her then, why was she acting like a Nervous Nelly now?

She wasn't sure. Maybe it was just Karl's warning. Or maybe it was the growing sensation—or rather, the expectation—that something was about to happen.

Something that *needed* to happen. Which made no sense at all.

She stared into the storm-locked night for a few

seconds longer, then resolutely dashed out into the thickness of it. The wind tore at her as she ran, making her stagger like a drunkard, and the rain fell so heavily that visibility was almost impossible. Her pants became plastered to her legs in an instant and her shirt clung like a second skin. Only in Melbourne could a day whose weather had started off so nice do a complete one-eighty and become a bitch.

And, of course, the closest parking spot she'd been able to find near O'Hearn's office was a block and a half down the street. Wetherton's office wasn't that much farther beyond that. She might as well run all the way, because by the time she got to her car, she'd be soaked anyway. Besides, she wasn't likely to find parking any closer to Wetherton's office at this hour. There was too much traffic.

She ran down the street, jumping over puddles and barely avoiding the other madly dashing pedestrians. Another flash of lightning lit across the stormy evening, and the power within it skipped across her skin, crackling like slivers of fire between her fingertips. Every breath she took sucked that energy inside her, until it felt as if it were surging through every pore, every fiber. Her whole body seemed more alive than it ever had been before.

It scared her. Terrified her.

And the fact that it felt so *right* made her fear it even more.

Overhead, thunder rumbled again. The power of it echoed through her, a force that filled her to breaking, completing her in a way she couldn't even begin to understand.

Then the lightning hit.

It felt like a gigantic hammer, smashing into her

head, driving through her body, snatching her breath, her strength, even as it knocked her to the pavement. Her knees hit the concrete with a sickening crunch, but she felt no pain, had no awareness of anything going on around her, because everything had become white. It was as if she'd stepped beyond this world into a place of fierce brightness, in which nothing else existed but that light and the power within it—and within her. The air itself burned with the intensity of that light, but not half as much as her skin.

And it felt *good.*

So very good.

Without thinking, she flung her arms wide, accepting the power burning around her, drawing it in even more. Flesh and bone seemed to burn away, until she was nothing more than a creature of energy, a being at one with the storm and the night and the intense heat of the lightning. And it called to her, that energy, wanted her, reaching for her like a lover might welcome a much-missed partner.

She raised her face to the skies she couldn't see, torn by the need to answer that call and the growing knowledge that something was wrong, that this wasn't good, no matter how good it actually felt.

"Samantha!"

The call ran around her—through her mind and past her ears. Yet it wasn't one voice, but two.

Samantha! You must resist. You are not grounded and will be lost. You cannot do this yet.

The internal voice was one she recognized. *Joe.* Always there when she needed help the most.

But the storm called her name, and the thought fled. She closed her eyes and enjoyed the caress of the power as she raised her arms a little more.

No! You cannot *lose yourself to the storm. It would kill us both.*

His fear vibrated through her, briefly stalling the flow of energy swirling around her. But it was a voice, a *real* voice, hard and loud, that shook her more.

"Sam!" Hands appeared through the maelstrom of energy, their flesh almost black compared to the brightness of the lightning-fed power. They grabbed her arm, her hand, and a shock more explosive than the storm ran through her. Suddenly she could feel the chill of the wind, the splatter of rain across her face, the throbbing in her knees and the ache in her mind.

And with that, the energy leapt away and returned to the heavens. The feeling of oneness was gone, the light was gone, and all that was left was weakness. Complete and utter weakness.

She fell forward into arms that were warm and solid and real, and she knew without looking that it was Gabriel. She didn't ask how he was there, or why he was there, and she didn't particularly care. She simply rested in the security of his touch as her body trembled and she gasped for breath.

His grip tightened slightly, as if he'd felt her need for closeness. His warmth began to seep into her, heating her skin, leaching away the last vestiges of energy and making her feel real again, rather than a creature of the storm. She closed her eyes, listening to the steady beat of his heart, feeling her own begin to echo its rhythm.

"Are you all right?" he asked, after a while. His breath caressed warmth across the top of her head and a tremor of desire ran through her.

Not a feeling she needed right now.

She nodded in answer to his question and pulled

back. His grip moved to her shoulders, holding her steady and preventing her from drawing away. His gaze searched hers, the green in those hazel depths glowing like emerald fire, as if the storm had somehow empowered him, too.

"What the hell just happened?" he asked.

She gave a shaky laugh and wiped a hand across her wet face—a useless gesture given the rain. "I now understand what Karl meant with his warning. And he was right."

He raised a hand and gently brushed bedraggled strands of hair from her cheek. She didn't see the point since the wind and the rain just flung them back, but she wasn't about to object, either. His touch was too comforting. Too good.

"Then you called the storm to you?"

She shook her head. "It called me." She hesitated. "It felt so right, so pleasurable, like I was coming home. It would have been very easy to get lost in that feeling, as Karl warned."

Gabriel frowned. "So what brought you back?"

"You did." She paused. "And Joe."

She'd half-expected her answer to annoy or anger him, but he merely raised his eyes. "Both of us?"

"Yes. Joe contacted me, briefly halting the call of the storm. And then you touched me, loosening the storm's grip and bringing me back."

He studied her for a moment, then said, "That would suggest that this mysterious Joe and I might both play a part in being your base. And yet, according to Karl, a walker has only one base."

She blew out a breath, her gaze searching his. "You know, I thought you'd be pissed off about that— about being my base, that is."

"I am, but there's no use raging against something I can do nothing about." He hesitated. "Besides, we still know very little about walkers as a race. Karl's journal may have proven useful so far, but it isn't as in-depth as we need it to be. Even *if* your dominant genes are walker, we'll still be uncovering information as we run through our trials and experiments. And it is by no means certain that I *or* this Joe are your base. Nor is it certain that you actually need one."

If what had just happened was *any* indication, she did. But he knew that as much as she did. "But if it *is* true, you could end up tied to me. And we both know you don't want that."

"I don't *need* that, true." He brushed his thumb down her cheek, lightly touching the corner of her mouth. Another tremor ran through her and, like before, it had nothing to do with the night or the rain or the fact that she was drenched. He half-smiled and added, "But if I have to be stuck with someone, then I guess I could do worse."

"Well, gee," she said dryly, glad the tremor running through her limbs wasn't evident in her voice, "that is such an overwhelmingly sentimental statement that I might just cry."

He chuckled softly and dropped his hand to her shoulder again. "Look, I've been a bastard the last few months, and I will undoubtedly be a bastard again in the future. I don't want a partner, be it you or the idiot they've saddled me with now. I play solo. I *have* to. It's not personal."

"None of which is answering my original concern."

"I know." His touch left her shoulders as he sat back on his heels, and the night suddenly felt colder.

"It's not that I don't want any sort of connection with you—"

"It's just that you're afraid of it," she finished for him.

A wry smile touched his lips. "Not afraid, just wary. The more people in my life that I care about, the more targets I give my enemies."

"That doesn't mean we can't be friends." Nor did it mean he cared about her. Damn it, she wasn't even sure if he was physically attracted. His touch tonight might have been nothing more than concern for a workmate. And she couldn't take his sister's words as gospel, either. After all, most families weren't above a bit of matchmaking if they felt the mix was right.

Not that she had firsthand experience of families and their habits, having never had a family herself. But she'd seen it often enough in her years as a cop, observing from the sidelines.

Gabriel rose to his feet in one smooth, almost elegant, gesture and held out his hand. "I think we'd better get out of this storm."

Which was a neat way of avoiding her question and not committing himself one way or another.

"We're drowned rats anyway, so it doesn't much matter whether we stay here or not." But she grasped his warm fingers and let him help her up.

Pain slithered up her legs as she rose. She glanced down and saw the rents in her pants and the scrapes on her knees. She must have hit the concrete harder than she'd thought. "Oh great. This is going to make such a wonderful first impression on Wetherton."

"As far as first impressions go, you can't get much better than saving the man's ass last night. Even if you weren't supposed to be there."

"If I hadn't been, all of Stephan's carefully laid plans would have been blown to hell." She plucked material from the wound on her left knee. Though the worse of the two, the wound wasn't deep, just nasty looking. "And besides, Wetherton was out cold when his ass was hauled from that car, so I doubt he's even aware of my involvement. Especially since Briggs handled all the follow-up interviews." Mainly because *she'd* been getting raked over the coals by Stephan for shooting their suspect.

"What time were you supposed to be at Wetherton's?" he asked.

She grimaced and glanced at her watch. "I start at six thirty, but I'd like to get there just after six and look around."

"Which leaves just enough time to buy a change of clothes."

"Sounds good. Wetherton doesn't seem the type to be impressed by drowned rats."

He grinned as he took her arm and began guiding her down the street. "Wetherton is the type to be impressed with anything that has breasts and a figure. Even drowned, I think you'd qualify."

She raised an eyebrow and looked up at him. "Have you had a personality transplant or something?"

His grin faded into a grimace. "No, but I saw that lightning hit you, and I guess I'm just relieved to see you're unharmed."

"I bet it hurt admitting that."

"I'm not an ogre, despite what my behavior may have made you believe."

"So you're saying the ogre actually does have feelings?"

"Very occasionally." He gave her a half-smile, but

there was a seriousness in his eyes that suggested his words were more a warning. "It doesn't mean that you—or anyone else—will see the other side all that often. I will never get more than casually involved with someone again."

"Sounds like you're setting yourself up for a very lonely old age, Assistant Director."

"If I make it to old age, I'll worry about it then." He paused. "What can you tell me about this Joe?"

Meaning the subjects of his emotions and his life were officially closed—for now, at least. She shrugged. "He's been around for a while. He mostly used to talk to me in dreams, but lately we've been in contact through direct telepathic thought. He seems to know a lot about my past."

"And have you questioned him about his identity?"

"Of course. He's more than a little cagey." She hesitated. "There is a connection between us, a bond that goes beyond telepathy. I just don't know what that is as yet."

"Could he be another of Hopeworth's rejects?"

She glanced at him. "We're not actually sure that I'm a reject yet."

"No." He paused. "Is he military?"

She remembered the time they'd had coffee. Remembered the way he walked, the military-like alertness. "If he isn't now, I'd say he has been."

"What does he look like?"

"Brown eyes, big build, about your height. Very scruffy and very hairy." She shrugged. "He reminded me somewhat of a bear."

"Could you work up a facial composite? That way, we could search military records and see if we find a match."

"Hopeworth is not likely to allow you to do a search of their personnel—past or present."

He raised a dark eyebrow. "You think he's from Hopeworth?"

"Yeah. Everything else seems to be tied back to that place. I can't see why he wouldn't be."

"If that's the case, he might be a means of keeping an eye on you."

"And yet Hopeworth seemed to have no interest—no idea that I even existed—until I contacted them about the Generation 18 murders."

They reached a department store. As the front doors swished open, he ushered her through. The air in the store was so warm it felt like they'd stepped into a sauna. She resisted the urge to strip off her soaked sweater and dripped water all over their shiny floors as she made her way toward the women's section.

"That could be because all evidence of the Penumbra project was destroyed," he said, watching as she sorted through the racks of clothing.

"Or it could mean that I was never a part of that place and came from somewhere else."

He raised an eyebrow again. "Do you believe that?"

"No." They might not have gotten a whole lot of concrete information about the project or her part in it, but the little they *did* have was convincing enough. Plus, there was now the fact that—according to O'Hearn and all the tests done so far—she wasn't human. And not only wasn't she human, she wasn't a creation of nature, either. Which invariably led to the conclusion that she *had* to be lab-created. And the fact was, there weren't many labs around capable of supporting such a long-term commitment as developing a being—either timewise *or* moneywise.

Only the military. And perhaps other covert government departments they didn't know about.

Her search through the racks eventually turned up suitable pants, a warm sweater, shoes and a hooded, waterproof jacket. Once she'd paid for them, she went into the dressing room, stripped off her soaked clothes and changed. After brushing her hair, she almost felt human again. Although *that* term was apparently relative.

"The drowned rat has vanished," Gabriel noted, his gaze sweeping her as she came back out. "Though I bet Wetherton would have preferred the wet—and therefore see-through—blouse to the bulky sweater."

"If that old lecher comes anywhere near me, I'm going to punch him." Sam gave him the plastic bags of wet clothes to hold while she donned her jacket. Now that she was beginning to warm up, she didn't want to step outside and get drowned again.

"Like that would get the two of you off on the right foot."

"Well, at least he'd know the boundaries."

His smile faded. "Be careful with Wetherton. He might be a Hopeworth plant, or he might be one of Sethanon's, but, either way, he's going to be dangerous."

She zipped her coat, pulled up the hood and grabbed her bags back. "Is that why you've placed a twenty-four-hour watch on me?"

He had the grace to look guilty—but only briefly. "How did you find out?"

She snorted softly. "I've been a cop for more years

than I care to remember. Why on earth would you think I *wouldn't* notice a tail?"

She pushed the door open and stepped back into the storm-held night. The wind seemed even stronger than before, buffeting her sideways until Gabriel touched her arm and steadied her. But unlike before, the power in the storm seemed muted. She could feel it, but it was distant, no more than an electric murmur in the background. Yet one that could sharpen instantly given the slightest provocation.

"I had some very experienced people following you," he said, as the doors swished shut behind them. "I just didn't think you'd spot them so quickly."

"Those experienced people were your sister, her husband and you." She squinted up at him. "Did you actually plan to sleep anytime?"

His hazel eyes met hers, the green-flecked depths showing little in the way of emotion. The caring, sharing version of Gabriel Stern she'd enjoyed for the last few minutes had all but disappeared. This version she knew all too well.

"I'm a changer. We can survive on very few hours of rest," he said.

"Not long-term."

"I was hoping it wasn't going to be long-term."

"Ah." She glanced ahead, noting with a little annoyance that Wetherton's office building was less than half a block away. "And if it was?"

"I would have dealt with the problem when it arose."

Which was not very practical. "What if your solution isn't the best solution?"

He frowned. "What do you mean?"

She hesitated. "It's just a thought that occurred to

me when I was talking to Jessie. All roads are leading
to Hopeworth, so would it not be better—"

"No," he cut in instantly.

"But it may be our only chance to get any sort of
answers. For all we know, Sethanon might be—"

"No!" he cut in again, more forcefully this time.
He took a steadying breath, then said, "It's too damn
dangerous. Heaven only knows what that place would
do to you if they got hold of you. I can't risk it, Sam.
I won't."

He couldn't risk it. Not the SIU, not the Federation.
Him. Surely that was a sign he cared far more than he
was admitting? Or was it simply that he had no intention of losing her until he knew what she was capable
of and how they might use her growing abilities for
the benefit of the SIU and the Federation?

And why did she even care? Hadn't she just made a
resolution to stop centering her life around her work
and her partners?

The trouble was, he'd touched her. Brushed the hair
from her face and run his fingers down her cheek to
her lips. And those two actions had her long-ignored
hormones dancing.

From the very beginning she'd been attracted to
him, and while they might not have shared anything
more intimate than a brief hug, that attraction still
flared up at the slightest provocation. And no matter
how angry she might be with him, it appeared that
the attraction wasn't going away. Ignoring it might
work in the long run, but only if she wasn't seeing
him regularly. As long as he was still in her life, she
was stuck with it.

And since *he* obviously wasn't going to pursue it,

maybe she should just bite the bullet and do as Jessie suggested. Become the hunter.

Could she do it?

She didn't know. She'd never actually pursued *any* man, whether it was for sexual or emotional pleasure. Which wasn't to say she hadn't indulged in either—she had, and had enjoyed herself immensely. But in the past, she'd always allowed men to do the pursuing, and she always knew going in that neither the man nor the relationship—however good or emotional it felt at the time—would last.

Why she'd always been sure of that she couldn't honestly say. Nor could she say why she was so sure that her attraction to Gabriel was more than just the natural attraction of a female to a sexy male.

Maybe it had something to do with the walker gene and the bond that might be between them. Maybe it didn't. Or maybe it was nothing more than wishful thinking on her part. Whatever the reason, perhaps wondering if she *could* pursue him wasn't the right question. Maybe what she *should* be asking was what she actually wanted from him. What did she expect? Just another good time? Just another physically satisfying month or two in her life?

No.

Whatever this thing was between them, it definitely felt bigger. Which in turn meant she was expecting something more than a month or two of mutual pleasure. Something deeper than just caring.

But given his stance against any emotional commitment in his life, wasn't she just setting herself up for heartache? If he could keep his twin—his own flesh and blood—at arm's length, what made her think his connection to her would be any different?

So maybe that was the *real* question she needed to ask herself. Was she ready to face that heartache if it went belly-up? And could she live with it, face being around him day in and day out if he did in fact prove to be her base?

Probably not.

But maybe she had to try, anyway. Because surely it was better to attempt a relationship on her own terms, in her own time, than to be forced into it by genes and fate.

At the very least, if she seriously tried to start something between them that went beyond friendship and duty, she'd know for sure whether Jessie was right about the attraction going both ways. Which was far better than realizing sometime down the road that he was with her only because he had no other choice.

Freedom of choice was important, no matter what fate and the future planned for them both.

"Earth to Sam. Are you still with me?"

She blinked and looked up at him. "What?"

"I've been talking to you for the last few minutes. Did you hear anything I've said?"

"Ummm . . . no. Did you say anything important?"

He rolled his eyes. Amusement touched his lips, yet his concern whipped around her, as chill as the wind, and his grip on her arm tightened a little. "Is the storm calling again?"

"Not really." She shrugged. "I was just thinking about Wetherton and how little I actually want this assignment."

"Then why accept it? You had the choice to refuse, you know."

She stopped and turned to face him. "How could I *not* accept it? At least it got me out of the broom closet and let me do some real police work. You're not the only one who hates being confined indoors, Assistant Director."

He grimaced. "You know why I was doing that—"

"Yeah, because you're an ass who would rather force an unwanted situation to go away than be up-front and talk about it. Cowardice is not a trait I expected from you, but you've been consistently proving me wrong for three months."

Anger flicked through his eyes. "I had no choice in taking you on as a partner. And the only way the situation could have been altered was if you had requested a transfer."

"So why not come out and say that straight off the bat? Between the two of us, I'm sure we could have come up with a strategy that would have changed Stephan's mind. But no, you found it easier just to stick me down in the dungeons and ignore me."

He thrust a hand through his wet hair. "Damn it, I was doing what I thought was right—"

"No, you were doing what was easier for you," she corrected. "You knew it wasn't right, or you wouldn't have apologized for being a bastard. Or didn't you mean your apology?"

"I did—"

"Then prove it."

He raised his eyebrows. "How?"

"Take me out to dinner. To a nice, expensive restaurant."

"And how, exactly, will that prove anything?"

He looked a little confused, which was good, because she had a feeling confusion was a state she'd have to keep him in if she was going to get anywhere with this seduction.

Not that she had a specific plan. Right now, she was just jumping at an opportunity that had presented itself.

"Well, in the brief time I've known you, you haven't exactly been free and easy when it comes to money. And word around the office is that you're a first-class tight-ass—"

"It is?" he asked, his surprise evident in his voice.

"Yes. So, if you go to the trouble of buying me dinner at an expensive—and I do stress the word *expensive*—restaurant, then you're putting your money where your mouth is. And that, in turn, means you really *are* sorry." She couldn't help the smile playing around her lips. "In which case, your apology will be graciously accepted."

"This sounds to me like a sneaky method of getting an expensive meal without having to pay for it."

"Are you saying I don't deserve it? Even after the way you treated me?"

"No, I'm just saying that this will be a one-time apology. Don't be expecting future apologies." He paused. "Or dates."

"I'm not after a *date*, Assistant Director—not now *or* in the future. I don't date men I work with." Which was true, up to a point. She'd certainly never dated Jack, her partner in the State Police, though she *had* dated cops in other divisions over the years. She raised an eyebrow, silently challenging him to answer honestly. "Why would you think I'm after a date? Especially after the way you've treated me for the last few months?"

He didn't take up the challenge. No surprise there. "I have no idea." He motioned her to move on. As she did, he added, "So, dinner at an expensive restaurant. When?"

She shrugged. "I'm on the night shift now, so it'll have to be during the day."

He raised a cynical eyebrow. "Meaning lunch? How about tomorrow, then?"

"Get the ordeal over with as quickly as possible, huh?"

He smiled but didn't deny it. Boy, was she ever going to have some fun attempting to shock this man's starched sensibilities! She might end up in tears, but at least the journey would be interesting. And at least she'd see if Jessie's assessment was correct.

"Give me a call when you finish your shift tonight," he said. "We can make arrangements then."

She glanced ahead and saw that Wetherton's office was only two doors away. *Damn.* She looked back to Gabriel. "Who's watching me tonight?"

He hesitated, then said, "Alain."

"After which?"

"Jessie takes over. Though since we now might be having lunch, I'll probably step in and let her rest."

"You're expecting a bit much of your sister and her husband, aren't you? They have their own lives to live, too."

"No one in my family has their own life. Everything revolves around the Federation."

The edge of bitterness is his voice surprised her, but she didn't question him about it. He wouldn't tell her anything. When it came to family, he was tighter than a clam. "But I'm not involved in this Federation of yours."

Hell, even though she knew the historical facts

about the Federation's origins—that it was formed to protect the political and legal interests of nonhumans after the Race Wars—she had no idea what it truly did these days. The few things he had said about it, however, suggested that not only were they still very much involved in protecting the interests of non-humans, but they were also some kind of undercover, independent spy agency.

His gaze met hers briefly. "No, but who you are, and what you are, might very well affect the Federation and its operations in the future. So, in that respect, you warrant Federation involvement."

"So why hasn't Stephan assigned other—" She paused, remembering what Jessie had told her. The urge to grin was almost overwhelming, but she somehow kept a straight face. Which didn't mean she could resist the temptation to pull his chain a little. "He doesn't know you've assigned me guards, does he?"

"No."

"So, you're having me guarded twenty-four hours a day against your brother's direct orders, but you refuse to admit there might be anything more than professional interest motivating you?"

He glanced at her. "That's about it."

Anger rose so fast she could barely restrain it. He *knew* there was something between them, something that needed to be sorted out. Something that was more than just a fluke of DNA. Why couldn't he give her at least *that* tiny crumb of admission, even if he never intended to pursue it?

"You're so full of shit, Assistant Director, that it's almost scary." Sam stopped as they reached the front of Wetherton's office building. "And you know what?

Call off your guards now, or I'll let Stephan know what you're up to."

Annoyance flashed through his eyes. "But Hopeworth—"

"As I've already said, let them come. I want answers. I want this mess sorted out so I can finally get on with the rest of my life."

"There may not *be* a 'rest of your life' if Hopeworth grabs you!" His anger all but seared her senses. But underneath it, there was also fear. "If they kidnap you, we may not be able to find you, let alone rescue you. The whole Wetherton operation last night went to hell, so it's possible this will, too."

"Your brother isn't a complete fool. I have trackers on me, so they can find me no matter where I'm taken."

"But the danger—"

"Walking across the street during rush hour is dangerous, but I do that every damn day. Back off, Assistant Director. If you wanted to be involved in this operation—and my life—you shouldn't have pushed me away."

"That is beside the point . . ."

"No, it's not. It is precisely the point. I have no desire—and no need—for a babysitter. Especially when that person isn't courageous enough to get over the past and get on with his life." And with that, she turned around and walked into the building.

SEVEN

GABRIEL SWORE TO HIMSELF AS Sam walked away. No one looking at her slender figure right now would guess at the steel and determination hidden within that slight frame.

Or the depth of sheer, damn foolhardiness.

There was a *huge* difference between acting as bait and walking into a situation seriously underprepared. No matter what she or Stephan thought, she *couldn't* handle this sort of job alone. There were just too many angles they could neither guess at nor cover.

As for her last jibe, where the hell did she get off accusing him of cruising through life when she was basically doing the same thing? God, at least he had a family . . .

He stopped the thought. That was hardly fair. And she couldn't exactly be blamed for her reluctance to have backup. She'd been abandoned as a teenager and, for all intents and purposes, had grown into adulthood alone. She'd spent half her life having few friends and depending on no one but herself. It wasn't entirely surprising that she would reject his offer of help now.

What was surprising was the fact that she still wanted to see him socially, even after all he'd done to her.

He blew out a breath, then he spun on his heel and hitched the collar of his jacket up in an attempt to stop the rain from dripping down his neck as he walked across the street. He'd spotted Alain as he'd followed Sam from O'Hearn's office earlier, and the big man had been their distant shadow ever since. He was glad Sam hadn't spotted Alain. Undoubtedly, that would have made the situation worse.

Lightning split the wet darkness—a blinding, ragged streak whose power seemed to echo right through him. He frowned. When he'd stepped out into the storm earlier, he'd felt the energy in the night. It was a sensation similar to walking underneath high-voltage power lines—the crackle of electricity was very audible, and static had caressed his hair and skin. If he *had* been standing under high-voltage lines, and if he *were* stupid enough to climb the pylons, he could have touched all that power, felt it running through him. And died in the process.

The storm had felt like that—power that was both enticing and dangerous. Power he could reach out and touch if he wanted to. Power that would kill him if he tried.

He glanced at his hands. There were no burn marks, despite the fact that he'd shoved them into the middle of the lightning strike. Neither he nor Sam had been hurt, and that in itself was a miracle.

Or maybe it wasn't. Maybe it was just another sign that Karl was right. She'd used the storms before and was certainly no stranger to that sort of power running through her. Maybe touching her had somehow protected him.

Or maybe, as Karl had stated, he and Sam had a bond in which the storms were a major component—one they couldn't yet understand, and maybe never would.

For someone who didn't want bonds of any kind, he seemed to be gaining more than his fair share. And there wasn't much he could do to stop it. Ignoring the bond—and trying to push her away—hadn't worked.

Actually, he pretty much suspected that, despite her words to the contrary, he'd only made her more determined to force the issue.

And he wasn't actually sure how he felt about that.

He didn't *want* bonds of any kind; he'd been telling himself that for half his life. Yet part of him now hungered for it. Hungered for the closeness his brother and sisters had.

Maybe the lightning *had* affected him. Short-circuited a brain wire or two.

He hurried inside the small café where Alain had settled. His brother-in-law sat at a table to the left of the entrance, out of immediate sight but with a full view of the road and Wetherton's building. Gabriel took off his coat and shook it out as he walked over. Droplets of moisture scattered over the nearby chairs and tables, but since the café was almost empty, it didn't really matter.

"I ordered you a coffee," Alain said, sliding one of two steaming cups across the table.

"Thanks." Gabriel slung the coat over the spare chair and sat down. "You saw what happened?"

Alain nodded. "It was pretty damn scary, too." He glanced down, his gaze skimming Gabriel's hands. "You don't appear to be suffering any side effects from the strike. How did Sam fare?"

"Much the same." Gabriel shrugged, not wanting to get into explanations when he really didn't have them. "But we have a bigger problem."

"What?"

Alain picked up his coffee and sipped it, but there was the faintest touch of amusement in his brown eyes. Which, knowing the man as well as he did, suggested to Gabriel that his next comment would come as no surprise. "Sam knows we're following her. She wants you both to stop, or she says she'll call Stephan."

"So what are you planning to do?"

"Nothing. I want you and Jess to keep watching as planned. Except for tomorrow. I'll take over the day shift."

"Will she go through with her threat if she sees us?"

"Most likely, so you need to be careful."

Alain raised a bushy eyebrow. "Stephan will not be happy if he discovers what we've been up to."

"Undoubtedly." Gabriel picked up his coffee and gulped down some of the steaming liquid. "But I don't care."

"So, basically, you're saying the only thing you *do* care about is Sam's safety." Alain paused, a grin stretching his lips. "One could take that as an indication of emotional interest."

"Or professional interest. Especially if she proves to be our link to Sethanon."

Alain put down his cup and crossed his arms. "And

do you believe that she is the link? After all these years of successfully avoiding us, do you seriously think Sethanon will come out of hiding for one woman?"

"Seriously? Yes."

"Why?"

"Because I don't believe he would have placed a watch on her if she was of no use to him."

"True." Alain paused. "But he might have intended to cultivate her, as he had her partner."

"No. Kazdan's orders were to watch her, to keep her safe. That implies interest, not cultivation."

"And yet Kazdan was trying to recruit her."

"For himself, for his own takeover bid. Not for Sethanon."

"You can't be sure of that."

Yes, they could, because that was exactly what Kazdan had told Sam. She believed it, and so did he. Still . . . "We can't be sure of anything until we know for sure who she is and where she came from."

"Is that why you won't admit to feeling anything for her?"

Gabriel snorted softly. "No, I'm not admitting anything because there is nothing to admit." And even if that wasn't the entire truth—even if there *was* destined to be a bond between them—he'd successfully contained the link with his twin and he had every intention of doing the same with Sam. No matter how much a part of him might wish it otherwise.

The truth was, while he couldn't deny his attraction— at least to himself—he would *not* break his vow to never get involved. He wouldn't do that to someone ever again. And if, as Jessie predicted, he became a sad and lonely old man, so what? He could at least rejoice in the fact that he'd actually lived long enough to become sad and lonely. That another human being hadn't been killed simply because he had made her a target.

"So," Alain said thoughtfully, "that look of horror and panic on your face when she was hit by lightning had absolutely no emotional basis whatsoever?"

"None at all." Gabriel couldn't actually remember much about that moment, because when the lightning hit her, it had echoed through him, burning away all thought and emotion. He'd reacted instinctively, without really knowing what he was doing or saying until his hands had touched her.

But before he could actually reply further, his wristcom rang. He breathed a silent prayer of thanks for the timely intervention. No matter how he answered Alain, his brother-in-law would have twisted his words.

He retrieved his phone from his coat pocket and hit the receive button. "Agent Stern."

"Hey, Boss." Illie's usually cheerful expression looked subdued. "We've got a problem."

"Just one? That would be a minor miracle." Gabriel rubbed his eyes wearily. "What's up?"

"You remember Kathryn Douglass?"

"It was only yesterday that we visited the Foundation, Illie. I may be older than you, but I am not senile."

His would-be partner snorted. "Yeah, well, the SIU just received a call from the State boys. It appears Kathryn Douglass has been murdered."

"What?"

"Yeah. It happened last night, at her home. State

called us because there was no entry or exit point. They're saying there's clear nonhuman involvement."

Gabriel glanced at his watch. "I'll meet you there in fifteen minutes. Did you manage to interview Pegasus's security guards?"

"Some, but they weren't able to add anything to what we already know."

"Have you scheduled time with the others?"

"I have. See you in fifteen." And Illie hung up.

Gabriel looked at Alain. "I've been called to a murder scene. Make sure you keep out of Sam's sight."

Alain gave him a grin that held very little humor. "I've been doing this for more years than she's been alive."

"Yeah, but she's a whole lot cleverer than most of our usual targets." Gabriel drained his coffee and stood. "If anything happens, call me immediately."

"Don't worry. I won't let anything happen to your lady."

Gabriel didn't dignify the comment with an answer. He just turned around and headed back out into the weather.

SAM LEANED AGAINST THE ELEVATOR wall and watched the numbers roll by. Wetherton, despite his supposed fear of heights, had moved his office from the third floor to the twenty-fifth floor, claiming a good third of the top floor for his boardroom, office and waiting area. If anyone in the government or press thought this was outrageous—or out of character—they weren't saying anything. Maybe they were just so used to the excesses of government ministers that they simply didn't bother questioning them anymore.

Or maybe Wetherton was simply paying off the right people. It certainly wouldn't be the first time something like that had happened.

The elevator stopped and she walked out. The standard blue carpet in the lobby gave way to a plusher, more luxurious plum once she'd pushed through the doors leading into the minister's suite.

A buxom blonde looked up and gave her a practiced but totally false smile. "Good afternoon. How may I help you?"

Sam dug out her badge and showed it to the woman. "Samantha Ryan, SIU. I have an appointment to see the minister."

"Ah, yes. If you'll just have a seat, I'll let him know that you're here."

The blonde picked up the phone. Sam sat on the nearest pale lemon couch and let her gaze roam. The first thing she noticed was the security camera in the corner to the left of the reception desk. It was pointed at her rather than at the doorway, meaning that someone was probably watching her.

Or maybe *all* visitors were scrutinized this intently. Paranoia surely was uppermost in the life of a clone who was trying to masquerade as the genuine object.

Or did the clone actually *think* he was original?

If, as she and Gabriel had theorized, someone had successfully found a way to transplant a brain, then it was certainly possible—especially if you believed the brain was the center of not only personality and memory, but also the soul. Maybe the real Wetherton *was* inside that clone somewhere.

But if he was, why the abrupt change in personality?

It was certainly a line they needed to explore—particularly since it was obvious that whoever was making these clones had successfully traded one of his creations for an original, and had tried to do the same with the Prime Minister himself. If Sethanon was involved with Hopeworth, as Gabriel and the Federation presumed, then these attempts to replace government ministers weren't going to end here.

Sam let her gaze move on, studying the two other doors leading off this main room. One was a standard door, the other a double set with plusher handles. Wetherton's office, obviously.

But as her gaze rested on those doors, the feeling hit. A wash of heat, followed by the certainty that there was a shifter inside—a shifter whose very essence felt malevolent.

A tremor ran through her—and not so much because of the thick sensation of evil, but because she'd felt this particular brand of filth before.

In her dreams of Joshua and fire.

The man with the gray eyes was in the room with Wetherton.

Her heart accelerated and her stomach began to churn. She licked her lips and tried to get a grip. Damn it, she'd seen Gray Eyes last night, had even interacted with him, and she hadn't felt anything *close* to this.

So why now and not then?

It didn't make sense. Maybe her psychic wiring had been short-circuited by the lightning strike. Or maybe there'd been too much other shit happening last night and she simply hadn't had the time to notice the psychic sensations.

"The minister won't be too long," the blond secretary said into the silence.

Sam jumped, just a little, but managed to fake a smile of thanks. *God,* this was ridiculous. Anyone would think she was a green trainee, not a cop with years of experience. She crossed her legs, tapping her foot impatiently as she waited.

After another five minutes or so, the doors opened and two men walked out, both of them wearing that happy-to-have-met-you smile that was obviously as fake as the secretary's.

Gray Eyes was dressed in military blue that made his silver hair stand out all the more. Just watching him—watching the calm, assured way he moved—sharpened Sam's perception of evil until it felt like her entire body burned with his wrongness. Looking at him was making her physically ill, but she wasn't entirely sure whether it was a result of psychic distaste or a reaction left over from her dreams.

Wetherton stuck his hand out to Gray Eyes and said, "I'll certainly mention your concerns when the matter comes up in Parliament, General Blaine. Thank you for speaking with me today."

General Blaine? It wasn't a name she'd heard before, but then, given the security surrounding the military base and its projects—old or new—that wasn't really surprising.

So was Blaine one of the scientists involved in the Penumbra project, as her dreams seemed to indicate? And if so, how had he escaped the fire that had killed nearly everyone else?

And why was there no sign of a cut or burn marks

on the left side of his blunt features? Last night, when he'd climbed out of the car with the woman, the wound on his head had looked nasty—and if the amount of blood that had been pouring down his face was anything to go by, it had been deep. Wounds like that didn't disappear overnight. Not without a trace, anyway. Shapeshifters and shapechangers *did* have the ability to heal wounds fast, but even they were usually left with scars.

Her gaze flicked to Wetherton. His spudlike face bore several nasty scrapes, and he had an egg-sized lump near his right temple. No anomalies there, at least.

Gray Eyes nodded and shook Wetherton's hand. "I appreciate that, Minister. The military cannot afford to have our funds cut for the third year in a row. Several projects vital for national security could be in jeopardy if they are."

"I'll put your case forward, General. I can't promise more at this time."

Blaine nodded and turned for the exit. Then his gaze met Sam's and he paused. Deep in those gray, soulless depths, she saw surprise. Maybe even shock.

The sort of shock that came when you suddenly and unexpectedly met someone you knew but hadn't seen for a very long time.

Which again didn't make sense, given the events of last night. If he *did* somehow recognize her, if he did know her from the projects, why hadn't he reacted last night?

"Do we know each other?" he asked, eyes narrowing slightly.

Yeah, she wanted to say. *I helped save your ass last night.* But something inside stopped her from utter-

ing the words. Instead, she simply said, "I don't believe so."

He stepped closer and she resisted the urge to sink
back into the sofa. This close, the sensation of his evil
was so strong that her insides felt like they were trying to claw their way out of her body.

"Are you military? Ex-military?"

Energy crawled around her—a sensation wholly
different from the evil of his soul but just as sickening. That pressure seemed to build around her, as
if the energy were trying to crawl into her mind.
Telepathy, she realized. He was trying to read her
thoughts.

And while the fact that she couldn't actually feel
him *in* her mind suggested he wasn't having any immediate luck, she wasn't about to give him the time to
succeed, either.

"No, I've never been in the military, General." She
rose, retrieved her badge from her pocket and flipped
it out for him to see. "Samantha Ryan, SIU. If you
have questions, please ask them. I do not appreciate
your attempts at mind reading."

"Mind reading?" Wetherton said, voice all bluster
despite the quick flick of concern he cast the general's
way. "This office is fully shielded against such intru-
sions, so you must be mistaken, Agent Ryan."

"No," she said, her gaze not leaving Blaine's. "And
shielding is not always one hundred percent effective."

Wetherton's expression didn't give much away, but
she had the distinct feeling, just from the way he was
looking at the general, that the news that the general
could read minds horrified him. Which meant that
maybe Wetherton *did* have secrets he had no wish for

the military to uncover. It also meant that there was a whole lot more going on here than what Stephan and the SIU presumed.

The general's smile was slow and cold. "No, psi shields are never one hundred percent effective. But you are wrong, Agent Ryan. I was not trying to read your thoughts."

So what the hell *had* he been trying to do? She shoved her badge back into her pocket and decided to tackle Blaine head on. "So, General, do you work in the same division as General Frank Lloyd?"

He raised his eyebrows. "You know General Lloyd?"

"Yes. I had a brief conversation with him about some former military employees that were getting murdered."

"Ah, yes, the retired scientists."

"And the retired specimen donors. Don't suppose you know anything more about the projects they were involved in, do you?"

"No. I was never involved in that side of the operation."

"Then what were you involved in?"

"Why do you want to know?" he countered. "You caught and killed the people involved in those murders, correct? So the case is now closed."

"Actually, no, it's not, because one of the murderers is still loose. The kite." It was risky mentioning it, because few people had any idea they existed. The SIU hadn't yet released an all-points about their existence.

"Kite? What the hell is a kite?" Irritation was very evident in Wetherton's voice. He had no idea what was going on, and he didn't like it one bit. But if he was the military's puppet, shouldn't he have had some clue? "Beyond something flown on a string, that is."

Blaine didn't react to the mention of the kite. He didn't do anything more than stare at her in that flat, calculating way. Either he knew about the kite and wasn't about to give her any information or he didn't know anything and wasn't going to admit it.

She ignored the minister and added, "The kite might yet come after you and Lloyd and anyone else involved in those projects. We'd like to prevent that, and would appreciate the military's cooperation."

"The military takes care of its own, Agent Ryan." He tilted his head a little, his gaze intensifying, as if he were trying to see into her head and her memories without actually using his psi skills. Or maybe he was simply recalling the past and juxtaposing his memories of a flame-haired child against the woman who now stood in front of him. Comparing the two and drawing God knows what conclusions. "And my involvement in those projects was in the area of training, as I'm sure you're already aware."

A chill prickled across her skin. His words were an indication that his comparison had drawn the obvious conclusion. But for now, it was one she had to let ride.

"General, getting information out of the military is harder than getting blood out of the proverbial stone. So no, I have no awareness of either your or General Lloyd's position in Hopeworth."

"I would be surprised if that was the truth, Agent Ryan." He glanced at Wetherton. "If you wish to discuss the funding matter any further, please call."

Wetherton nodded, his expression still a mix of

confusion, irritation and concern. And Sam had every intention of finding out why.

Blaine met her gaze again, gave her a remote smile that sent another bout of chills down her spine, then turned and walked out the door.

She didn't relax, and she didn't move. Not until she heard the soft ding of the elevator button and then the electronic hum of machinery as the elevator moved down.

"Would you care to explain what the hell was going on between you and General Blaine, Agent Ryan?"

"I'm afraid that would involve revealing details of an ongoing case, Minister, so no, I can't discuss it."

He grunted, his expression suggesting he was far from happy.

"Well, come into my office and I'll give you my schedule for the next few weeks." Then he spun on his heel and stalked back into the office. She followed him in. It was a huge expanse, filled with the latest chrome-and-glass furniture and plush leather sofas. The minister was a man with expensive tastes, obviously. His office was situated in one corner of the building, so two of the walls were all glass. The view over the city and the bay would have been truly amazing—a vista of fading sunlight, sparkling lights and blue-gray ocean—if not for the rain still sleeting down.

Wetherton stalked over to his desk and picked up a folder. "My schedule. You'll notice I have several important meetings at various restaurants in the evenings. During these events, you will keep an eye on proceedings from a distance."

Which was standard procedure, but she wasn't about to point that out. What it did mean was that she might need to place a bug on Wetherton himself. He obviously had secrets he didn't want her to overhear. She stopped in front of the desk and accepted the folder. "Why was the general here?"

"As you probably heard, he was here to discuss military funding."

"Did he ask anything else? Or mention anything else?"

Wetherton sat down on his plush chair and frowned. "What he and I discussed is really of no importance to you. You're my bodyguard, nothing more."

Despite his arrogant tone, she gave him her politest smile—even if all she wanted to do was smack his dumb ass. But since she'd probably have to work with this man for several months, she knew she'd better play nice. At least for a little while.

"And as your bodyguard, I have the right to question you about certain people. General Blaine was with you last night, and yet he shows no obvious sign of injury. I think that's a little odd, don't you?"

Wetherton's frown deepened. "Not really. All it means is that he wasn't injured in the attack."

She picked up the newspaper lying on his desk and threw it across to him. "So you're telling me that photo—the one that shows blood pouring from a wound on his head as he's carrying you away from the car—is fake?"

Wetherton picked up the paper and studied it. "It might not be his blood."

"Minister, I was there last night. I was one of the two people who helped save your ass. I know for a fact that the general was injured. So, I ask you again, what was the general doing here and what did you talk about?"

"I told you—just the military budget." Wetherton threw down the paper. But despite the calm assurance in his voice, the hint of concern in his eyes was stronger. Which meant that maybe he recognized something *had* happened here this afternoon, even if he didn't know what it was.

And did he not know because his memory had been erased? Blaine had been able to use his powers despite the deadeners, so that was more than likely.

"What time did he arrive this afternoon?"

"He had a five o'clock appointment."

She glanced at her watch. "So, you discussed the military budget for just over an hour?"

"Yes."

"And is that usual?"

Wetherton shrugged. "It all depends."

On what? On how much information the general needed to siphon from him? Why could he not see that something was very wrong? Or could he see it and just wasn't about to admit it to her? And if that was the case, why not admit it when she was the person being paid to protect him?

Nothing about this situation was making any sense—including her two vastly different reactions to a man she could remember seeing in her dreams but not in real life. Until now, that is.

She frowned and tried a slightly different tactic. "Why was Blaine in the car with you last night, anyway? Are you friends?"

Wetherton hesitated. "Not really. But my wife knows his wife, so we occasionally see each other during social events."

"What is his wife's name?"

"Anne Blaine."

"I mean before she married him."

He paused. "I think her surname was Grantham, or something like that. I'd have to ask my wife to be certain."

Sam nodded. "Was his wife in the car last night?"

"No." He hesitated, and she had a sudden feeling that he was searching for the "right" answer. Odd, to say the least—especially since she'd sensed no outright lies so far. Just avoidances. "He said she was ill, but they had the tickets and he didn't want to waste them. He'd come by taxi, so I said we'd take him home. He doesn't live that far from us."

"You mean not far from your wife's house and not your Collins Street apartment?"

"Yes." He paused. "I'm afraid my wife wasn't able to cope with the long hours I worked, nor did she like the constant media attention that came with being the partner of a politician."

And wasn't that a well-rehearsed excuse? "I'm sorry to hear that, Minister." No sense in totally annoying him, as tempting as that might be. "So, getting back to my original question—why was the general here, talking to you about the military budget, when you're the Minister for Science and Technology, not the Minister for Defense?"

"Easy. Certain military research allowances come out of the Science and Technology budget."

"But why? Isn't that why there's a defense portfolio? To assign and control the military budget?"

"It's the *defense* portfolio," he said patiently, as if he'd answered this question a million times. Or as if he were talking to a simple child. "Therefore, it concentrates on defense items. Personnel, big hardware items, small hardware items, et cetera. The research section of the military is lumped in with my portfolio."

Well, there you go; she'd learned something new. "Just one more thing, Minister, and I'll let you get on with your work."

"Good."

"I need to do a sweep of your office, just to make sure there are no bugs or anything."

"I can assure you, this office is swept regularly, and nothing has ever been found."

"I'm sure it hasn't, but it's still part of my job to check."

He muttered under his breath, then stood up. "I can go get a cup of coffee, I suppose." He paused. "And the door will remain open."

"Minister, if I wished to snoop through your paperwork or filing cabinets, I'd simply pick up the phone and get a court order."

He grunted and walked out. Knowing she was in full view of the secretary, she began her check, searching quickly and efficiently. She didn't find any bugs, but she did manage to place her own.

All she had to do now was sit back and hope it picked up some clue as to what the hell was going on with Wetherton—and what his true connection was to Blaine.

EIGHT

GABRIEL SHOWED HIS ID TO the black-clad police officer keeping watch and ducked under the yellow crime-scene tape. The rotating red and blue lights of the nearby police vehicles washed across the night, splashing color across the white-walled ten-story apartment block directly ahead. The building had million-dollar views over Albert Park Lake, which became part of the Grand Prix racetrack when Formula One was in town. Douglass might not have had much money in her accounts, but she *did* have this apartment. Maybe she owned others; it wouldn't be the first time someone had invested in property rather than put up with the low interest from banks.

"There are three apartments on each floor. Douglass lives in 1003, which is the one with the lake view." Illie was looking at his notebook more than where he was going, and Gabriel rather churlishly hoped he'd run into something. But the man seemed to have a sixth sense when it came to objects in his path and sidestepped each one at the last moment. And all without actually looking up. "The building has keypad number and thumbprint code security in place, and the system records all visitors."

"You've checked the records for her apartment?" Gabriel flashed his badge at the officer standing at the heavily barred front door and nodded his thanks when the officer keyed the door open for them.

"Yes. No visitors recorded for the last forty-eight hours," Illie said. "She left her apartment at five forty-five this morning and returned at two thirty this afternoon. She was alone both times."

Another State Police officer stood at the elevator. Gabriel again showed his badge and asked, "Who's the officer in charge up there?"

"Captain Marsdan."

Who was the head of Sam's squad when she'd been a State Police officer, and a man with no real liking for SIU interference. But he was an excellent cop and, despite his adverse opinion of the SIU, he was probably the reason they'd been called in so fast.

They made their way up in the elevator. Illie shoved his notebook in one pocket, then retrieved a small crime scene monitor from another.

Gabriel watched with mild amusement as Illie activated it, then tossed it into the air. It was always easy to tell raw recruits from those who had been with the bureau for years, simply because the newbies followed the rules to the letter. Those who had been around for a while recorded information only when there was actually something to record. And in cases like this one, there'd be a CSM in place anyway, so there was really no point in doubling up.

Black uniforms dominated the fifth floor, several interviewing neighbors and others guarding Douglass's door. Gabriel flashed his badge yet again and stepped inside the apartment.

A spherical CSM hovered in the middle of the living room, red light flashing to indicate it was recording. It swung around as he entered. "ID, please."

"Assistant Director Gabriel Stern, SIU, and Agent James Illie, SIU," Gabriel said almost absently as he looked around.

Douglass might have made a ton of money, but aside from the location of her apartment, there was little to indicate wealth of *any* kind. In the living room there was only a small TV, a coffee table and a brown leather sofa that had seen better years. The pale gray walls were bare, and the claret-colored, heavily brocaded curtains had that aged, dusty look that only came after years of neglect.

"A woman of minimalist taste, isn't she?" Illie commented. "Hard to imagine, given the image she'd presented at Pegasus."

"Yeah, it is. Do you want to check out the rest of the apartment, see what you can find?"

Illie nodded, and Gabriel looked around as a balding man in his mid-forties came out of a doorway to his right. The captain himself. Surprise flickered briefly through Marsdan's small brown eyes. "I didn't think this case was big enough to bring out an assistant director."

"It is when the case has links to an investigation already underway." Gabriel walked across to the doorway Marsdan had exited through. It led into a bedroom—the place where Kathryn Douglass had met her death.

And it hadn't been an easy one, if the evidence indicator tags were anything to go by. There were at least ten of them, but only five of those caught his immediate attention. They were spread across the room, each one joined by a trail of blood that was already beginning to dry and darken. They were an indication of where the body had lain. Kathryn Douglass had been torn apart.

His gaze rose. A warning had been painted—in what looked like blood—on the wall.

Do not revive Penumbra. Douglass was warned. She chose to ignore it.

Something inside him went cold. Penumbra—the project that seemed most likely to have produced Sam.

What the hell did Kathryn Douglass have to do with *that* project? She was far too old to be one of the children raised from those projects. And according to her records, she'd never been a part of the military, even if the foundation she controlled had deep military links.

So who was the warning aimed at? The military? The SIU? Or someone else entirely?

Someone like the mysterious, ever elusive Sethanon? But what did he have to do with someone like Kathryn Douglass?

Or was it, he thought, reading the message again, nothing to do with Penumbra itself, but rather Douglass—perhaps in partnership with the military—attempting to revive that project in some manner? Was that why only some files had been destroyed during the break-in at Pegasus?

And was it a coincidence that not only had a fire destroyed the Penumbra project, but whatever project Douglass might have been working on? Again, he seriously doubted it.

"Who reported the murder?" He walked over to the wall, carefully avoiding the outlines, blood trails and evidence markers.

"A neighbor. Apparently she heard screams and strange thumping."

"Did she hear any voices? Or see anyone enter or leave?" Gabriel stopped and looked a little closer at the writing. It smelled like dried blood to his hawk-sharpened senses, and given the almost scraped effect of each letter, it appeared something other than fingers had been used as a writing tool. He'd guess rolled-up paper, or something like that. It certainly wasn't the type of effect achieved with cloth, though there'd obviously been plenty of blood-soaked material lying about.

"The neighbor didn't hear the elevator or any other voices, but these apartments have very good sound-proofing," Marsdan said. "The screams would have to have been extremely loud for the woman to have heard them at all."

"How many minutes passed between the report and a squad car arriving?" Gabriel stepped back to take another overall look at the writing. The letters sloped to the left rather than the right, which was usually a good indication that the author was left-handed. Not that that meant anything in itself. A good percentage of the population was left-handed these days.

"The report came in at three fifteen. The squad car was here by three twenty-one."

Gabriel looked around. "That's fast work, Captain."

"There was a car in the area." Marsdan shrugged. "They saw no one coming out of the building, and after gaining access to the apartment via the building's super and finding the body naked and in pieces, they immediately secured the main door."

Gabriel raised an eyebrow. "Naked?"

Marsdan nodded. "The bedding was rumpled. We've already sent it to the lab to test for body fluids and DNA."

Meaning Douglass might have known her attacker *extremely* well. "Is there a fire exit?"

"Yes, but it's alarmed. No one has come in or out of it."

"No broken windows or anything like that to indicate entry from the rooftop?"

"No, sir."

Then how had the murderer gotten in or out? There had to be *something* here, some access point Marsdan and his men had missed. "What about the air-conditioning ducts or vents? Does the building share a single system, or does each apartment have separate air-conditioning units?"

"The second option, I'm afraid." Marsdan paused. "And so far, the only prints we've picked up are the victim's."

"Not surprising. Whoever did this obviously had it well planned." Gabriel paused, remembering what Douglass had said about bringing research home. "Has she got an office? Or a safe?"

Marsdan raised an eyebrow. "Both. The safe was open, but our murderer set fire to the contents rather than snatching them. We've asked Forensics to sift through the ashes and see if they can discover what the safe might have held."

Gabriel suspected they wouldn't find very much at

all. He looked past Marsdan as Illie came to the door. "Yes?"

"I found something you might want to look at."

"What, exactly?" Gabriel asked, as he and Marsdan followed Illie through the living room.

"This apartment has a guest bathroom as well as a regular bathroom. It's little more than a toilet and washbasin, but it's situated on an outside wall and has a small, wind-out window which I presume is meant to give ventilation." Illie glanced over his shoulder. "The window was open."

"Big enough for someone to get in?"

"Someone? No. Some*thing*? Yes."

Illie stopped in the doorway and Gabriel stepped past him. As his partner had stated, the room contained nothing more than a toilet and a basin. The soap sitting on the edge of the small metal basin was old and cracked, suggesting this room hadn't been used in quite a while, though the toilet itself was spotless. The window above it was roughly two feet in diameter, which was certainly big enough for someone to crawl through if they weren't so high up. With the winder in place, though, the amount of space the window could open was severely restricted. Windows and winders could be broken, of course, but this one was still intact. And right now, it was open only a couple of inches.

"Seems your people missed this," he commented, without glancing at Marsdan.

"The open window was noted, but we are duty bound to assume human intervention first. Our searches are for more conventional clues and entry points." He hesitated, expression annoyed. "We called you as soon as the other options were eliminated."

Gabriel squatted and looked behind the bowl. "I would have thought the fact that she was torn apart precluded human involvement."

"She was ripped apart?" Illie said, surprise evident in his voice.

"Yeah."

"There are not many folks in the paranormal community who have the strength to do that," Illie said. "I mean, bear changers would, but a bear changer couldn't get through that window."

"Nor could any of the big cat changers, though they certainly could tear someone apart. But there would also be tooth marks, and I presume our good captain would have mentioned it if something like that was evident."

"He would," Marsdan confirmed. "It wasn't teeth, but the separation also wasn't clean enough to suggest a blade."

Gabriel shifted to get a better view of the S-bend area and saw something odd—a feather. A *black* feather. He frowned. Sam had mentioned that the man in her dreams was a crow shifter—coincidence? He tended to think not.

"Though of course," Marsdan said, "the coroner still has to make her report."

"I found something." Gabriel leaned a shoulder against the wall and said, "Crimecorder, record image and location of feather for evidence."

The black sphere responded immediately, zipping into the room to hover inches from his head. "Image recorded," a metallic voice stated.

"Resume original position."

Gabriel put on a glove, then reached in and grabbed

the dark feather. "It would appear our murderer is a crow."

"A crow shifter wouldn't have the strength to tear someone apart."

"This one obviously did—unless Douglass herself is a changer."

"She's not listed as one." Illie frowned as he handed Gabriel an evidence bag. "A crow is a fairly large bird. Would it even be able to get through a gap like that?"

"Obviously, since that feather is inside rather than out. Crows don't exactly make great pets, so why else would the feather be here? Besides, there's blood on some of the quills. Could be an indication that he or she injured themselves coming in."

"Or going out."

Gabriel nodded. "Are any of Douglass's known associates shapechangers?"

"Not that I've discovered." Illie hesitated as Marsdan's phone buzzed. He gave them an apologetic look and stepped away. Illie continued. "I requested a computer search through Pegasus's employee files. So far, there are several shifters listed, but none are crows." He paused, eyeing Gabriel critically. "You're not expecting a result, are you?"

Gabriel rose. "No."

"Why not?"

"Because this attack came a little too soon after the attack on us. I think someone is either covering his tracks or sending a warning. Maybe even both."

Illie raised his eyebrows. "How did you come to that conclusion?"

Gabriel told him about the message on the wall. "Penumbra is an old military project whose records were all destroyed in a fire. Given Pegasus's military links, it's possible that Douglass knew something about the project." Especially given her request that he and his partner investigate a break-in and her obvious disappointment—or concern—that the partner he'd turned up with was male. They'd wanted Sam there. Wanted her to do those tests. Douglass might have known why, but her death certainly ensured they'd never be able to ask her.

It was just too damn convenient.

And yet, if the military *had* killed her to prevent her from talking, why would they leave a message about Penumbra? That just didn't make sense.

But if not the military, then who?

Sethanon? But what reason would he have to kill Douglass and stop the military from revisiting an old project?

Though if he *did* know of Sam's history, maybe he was still trying to protect her. But why would a man who possessed a ruthless and bloody determination to start a war want to protect someone like Sam? If he planned to use her abilities for his side, why wouldn't he have snatched her long before she'd come to the notice of the SIU or the military?

What was the damn connection between the two of them?

No one knew, not even Sam. Though given what she'd admitted this afternoon—that she was in telepathic contact with a man she recently met—maybe she wasn't being as truthful as he'd presumed.

And that made it more important than ever that he keep an eye on her. If Sethanon was looking out for her, then maybe his brother was right after all. Maybe she would lead them to the one criminal they'd never been able to see, let alone catch.

"So you think the military was behind the murder?" Illie asked, his voice holding a hint of skepticism.

"No, actually, I don't." Gabriel glanced past Illie as Marsdan walked toward them. "Yes?"

"Seeing as you SIU boys are taking over this one, I thought you might like to handle this. We've two military men outside who want to come in and view the scene."

"Talk about timing," Illie muttered.

"Let them up, Captain. I'll talk to them."

"And the first question that has to be asked," Illie commented, as they followed Marsdan back into the living room, "is how they found out about the murder so quickly. Hell, the press aren't even here yet."

"Maybe they were coming to see Douglass anyway. Why don't you see if you can find an appointment book?"

Illie's wry grin flashed. "In other words, 'Get lost while I interview the military men.'"

Amusement ran through Gabriel. "Basically, yes."

"All you had to do was ask, Boss." And he walked away.

Gabriel shoved his hands into his pockets and waited for the two men. He had every intention of taking them into the bedroom to view the murder scene and watch their reaction, but first he wanted to assess them.

Within a few minutes, the apartment's front door was opened and a police officer escorted the two men in. The first was about six feet tall and broad shouldered, with a shock of silver hair that was accentuated by the dark brown of his suit. His face was flat, hard, and the red of a barely healed wound marred its left side. The second man was shorter by several inches, yet had a more powerful presence. Gabriel recognized him instantly, even though he'd seen him only once, on Sam's com-screen. General Frank Lloyd from the Hopeworth Military Base. Was he here by coincidence? Gabriel suspected the answer was no.

The CSM spun around to record the two men walking in. "ID, please."

"General Frank Lloyd, from Hopeworth Military Base."

"General Michael Blaine, also from Hopeworth."

Gabriel raised an eyebrow. "Even with Pegasus's close military ties, surely it's overkill to send two generals to investigate."

"No more than the SIU sending an assistant director," Lloyd said and held out his hand. "I don't believe we've met officially."

"No, General, we haven't." Gabriel shook the man's hand. Power rose when their flesh touched, an electricity that felt oddly disturbing. "And since you specifically asked for me and my partner to investigate the Pegasus break-in, it should come as no surprise that we're now investigating the murder of the person who ran that facility."

"I guess not." Lloyd paused. "While General Blaine here also works at Hopeworth, it's not in the same capacity. His area of expertise meant he was in contact with Douglass more than I was."

Gabriel's gaze switched to the silver-haired man. "How much contact?"

Blaine's expression was polite, almost disinterested, and yet there was something in the man's gray eyes that had Gabriel's hackles rising. He was facing an enemy, even if they'd only just met.

"Not socially, if that's what you're implying. We were merely business acquaintances."

"Have you talked to her in the past few days?"

"Yes."

"And did she appear distracted? Concerned by anything?"

"Not that I was aware of."

"Not even by the break-in?"

Blaine smiled. "Aside from that, no."

Gabriel switched his gaze back to Lloyd. Of the two, he seemed the more approachable—which in itself had alarms ringing simply because the general had been of very little help in the past. Except, of course, when it suited him.

"Why are you here, General? This murder hasn't even hit the headlines yet, so how did you hear about it?"

"All of those scientists and team heads involved with military projects at Pegasus have emergency call buttons installed in their homes. As the director of the company, Douglass also had one. It was pressed at two forty."

Ten minutes after she'd arrived home. Thirty-five minutes before the neighbor heard the screams and called the police. Given what Marsdan had said about the state of the bed, did that mean Douglass pressed the buzzer and *then* seduced her attacker? Or were the seducer and the attacker two entirely different people?

"If Douglass pressed the emergency call button at two forty, why are you only responding now?"

"Hopeworth is a long way from St. Kilda."

"Not by helicopter." And there were military offices in the city itself. Why couldn't they have dispatched military police from one of them to investigate?

"Helicopters are not allowed to land around here, and, given the sensitivity of Pegasus's links with Hopeworth, we prefer to send out our own personnel." Lloyd studied him for a moment, blue eyes assessing. "Why do you suspect us of wrongdoing?"

"I'm an SIU agent and predisposed to be suspicious of everything and everyone. Especially those who have a vested interest in keeping their secrets."

Lloyd's smile was cold. "The military did not silence Kathryn Douglass, I can assure you."

Oddly enough, Gabriel believed him. "Where is the call button?"

"In the bedroom, beside the right bedside table."

"The police found her dead in her bedroom at three twenty-one."

"Meaning the murderer savored his time with her?" Blaine asked.

Gabriel glanced at him. There was an odd hint of amusement in the general's voice that rankled. "Given Douglass's body was torn apart, I doubt the murderer savored her death too much."

Blaine raised an eyebrow. "There are some in this world who get off on such things."

And the general was one of them. Why he was so sure, Gabriel couldn't say. Perhaps it was just the hint of hunger in the general's otherwise flat gaze.

"The police believe Douglass and her murderer had

intercourse before she was murdered. They're testing for DNA."

"So it could be nothing more than rough lovemaking gone extremely wrong?" Blaine asked.

"I seriously doubt it."

Blaine's smile was unexpectedly ferocious. "Oh, so do I."

Which was an odd thing to say when he hadn't yet viewed the room in which she'd been murdered.

"May we see the scene?" Lloyd asked.

"This way." Gabriel led them into the bedroom and stepped to one side so he could see their reactions. Neither man gave much away, but the tiny hint of amusement touching Blaine's mouth was disturbing, to say the least.

"What do you make of the message, General Lloyd? How is Kathryn Douglass connected to Penumbra?"

"She's not." Lloyd's voice was flat. "As you are well aware, Penumbra is not an active project, but one that was shut down years ago."

"Forcibly shut down by fire," Gabriel amended.

Lloyd's gaze flickered toward him. "Yes."

"But if the project was destroyed and Kathryn Douglass had no involvement, why would the murderer leave this particular message?"

"I don't know."

"Don't know, or won't tell?"

Lloyd's smile was flat. "I cannot withhold something I do not know."

Again, Gabriel believed him. "Were there any other survivors from the project that you haven't mentioned already?" He didn't have much hope of getting a direct answer, but the question had to be asked.

"Only the peripheral project support," Blaine said. "People like nurses, teachers, trainers, et cetera."

"And they have all been assigned elsewhere?"

"Many have retired or died," Blaine said, and there was something very cold in his eyes as he said it. "That project occurred a long time ago, and it has not been reopened or repeated since."

"And yet, evidence of it keeps appearing."

"Not through military means, I assure you," Lloyd said. He glanced at Blaine. "Though we should do a check of the surviving personnel. See if any had recent contact with Douglass."

"They haven't. I would have been informed," Blaine said.

Gabriel frowned. Again, there was something very strange in the way Blaine said that. "But if there has been contact?"

"We shall investigate and let you know the results." Lloyd held out his hand. "Thank you for your assistance, AD Stern."

Gabriel shook his hand and again felt that tingle of power. But if the general was trying to read him, then it wasn't through telepathic means. He would have felt any attempt to read his thoughts.

Blaine didn't offer his hand, but just gave him a curt nod before following Lloyd from the room.

Gabriel watched them leave, unable to shake the feeling that Blaine *knew* him. Knew him and hated him.

Which meant that, somewhere in the past, their paths had crossed, even if he couldn't remember it. He needed information on the man, and he needed it fast.

He glanced around as Illie came into the room.

"Do a full search on General Blaine. I need to see whatever you can find."

In the meantime, he'd contact his family and see if anyone had any memory of the man. Then he'd head to Federation headquarters and see if there were any files on him. Once all that had been done, he'd contact Sam. She needed to know that once again the Penumbra project had raised its head.

SAM REPRESSED A YAWN AND wished, for the umpteenth time, that Wetherton would just shut up and go home. Night watch always took several days—or rather, nights—to get used to, and she was tired as hell.

Right now, it was two in the morning and they were in a nightclub situated right in the heart of the King Street club scene. The place was packed with wildly gyrating teenagers and adults, and the music was so damn loud her body vibrated with it. The air was filled with an array of perfumes, the source of which was both male and female. When combined with the odor of sweating bodies, the result was stomach-churning.

The one thing the place *didn't* have was someone watching her. She'd spotted the man Gabriel had following her several times and had finally phoned Stephan about it. The big man had disappeared very quickly after that. As much as his presence had offered her some comfort, she'd meant what she said to Gabriel. She wanted this done, and if that meant Hopeworth snatching her, then so be it. She *needed* answers, because if there was one thing she was certain about, it was that she had to find her past before she could gain a future. Besides, she'd be damned if she'd allow someone to risk his life to protect hers. Especially when that someone was the husband of a woman she liked.

She stood in a corner opposite Wetherton's table and idly rubbed her arm. For some reason it had started aching a few hours ago, and although the pain was now easing, it still niggled. It was the sort of pain that came with a decent skin laceration, although she hadn't cut herself in any way, shape or form. It was just another piece of weird in a gathering pile of them. She looked around the room again. She was currently squashed between a pole and the wall, trying not to breathe too deeply. While uncomfortable, the position allowed her to watch both Wetherton and anyone who approached his table. Not that anyone *had* for the last four hours. She sipped on a juice and wished it were coffee. She had a feeling she was going to hit a wall soon, and at least the caffeine would have helped fend that moment off a little longer. But the bar didn't serve the hot stuff. And as much as she wouldn't have minded a mixer with the juice, her exhaustion and the fact that she hadn't eaten much today meant it would more than likely go straight to her head.

Not a good thing when she was supposed to be protecting the minister.

Although *that* was most definitely not the only reason she was here. She glanced at the other man at the table. Wetherton's meet was a tall, thin man who didn't appear to be another politician. His brown suit was rumpled, his face haggard and unshaven, and there was nothing polished or practiced about the way he spoke. On first sighting him, she'd thought he was a reporter. But after watching him for the last four hours, she'd revised that to criminal. There was something very guarded about the way his gaze continually roamed the room.

There was also something oddly familiar about him, though she'd swear she'd never met or seen him before. It wasn't even so much his looks as his feel.

If that made any sense.

She'd managed to grab a couple of shots of him with her wristcom and had sent them to Izzy, asking for a full search to be done. She figured the name he'd given her—Chip Braggart—was just a little too weird to be true. And she couldn't remember seeing him listed among Wetherton's known associates. Even as tired as she was, it was doubtful she'd forget a name like that.

And why was Wetherton, a government minister, meeting with the likes of Braggart? Was he a contact from the real Wetherton's past, or was he a part of the clone's very recent past? Or was he even, perhaps, the contact between the made man and the creator?

Very likely, she thought, studying the cold wariness in his dark eyes. This man was more than just a petty criminal. And there was something very familiar in the way he moved, the way he reacted.

She frowned, trying to chase down the feeling, but at that moment, the presence of evil crawled across her skin like foul electricity, making it hard not to react instinctively and draw her gun. She placed her glass on a nearby table and casually looked around.

For quite a few minutes she couldn't see the threat. The main dance floor was too crowded, and the table-lined edges were too shadowed. Then the strobe lights pulsed, briefly illuminating a group on the far side of the room and flashing off the hair of one man, making it gleam like a beacon of molten red.

The hair color of Hopeworth's creations. And the face of the man who had tried to kill both her and Wetherton last night.

Only it couldn't be the same man, because he was dead. And although this man's features were almost identical, his nose was just a little bit sharper.

Unlike the rest of the people in his group, he was neither talking nor drinking, but simply standing still as his gaze roamed the confines of the room. When his gaze neared where she stood, she ducked back into shadow, but she had an odd feeling he'd know she was there anyway—that he would feel her presence as easily as she felt his. When she risked another look in his direction, he was gone.

Fear shot through her. The hunt was on.

She pushed away from the wall and walked across to Wetherton. "I'm sorry, Minister, but we need to leave."

Wetherton glanced up, his expression annoyed. "I'm not finished here yet."

"Sir, I have reason to believe your life is under threat. Continue this conversation in the car if you must, but right now we need to move."

His scowl deepened. "It would be inopportune for Mr. Braggart and I to be seen together right at this moment."

"Minister, you asked the SIU for protection. If you do not wish to follow my advice, I can only presume you do not, after all, wish such protection."

Wetherton sighed, though it was more a sound of exasperation than compliance. "If you insist—"

"And I do."

He glanced at Braggart. "We'll continue this tomorrow night, then. Make sure you bring the information I requested."

Braggart nodded, but his gaze was on her and a chill ran down her spine. There was something in his eyes that suggested he saw more, knew more, about this situation and about her than she could ever guess. Yes, this man definitely *knew* her. How or why she couldn't say, but she had a feeling she'd better find out, and quick.

Wetherton downed the remainder of his drink in one gulp and dug a hand into his pocket. "I'll call my chauffeur to make sure the car is waiting out front."

Sam scanned the immediate area, but she couldn't see the flame-haired stranger. Yet she could feel him. His presence itched at her skin, stronger and closer than before. "Hurry," was all she said.

Wetherton made his call and rose. "Let's go."

She waved him ahead of her. She didn't have eyes in the back of her head, and with the crowded state of the nightclub, she wasn't about to leave his back unguarded. At least if she followed, she'd have a chance of seeing a threat coming from the front or the sides.

Wetherton shoved his way out of the club, seemingly oblivious to the angry retorts thrown his way. She followed, her gaze constantly on the move, watching and waiting. The foul energy of the flame-haired stranger followed them. He was close—very close. And yet, no matter how hard she tried, she couldn't pick him out in the crowded confines of the dance club.

The sooner they were in the car and away from here, the better.

They exited the main room and were striding up the long hallway to the front doors when Sam risked yet another look behind her. Though no one else had entered the hallway after them, the doors were still swinging, as if someone had. And she could certainly still feel him. A shiver ran down her spine. If the flame-haired stranger was a Hopeworth creation, who knew what other abilities he had? Invisibility might be a figment of fiction and comic books up until now, but if *she* had the capability to fade into shadow, then how much more of a step was it to create someone who could fade into shadow *and* light?

Not much, she thought, her gaze straying to the deeper shadows to the left of the swinging doors.

Was it her imagination, or did something stir in the half-lit corners?

Another shiver ran down her spine and she pressed a hand against Wetherton's back, pushing him a little.

He swore at her, but nevertheless moved faster. Two security guards opened the door for them and the cold night air swirled in, thick with the promise of rain. Sam shivered again—this time with the cold—and glanced around for the minister's car. It was up the street, parked in a bus zone, and was a little too close to the nearby alley and its encroaching shadows for her liking.

But the foul energy of the stranger was behind her, still in the nightclub, and the shadows ahead held no threat as yet.

It was just nerves, nothing more, that made her fear them.

She grabbed Wetherton's arm and propelled him forward as she slipped her other hand inside her coat and wrapped her fingers around her gun. The cool feel of the metal pressed against her flesh was comforting, and some tiny part of her relaxed a little.

It shouldn't have.

NINE

THEY'D BARELY REACHED THE CAR when the sensation of wrongness rolled across her skin. Not from the man who'd followed them from the club, but from the alley and the shadows. Sam whipped the car door open, thrusting Wetherton inside as the feeling of wrongness sharpened.

Something was about to attack.

She slammed the door shut, barely avoiding the minister's feet, and swung around.

She'd expected it to be the red-haired stranger.

It wasn't.

It was the vampire Stephan had unleashed to attack Wetherton. Sam drew her weapon and pressed the trigger, but the vamp moved so fast that the bright beam of the laser tore through his shoulder rather than searing his brains to dust.

The sharp smell of burned flesh filled the air and he snarled—a shrill sound of anger. Then he was upon her, spindly arms flying, face gaunt, his pupils mere pinpricks. *A junkie in need of a fix,* she thought, and wondered if it was just blood he needed or actual drugs.

She ducked his first blow and let fly with one of her own. Her fist sank deep into his stomach, but he didn't even grunt in response. *Too far gone,* she thought as he snarled, revealing elongated teeth.

A shout came from the direction of the club entrance—one of the bouncers, telling her to knock it off. Like that was going to happen! She blocked another of the vamp's blows, then hit him over the head with her gun as hard as she could. He staggered back, shaking his head and spraying blood in the process. It splattered across her coat and face, stinging like fine acid. But she ignored it and raised her weapon.

"Agent Ryan, SIU," she said, speaking loud enough that the rapidly approaching bouncers might hear. "Raise your hands and don't move, or I *will* shoot."

The vampire either didn't hear, didn't understand or simply didn't care. He just snarled and launched himself at her.

She pulled the trigger.

The shot hit dead center in the middle of his forehead and burned through his skull, cindering flesh and bone and brain matter along the way.

He dropped dead at her feet and didn't move. She didn't look down. She barely even dared to breathe lest the smell make her lose the control she had over her stomach.

Instead, she wiped her face with the sleeve of her coat, then got out her badge and showed it to the two horrified bouncers. They stopped immediately, the aggression that had been so evident moments ago slipping away. Then she tapped her wristcom and made a call to the SIU.

"Agent Sam Ryan, badge number 1934," she said, when Christine came on the line. "I need a cleanup team at my current location. And please inform Director Byrne that the escaped prisoner has been dealt with."

"Cleanup team three has been notified," Christine answered, her digital tones sexier than any computer-generated form had a right to be. "And I've sent a message to Director Byrne."

"Thanks, Christine." Sam hung up and glanced at the bouncers. "You want to keep the gawkers back for me?"

They nodded and began to deal with the gathering crowd. She stepped over the body of the vamp and opened the car door. "You all right, Minister?"

He nodded, his face a little paler than normal. "How did you know that vampire was outside?"

"I didn't. He was an entirely different threat than the one I felt before." She lifted her gaze and let it roam the street. No sense of anything evil or even out of place. Not until she looked past the crowd to the night-club's entrance, anyway. Braggart was there, watching, a hint of amusement touching his thin lips. And if the tingle running across her skin was anything to go by, the redheaded stranger was there, too, even if she couldn't see him.

Not that she could do anything about his presence right then. She didn't dare leave Wetherton alone. After all, the red-haired man might be nothing more than a decoy meant to draw her away from the minister's side. And though she wanted to get out of here as much as Wetherton did, she couldn't whisk him away until the SIU had arrived and the vampire had been dealt with. Protocol had to be followed, most especially in this situation.

She met Wetherton's gaze again. "I have to give my report to the SIU team I called in, and until then, I'm afraid, we'll just have to wait here."

He scowled. "Why can't I just go inside and continue my meeting? Braggart hasn't left yet, surely."

"He hasn't, no. But we're being watched, Minister, and I prefer not to take a risk right now."

"Watched?" A hint of emotion—not fear, not panic, but something in between—flitted through his eyes. He looked around briefly, then met her gaze again. "By whom?"

"I don't know." She briefly toyed with the idea of telling him their watcher was more than likely military, but let it go. Until she knew where, exactly, Wetherton's alliances lay, it was better not to give him too much information. For her sake, as much as his.

He grunted his displeasure, then reached forward and grabbed the car's phone. "Shut the door, please. I have a few personal calls to make."

Ungrateful bastard, she thought, as she slammed the door shut. Not even a thank-you for saving his life. But then, he probably figured she was only doing what she was being paid to do—risking her life to save his lab-made ass.

When she glanced back at the gathered crowd, Braggart had gone. She studied the street beyond the club but couldn't find any sign of him. Unusual for a human to move so fast in such a brief time—unless, of course, he was something more than human.

And she had a strange feeling Braggart was, even if she hadn't sensed him as such. Why she felt this, she couldn't say, but maybe it was connected to the odd sensation that she knew him. Knew the soul of him, if not the outer layer.

Which in itself suggested a shapeshifter of some kind.

She frowned but let the thought go, simply because it was just another question for which she had no answer.

As she looked back to the club's doorway, she noticed that the red-haired stranger had also slipped away. His presence was a fading tingle, getting more distant by the minute. And the night felt cleaner for his disappearance.

She put her weapon away and leaned back against the car, waiting and watching.

It took ten minutes for the cleanup team to arrive. Two men took care of the vamp's body, while the man in charge—an agent she didn't recognize—took statements from her, Wetherton and the driver.

As he moved on to interview the other witnesses, she opened the door and climbed into the car. "We can go now."

"About time," Wetherton muttered, glancing at the driver. "Henry, take me home."

She didn't comment on his tone or the implication that she'd delayed him on purpose, but simply leaned back in the seat and watched the lights flash by. Exhaustion washed over her, and it was all she could do to suppress a yawn. Thankfully, King Street wasn't that far from his Collins Street apartment. Once the driver had stopped in the secure underground garage, she climbed out and checked to make sure there was no one about, then signaled the driver to pop the trunk. She retrieved her overnight bag and com-unit,

then opened Wetherton's door. He grabbed his brief-
case, climbed out and headed for the elevator.

It turned out that the minister's apartment was on
the top floor, with good views of the bay. The apartment's living area wasn't huge, but the floor-to-
ceiling wall of glass made it seem otherwise. The city
stretched before them, an unending sea of twinkling
lights that merged gradually into the dark waters of
the bay.

She dumped her bags on one of the black leather
sofas, then caught Wetherton's arm as he walked past
her.

"Minister, I should check all rooms first."

"This apartment building is fully secure," he said,
exasperation in his voice. "No one could get in here."

"There's no such thing as a fully secure building.
All security can be breached, even that of the SIU."

He grunted, but waved her on irritably. She walked
to the nearest room, which turned out to be the bathroom. There was nothing out of the ordinary, despite
the marble tiling and the gold-plated taps. The same
could be said for the bedroom—though the silk-clad
bed had to be the biggest she'd ever seen. It dominated the room, leaving little space for anything else.
She walked past it into the walk-in closet and dressing area, noting with a frown that the minister's suits
were all top of the line. And there were enough of
them that he could wear a different one every day for
a month. Surely politicians didn't make *that* much
money. Between the apartment, the suits, the family
home and the family itself, Wetherton had to be
draining himself dry.

Unless, of course, he had a secondary source of in-
come no one knew about.

As she turned to leave, her gaze fell on a grate covering what looked like a large vent. The paintwork around one edge had been scratched, as if the vent had been opened recently, or often. Frown deepening, she knelt and ran her fingers around the covering's edge. It was loose. She pried it open and looked carefully into the hole.

Darkness and air rushed up at her and she shuddered, quickly drawing back. Small places had *never* been on her list of favorites things—especially when they were small places that seemed to drop down into unending darkness.

But why was this here? It didn't appear to be part of the air-conditioning system, as it seemed to go straight down. And if it was a laundry chute, why was it here rather than in the bathroom? And why wasn't there a proper cover?

"What the hell are you doing?" Wetherton appeared in the doorway, his expression darker than usual.

She sat back on her heels and indicated the vent. "What is that used for?"

"It's a vent."

"One whose cover has been removed many times."

He shrugged. "They're in the process of placing a laundry chute in the building. Workmen have been in and out all week, fiddling with the damn thing and generally being a nuisance."

Some of those scratches were more than a week old, but still, the explanation was reasonable enough.

So why did she sense that he was lying?

"It's a dangerous thing to have such an easy access point in your apartment, Minister."

Wetherton snorted. "No man could fit in that vent, let alone climb it."

"No man could, but a shifter is a different matter."

"A bird wouldn't have the strength to shift the grate with its wings or its claws, Agent Ryan. Now, will you just get out of my bedroom so I can go to sleep?"

"Only doing my job, Minister." She shoved the cover back into place, taking careful note of the existing scratches, then rose. "The agent assigned to the day shift will be here at seven. Do you wish me to wake you at that time if you're not already up?"

"Yes. Now get out."

She did, but she stayed near the closed door, listening. She wasn't entirely sure what she expected to hear, but there was something about Wetherton that scratched at her instincts. He was up to no good, she was sure of that. And it was something he didn't want *her* to know about.

But the soft sounds coming from the bedroom suggested he was doing nothing more than getting ready for bed. She gave up after a few minutes and walked over to the sofa where she'd left her com-unit. After sitting down, she pressed her thumb into the lock.

"Voice identification required," the unit stated.

"Sam Ryan, SIU officer, badge number 1934."

"Voice scan correct. Eye confirmation required."

She looked into the small scanner fitted into the left-hand side of the unit. A red beam swept over her eye.

"Eye scan correct." The unit clicked open.

Izzy's pink fluff form appeared onscreen. "It's a little early in the morning to be up and about, isn't it, sweetie?"

"Tell me about it," she said dryly, and barely repressed a yawn. "Has Hopeworth replied to our request for information about the gray-haired man?"

Izzy's feather boa twirled. "Not a whisper, sweetie."

"Well, his name is General Blaine, and he apparently does work at Hopeworth." She paused, looking toward Wetherton's room. The soft sound of steps indicated he was still moving around. But when bedsprings squeaked, she relaxed and looked down at Izzy. "See what you can find out about him. Use all channels available."

"Oooo . . . freedom to search where I please. Thanks, sweetness."

She snorted softly. "And did you do an identity check on that image I sent you?"

"I did. I couldn't find a thing."

"Then keep looking. There has to be *some* information about him somewhere."

Izzy's boa twirled faster. "Darlin', I can only do so many things at once."

"Izzy, you're a computer, not a human."

"That doesn't mean I'm without limits."

She grinned. They were definitely making these things too real. "You'll live, Iz. Let me know when you find anything."

She closed the screen and set the com-unit to one side, then lifted her feet onto the glass-and-chrome coffee table. Without really meaning to, she dozed.

A soft sound woke her. She blinked, briefly noting that it was still night as she glanced sideways at the clock on the wall. Four o'clock. She'd been asleep just about an hour.

She frowned, listening to the silence, feeling guilty about sleeping on the job and wondering what the hell had woken her. Then she heard it again—a whisper-soft bump of something against metal. It came from the direction of Wetherton's room.

She rose, reaching for her weapon as she padded toward the door. After grasping the handle, she carefully inched the door open. Wetherton was a blanket-covered, unmoving lump in the bed who made no noise.

She frowned and pushed the door open a little more, quickly peering around the corner. Nothing unusual. No reason for the sound she'd heard.

Pressing her fingertips against the door, she pushed it all the way open. The room was still and dark, and Wetherton's aftershave—a spicy, musky scent that was far too powerful for her liking—filled the air.

She stepped quietly into the room and looked around. Still no noise. No indication that anything was wrong.

Half wondering if the noise she'd heard was nothing more than a figment left over from stolen sleep, she took another step forward.

And realized it wasn't Wetherton in the bed, but pillows bunched together to take on the appearance of a sleeper if anyone happened to look in.

The man himself was nowhere to be seen.

She raised her gun and cautiously approached the walk-in closet, all senses alert. Another duck around the door frame revealed that Wetherton wasn't hiding in there, either.

What the hell . . . ? She lowered her weapon and looked around the room, then up at the ceiling. No trap doors, no windows. No Wetherton.

A man his size couldn't just disappear . . .

Her gaze went to the vent. It was open.

"Shit." She dropped to her knees and peered into

the dark hole. Fear rose, threatening to engulf her, but she ignored it the best she could and listened.

From far down came another thump and the soft squawk of a bird. Then silence.

She pulled back from the hole and sat on her heels. Wetherton wasn't just a clone; he was a shape-changer.

But if he was so afraid for his life, why would he leave this apartment—and her protection—so abruptly? Why put himself in danger like that?

Unless, of course, he needed to report to his master and this was the only way he could do it without raising suspicion. After all, the real Wetherton was human, not changer. And this Wetherton had been in a mighty hurry to get her out of the room so he could sleep.

She rose and left, closing the bedroom door behind her. Whatever his reasons, it was obvious that he didn't want her to know he was gone. And it certainly played better for her if he didn't know that she knew.

After shoving her gun away, she flopped back onto the sofa and opened the com-unit again. Izzy's fuzzy face came online instantly. "And here I was thinking you were sleeping."

"I was. Can you send an urgent email to Director Byrne? Tell him Wetherton is a changer. Tell him I need a tracer sent in with Jenna Morwood this morning, if possible."

"Request sent. Still waiting on search results."

"Ta, Iz." Sam shut the com-unit down and settled back to wait. It was an hour before she heard the soft sound of movement in the bedroom. After a few seconds, the door opened and Wetherton's tousled head appeared.

"Anything wrong, Minister?" she inquired politely.

"I thought I heard something," he said, in the best just-woken-from-sleep voice she'd ever heard.

"Nothing's moving. I'm struggling to keep awake, in fact."

"Make sure that you do," he snapped, and closed the door.

Ass, she thought, and wondered how the hell she was going to get through months of this tedium.

With a sigh, she leaned back against the sofa and watched the dawn break slowly across the night-held sky. Jenna arrived just before her shift started. She was a pretty woman of Spanish descent.

After checking her ID, Sam let her in and introduced herself. Jenna smiled, the merry twinkle in her dark eyes belying the hint of steel in her handshake. "Director Byrne sent this for you," she said, handing her an interoffice envelope. "What's Wetherton like?"

Sam glanced at the still-closed bedroom door. "He's a politician."

Jenna grimaced. "Says it all, doesn't it?"

"Yeah." Sam tore open the envelope. Inside were two small plastic packets. Stephan wasn't taking any chances—he'd sent two tracers, one for each of them. She got one out and handed it to Jenna. "He's also an unrecorded changer. He disappeared on me last night, but he doesn't know that I know. Keep an eye on him, and try to place the tracer on him without alerting him."

Jenna nodded, pocketing the packet quickly as Wetherton came out. When his gaze fell on Jenna, his whole demeanor lightened. Sam didn't know who she felt sorrier for—Jenna for being placed on a twelve-hour watch with a lecher, or Wetherton if he actually tried to harass her.

Though personally, she wouldn't have minded seeing Jenna kick his sorry ass to kingdom come.

She made the introductions, then donned her jacket, grabbed her bag and com-unit and got the hell out of there.

And discovered Gabriel waiting for her outside the building. She stopped briefly as surprise and something else—something close to excitement—ran through her.

He was leaning against one of the concrete columns, arms crossed, and looking as tired as she felt. "What's wrong?" she asked, stopping a few feet away from him. His scent ran around her, spicy and warm, stirring her longing.

And steeling her earlier resolve to pursue whatever it was between them. Whether or not she succeeded didn't matter. If she *didn't* do something, if she simply sat back and accepted his statement that his heart belonged to someone long dead, she'd regret it.

"I heard you requested information about a General Blaine." He shifted his hand, revealing a manila folder. "I thought you might like to share why over breakfast."

She raised an eyebrow. "Breakfast doesn't get you out of lunch, you know."

A wry smile touched his lips. "I guessed that. But this is a business breakfast, not an apology."

Of course. He wouldn't be here, otherwise. "Why are you curious about my interest in Blaine?"

"Because I met him last night. Since you saw him

when the Wetherton attack went down wrong, I wanted your opinion of him."

He motioned her forward, and then pressed his hand lightly against her spine to guide her toward his car. The warmth of his touch trembled across her skin. *Yep,* she had it bad. But if he noticed her reaction, he didn't say anything. Didn't react in *any* visible way himself.

"I know this sounds catty, but why does my opinion of the man matter?"

He slanted her a look as he opened the car's passenger door for her. "Because you have an innate skill for sensing evil in people. I want to know if you sensed it in him."

She waited until he'd climbed into the car before replying, "Yes and no."

He started the car and pulled out smoothly into the early morning traffic. Then he flicked on auto-drive and programmed it to head to the hotel where she'd been staying. She certainly hadn't told him she was staying there, so he'd obviously dug it out of her personnel file. If she wasn't so tired she might have felt annoyed, but right now all she felt was vague amusement.

"What does that mean?" he asked.

"It means that when Wetherton's car was attacked and I was trying to save his ass, I felt no sense of evil from Blaine. Yet yesterday afternoon, as he was coming out of Wetherton's office, my skin fairly crawled at the sight of him. And oddly, he had no trace on him of the wounds he had received in the bombing."

Gabriel frowned. "What time was that?"

"A little after six. Why?"

"Because when I saw him a little before seven, there were definitely traces of wounds on his face then."

Sam felt a shiver run up her spine. "So what are you saying, that there are two different Blaines? Like a clone?" Though it certainly made sense, given her differing reactions to the man.

"Or a shifter impersonating Blaine," Gabriel added. "Do you know why he was visiting Wetherton?"

"Something to do with military funding. But why would someone bother to impersonate Blaine just to beg for money? If your Blaine had the wounds and was with Lloyd—who presumably would be able to spot a fake—then clearly he was the real Blaine." So why was *her* Blaine—the fake Blaine—the evil one? It made no sense. Then she frowned. "And why were they both turning up at a murder scene, anyway?"

"Because the woman murdered was Kathryn Douglass, director of the Pegasus Foundation, which has strong military ties."

"But that doesn't explain why Lloyd and Blaine would turn up."

"Many of the projects Pegasus was involved in came from Hopeworth. Blaine was Douglass's military contact."

"But . . ." Sam hesitated, mulling over the little she'd heard or read about Pegasus. "Don't they make big hardware, like fighter planes and stuff?"

"Yes, but they also work on smaller, more experimental weapons for Hopeworth. Illie and I were called in there yesterday to investigate a break-in."

"Illie being your new partner?" Meaning he didn't have something against partners, just against her?

Gabriel scowled. "Not by choice, I can assure you."

His gaze met hers for a long moment, and she saw not only annoyance but a loneliness and a longing that was as deep as anything she'd ever felt.

If ever she needed encouragement to carry on with her crazy seduction plan, that was it. The problem was, how far should she push? And how soon? Given the situation—and her reassignment—it wasn't going to be easy, no matter what she decided.

Which meant that maybe she needed to seduce him sooner rather than later—and hit him hard and fast. Give him no time to think, just react.

She looked out the window and wondered if she could even do that. Wondered if she'd do nothing more than make a fool of herself. Lord, she hadn't even kissed the man, and here she was, thinking of full-blooded seduction. And she had only her hormones and his sister saying that he *was* interested. Because while she might see loneliness and need in his eyes, it didn't actually mean that either was aimed at *her*.

"Sam?"

She jerked out of her thoughts and met his gaze. "Huh?"

He studied her again, his gaze shrewd and almost judgmental. "I said the problem was, Illie wasn't the partner they were hoping to see."

She frowned. "Meaning they wanted me? Why?"

"According to Illie, it was some sort of test." He hesitated. "A test they went through with regardless."

Alarm ran through her. "Why would they do that? What sort of test was it?"

"There was an explosion, followed by a fire hot enough to melt the walls and damn near kill the both of us."

The alarm got stronger. In her dreams, they'd tested *her* against fire, too. She swallowed heavily and said, "How did you survive?"

"We were lucky—the room had several fireproofed cabinets." His gaze met hers. "Why would they want to test you against fire, Sam? Do you have any idea?"

"No." She paused. "But in a recent dream, someone was trying to force me to control fire."

"Who?"

Sam hesitated, but something in the way he was looking at her suggested this was a pivotal point in their relationship. That if she lied about this, she could forget about the future and whatever plans she might have. "I don't know who they all were, but I recognized one of them—Blaine."

"How?"

"From my dreams."

His eyebrow rose. "And what was he doing in those dreams?"

She blew out a breath, battling a sudden reluctance to talk about it. What if the dreams were false? What if they were nothing more than images of an overactive imagination?

What if they weren't?

If she wanted to know the truth, she had to start trusting someone with her nightly journeys. Someone other than Joe, whom she might not be able to trust.

"They were training me to use gifts I don't appear to have."

"Hopeworth was?"

"I can't say for sure it was Hopeworth, because the dreams never included a location. It was just a room—or rather, an arena—with the scientists in an observation room above me."

"And was it just you in the dream?"

"In the training arena? Yes." She hesitated. "But I am never alone in the dreams. Joshua is always with me."

"And is Joshua this Joe Black you mentioned earlier?"

"In all honesty, I don't know. Joe looks nothing like the boy in my dreams. His coloring is completely different, for a start."

"But he could be?"

"I guess so. Anything is possible, especially when I don't even know if the dreams are real or a figment of a warped imagination."

He considered her, his hazel eyes shuttered. "Is Joe real?"

"I've already said yes to that question. But I do know Joe is not his real name."

"Do the dreams feel real?" Gabriel asked.

"Yes." Too real and too painful—even if she didn't entirely believe them.

Or maybe that should be even if she didn't entirely *want* to believe them.

"If you are so sure, why have you never mentioned them?"

Sam hesitated. "Just because they feel real doesn't mean they *are* real. For all I know, they could have been planted in my subconscious for some nefarious reason." She looked ahead as the car began to slow and saw that they were nearing the hotel. She returned her gaze to his. "That's what you were thinking, isn't it?"

A smile fleetingly touched his lips. "At first, yes. But I think it's becoming increasingly obvious you're from one of the Hopeworth projects, though whether that project is Penumbra or something else is anyone's guess. That being the case, you've obviously slipped their noose until now. Which means you had help."

"Because a teenager could not escape the might of the military alone."

"A normal teenager, no. But you are not normal, Sam."

"And if that wasn't apparent before, it sure is now." She smiled to counter the bitterness in her tone. "But even so, my memories—or lack thereof—and the fact that there has been a careful 'refinement' of my past suggests that someone, somewhere, knows who and what I am. And they have gone to great lengths to conceal it."

"Yes." Gabriel paused. "Have you asked this Joe about it?"

"He says I will remember when I need to remember."

"Helpful."

"Yeah. And when I've asked who he is, I get the same response."

"Then perhaps you need to find another source."

She raised her eyebrows. "You don't think I've been trying?"

"I meant another Hopeworth source. Have you ever gone back to see that woman who claimed to be your nanny in Hopeworth? The one who called you Josephine?"

"No."

"Then perhaps we should."

"What? Now?"

"Is there anything else you particularly want to do?"

"How about sleep?"

He looked at her for a moment, then he laughed a

little sheepishly. "Yeah, I guess you would. How about I come back later this morning?"

How about you come join me in bed? She rubbed a hand across her eyes and tried to ignore the impulse to say the words out loud. For all that she wanted this man, it wasn't the right time for a seduction. And in all honesty, her planned lunch probably wasn't the best time, either, though she had a feeling there was never going to be a "good" time.

But if she wanted to know for sure whether that something between them was more than just a side effect of genetics, of breeding, then she had better force her reluctant feet forward and at least *try*, wrong time or not.

"No. Let's do it now; then I can sleep for the rest of the day."

He raised his eyebrows. "And the apology lunch?"

"Can become an apology brunch. Unless you are willing to take a rain check." She leaned forward and programmed the nursing home's address into the auto-drive. The car shot back into traffic and drove on.

He didn't comment, just nodded. She wasn't getting much from him at the moment—not even little insights via body language, which meant he was controlling himself very tightly.

No surprise, really. He'd been doing that from the first time they'd met.

"So," she continued, "what did *you* learn about Blaine?"

"Not a great deal. Basic information on family and education. Information that all but ceased when he went into the military at eighteen."

"Did he go straight into Hopeworth, then?"

"No. Records show he enlisted in the army and went through basic training. The records are listed as high security after that, though."

"I thought Stephan's security listing was high enough to get access to such records."

"He has access to everything but Hopeworth. That is a law unto itself."

Sam snorted. "I'm thinking that's not exactly wise."

Gabriel grimaced. "The military would argue that, given the sensitive nature of much of their research, it is a necessity."

"So, if Stephan has access to all but Hopeworth, why haven't you got the rest of it?"

"Because Stephan is currently home with Lyssa and his new son."

"Lyssa's had her kid? Hey, send her and Stephan my congrats! What did they name him?"

"Devyn Charles Oswald Stern."

She blinked. "That's one hell of a moniker for a little kid to carry."

Gabriel grinned. "He's the first grandson, so he was destined to carry the first name of both grandfathers. It's something of a tradition."

"And a nice one. The past is never forgotten that way." There was sudden sympathy in his expression and she knew he was thinking about her lack of a past. Given that she didn't particularly want to dwell on the reasons for that right now, she rushed on before he could say anything. "She didn't have any problems, then?"

"Not as many as we expected. She's had a bad pregnancy and isn't strong—as you know, because you've met her—and it was an extremely long birth. But she's fine. Tired, but fine."

What *she* knew was that Lyssa was stronger than her family was giving her credit for. She *had* met the woman, and beneath that pale, frail build was a steely determination that was breathtaking. Anyone who could handle being kidnapped and isolated for six months and still come out of it sane could certainly cope with anything else life threw at her.

"So has the proud uncle been to see the newest addition to the family yet?"

He hesitated, and darkness flashed through his eyes. "Not yet."

"Why not?"

"Because sometimes there are things more important than family."

"Nothing is more important than family." *Says the woman who hasn't got one,* she thought with resignation.

"Some things are."

And the brief glance he gave her made her pulse skip, then race. Did that glance imply what she thought it implied? Or were her overactive hormones making her read far too much into it?

"Like what?" she asked, as casually as she could.

"Like stopping a madman intent on starting a war."

Amusement and perhaps a touch of disappointment ran through her. So much for her fantasies, she thought wryly. "So, you still think Wetherton has connections to Sethanon?"

"Do I believe it? Yes. Do I have any proof? No. Other than the body of the real Wetherton, and the fact that Sethanon was behind the attempt to replace the Prime Minister with a clone, that is."

"And Wetherton's connections to Hopeworth?"

"Could be a means for Sethanon to keep track of what is going on in there. Or maybe Wetherton is merely the go-between for Sethanon and his military source."

She raised her eyebrows at that. "You think Blaine is working for Sethanon?"

"It's not beyond the bounds of reason. I certainly don't think it's a coincidence that it was Blaine's image the multi-shifter used."

"Why?"

"Multi-shifters need to come in constant contact with someone to take that person's shape. It takes a little time for cells to reconfigure, and the longer the contact, the more exact the image."

"Really? Does it work the same for shapechangers? Or shapeshifters?"

He shook his head. "Shapechangers and shifters are born with their secondary form programmed into their cells. Multi-shifters have adaptable cells."

"Fascinating."

"Very."

His voice was dry and she smiled. "Maybe not to you, because you grew up with it. Who actually knows what, exactly, I grew up with?" She paused, frowning a little. "You know, it seems odd to me that you all fear Sethanon, and yet you haven't been able to find out a great deal about him in all the years you've been hunting him."

"We *do* know a lot about his organization. We just don't know much about the man himself."

"Why not? I mean, you've captured his people, interrogated them, so surely they were able to give you something more concrete."

"Only concrete in terms of his organization, his contacts, stuff like that. No one seems to know much about the man himself."

"Don't you find that a little surprising?"

"Not really. We're talking about someone who can change his identity at will. It's hard to trace someone when you can't even pin down his true identity." He grimaced. "Hell, for all we know, he could be one of the contacts we have under observation. Anything is possible when your form is mutable."

She raised her eyebrows. "So he suddenly appears on the scene sixteen years ago and starts taking pot shots at the Federation and the SIU?"

"It's a little more than potshots," Gabriel said, his voice a little testy. "And his agenda—which he's made perfectly clear in several messages he sent us—amounts to war."

"And yet if he intended war, why hasn't he just started it? Why warn you at *all*?"

"Because he enjoys an audience." Gabriel shrugged. "And he probably enjoys watching us run around trying to find and stop him."

"And it's hard to stop someone when you have no idea who and what he is."

"Exactly."

She considered him, thinking about what she'd said, what he'd said, and drawing conclusions that she really didn't like. Such as the fact that Sethanon's appearance seemed to coincide with hers. True, it *was* probably little more than a coincidence, especially given the appearance of other Hopeworth rejects over the years, but it was still a disturbing thought. After a moment, she said, "It still doesn't make sense, you know. I mean, if he wants a war, he could have started it years ago. What is he waiting for?"

"Who knows? It could be something as simple as the fact that it takes time to build a fighting force."

Something inside her clicked, and her eyes widened. "Hopeworth."

He frowned. "What?"

"Hopeworth is the key." She reached out, grabbing his hand and wrapping her fingers around his. "*That's* what he's waiting for. Hopeworth has spent years making the perfect soldier, and from what we've seen recently, may finally be succeeding. *That's* what he's waiting for. This Sethanon of yours is planning to take over Hopeworth."

TEN

GABRIEL STARED AT SAM FOR a moment, then said almost automatically, "He couldn't."

And yet even as he denied it, his mind raced with the possibility. It was something they'd never even contemplated. Yet, in a twisted way, it made perfect sense. If Sethanon intended to start a war against a well-armed, well-informed alliance of nonhumans like the Federation, then it would pay to get fighters that were stronger, faster and better than those nonhumans. And that's *exactly* what Hopeworth was breeding.

"He could if he's a multi-shifter," she said, her eyes bright in the pale light. "Remember, we have two Blaines running around."

"Yeah, but that's not something that could be done long-term."

"Why not? Stephan's been doing it for years to stay in charge of the SIU, hasn't he?"

"Hopeworth is an entirely different beast than the SIU. I doubt an imitator would go unnoticed for very long in an installation that specializes in interspecies and psi-talent development. Especially when the original is still running around."

"But if he's got people on the inside and the outside—people like Wetherton—tracking Blaine's movements, then it is totally possible."

"Only if Blaine didn't live on the base, and he does."

"But he doesn't stay on the base all the time. And who says this Sethanon of yours isn't also living on the base? You're the one who said whoever is posing as Blaine has to be in close contact to ensure a good replication."

That was true. And it was definitely an idea they would have to investigate. Though given the tight security on all Hopeworth information and records, it was going to be nearly impossible to get any information there. But the base itself was an entirely different proposition. They could certainly watch all the comings and goings. Gabriel shifted so that he was facing her full on, but he didn't dislodge her grip on his hand. There was something almost comforting in her touch—comforting in a way that was sexual and yet not.

In the early morning light, her skin was almost as luminous as her eyes. With her fiery hair covered by the hood of her dark coat, she appeared almost ghostly. His grip on her hand tightened a little, and the fingers of his free hand itched with the sudden need to caress her cheek. To feel the softness of her skin. To reassure himself that she was real and here, and not already beginning to fade away into nothingness as Karl had warned.

"Why are you so positive about this?" he asked.

When she hesitated and looked away, he reached

out and touched her chin, drawing her gaze back to his. She licked her lips, and he found his gaze drawn to the movement. *Not good,* he thought, and yet he couldn't pull his gaze away.

"How the hell can I be sure?" She hesitated again. "But I'm right. I know I'm right."

"Because you were at Hopeworth with the man who is now Sethanon?" The question came out of nowhere, and he had to wonder if it was an instinctive reaction to the pull he was feeling toward her.

And yet, at the same time, it *was* a natural question. She was obviously connected to Hopeworth, and there was definitely a connection to Sethanon somewhere along the line. Otherwise, why would the man have spent so much time over the years keeping an eye on her? Maybe even protecting her?

She gasped and jerked away from his grasp. Part of him regretted the loss of her touch. Part of him didn't. And he couldn't help noticing that, despite her reaction, there was no hurt in her eyes, no surprise, which suggested she'd contemplated the question herself, however lightly.

"That's not true," she said. Yet her eyes said, *Please don't let it be true.*

"Sam, think about it. Your memories started at the age of fourteen. At that very same time, Sethanon made his first appearance. And, coincidentally, just before either event, a project named Penumbra was destroyed by a fire to the point that there were absolutely no records left. There wasn't even enough DNA left to identify who, exactly, died in that fire. Normal fires don't burn that hot. Not without help."

She was staring at him, eyes wide and somewhat distant, like she was seeing things he couldn't even begin to guess at. He wondered what she was remembering, wished that she'd tell him. But he'd done very little in recent months to encourage trust, and for the first time he regretted it. Truly regretted it.

"Fire is not my element."

The words were said softly, almost automatically. He frowned. "Were they Joe's?"

She blinked, and life came flooding back into her eyes. "Joe was never at Hopeworth. At least, the man I know now as Joe wasn't. Joshua was."

"What if Joe is a shapeshifter? He could have been there as someone else."

"He's a shapechanger. A crow. Are you saying he's one of those rare types who is both shifter and changer?"

"Maybe." And what if it went beyond that? You could be a multi-shifter and, on rare occasions, even a multi-changer, but he'd never heard of a multi-shifter-changer.

But then, up until Rose Pierce began killing off Hopeworth rejects, he'd never heard of a male-female shifter, either.

"Hopeworth doesn't traffic in the normal," she said.

"No, they don't." He hesitated. "Your dreams haven't made any connections between Joe and Joshua, have they? Was Joshua one of the instructors?"

"No, and no." Her sudden smile held very little warmth. "If I can believe the nanny, Joshua is actually my twin brother."

He raised an eyebrow. "A test-tube twin, or the real thing?"

Sam shrugged. "Considering I have no idea about

the manner of my birth, I can't really comment. And Mary never said either way. Nor did I think to ask."

"But what do your instincts say?"

"My instincts and my dreams make me believe that Mary is telling the truth—that he's my brother. My *real* brother. The other half of me." She hesitated. "But since I still don't know whether my dreams can be trusted, I wouldn't rely on them as the truth just yet."

"But what if they *are* the truth?"

She stared at him for a moment, then looked away again—but not before he'd seen the sheen of tears in her eyes. "I don't want them to be the truth. I don't want to be just another product from some mad scientist's production line."

He gently forced her to look at him again. "Whether you are or not doesn't matter, Sam. The scientists may have given you life, but they haven't made you what you are."

"And just what am I?" she said, and for the first time there was a hint of desperation in her voice. "Am I a military weapon gone wrong, or one that is merely waiting for the right trigger?"

"What you are," he said softly, "is a warm, bright woman with a past that is undefined. But military creation or not, you are *not* the sum of your making. You have a mind and a soul that are all your own, and they are not evil. You could never be evil."

Her gaze searched his. "Are you sure of that? Truly sure? Because if my dreams are to be believed, I did some pretty horrible things in that place."

Maybe it was a trick of the light, or maybe the car had somehow shrunk, because suddenly her face seemed nearer to his, her lips nearer still. The urge to close the gap between them, to caress her mouth with his own, rose with a vengeance from somewhere deep inside. Suddenly he was drowning in the desire to kiss her and fighting for control.

"We all do what we must to survive," he said softly and gently brushed several strands of hair away from her warm cheek. She trembled slightly under the caress, but her gaze didn't leave his. And there was a challenging light in her eyes, as if she were daring him to acknowledge what was happening. Daring him to do what he wanted to do.

He didn't. He just said, "In your case, I doubt you would have done anything that you were not forced to do."

"I'm not so sure about that."

"I am."

And with that, he gave up the fight.

He kissed her slowly, passionately, as if he had all the time in the world and this kiss was not their first, but rather one of many. And it felt fantastic. As her smell entwined him, filling his every breath with the richness of vanilla and cinnamon, he groaned and deepened the kiss, wanting, needing, to taste every inch of her. As his desire fled south, she answered in kind, her hands sliding up his chest and around his neck, until she was holding him as if she never meant to let him go. It made him hunger to taste her more fully, to skim his tongue across her warm, pale skin, exploring and savoring every bit of her.

God, this kiss felt so right, so scarily right, unlike anything he'd ever experienced before—even with Andrea—that it shook him to his very core. Andrea had been his soul mate; he'd been *so* certain of that all his life. But if that were true, he shouldn't be feeling the completeness he was feeling with this kiss, this woman, no matter how deep the attraction.

And yet he was.

So had he been wrong so long ago, as Jessie had said, or was *this* connection, this rightness, something altogether different? Perhaps something due to the storm bond and the shadow walker genes that ran in her blood and apparently in his?

He didn't know.

But one thing was certain. Now that he'd experienced it, he *had* to explore it. He had no option. He was a shapechanger, and part of that heritage was the fierce desire to find the one woman who was his other half, his destiny. This kiss had woken that part of him, and there was no turning away. Especially after all these years of being convinced that his soul mate was dead and buried.

And while now was not the time for such thoughts or such explorations, the fact was, he could no longer ignore what was between them, could no longer push her away.

But could he breach the fences he'd spent so long creating?

He pulled back from her just enough to allow some breathing room between them.

"I'm sorry—"

She placed a hand on his lips, stopping the rest of his words. "Don't apologize for something I've wanted for a long time now."

He wasn't apologizing for the kiss, despite his reservations and uncertainty, but rather his timing—which pretty much stunk—and his treatment of her over the past few months. One kiss *shouldn't* have changed anything, yet it had. But really, what was the point of explaining that? She probably wouldn't believe him anyway. Hell, *he* was finding it hard to believe. "Then I won't."

She smiled. "Good."

He glanced at the road ahead and saw, with surprise, that they were almost at Greensborough. The nursing home where Mary Elliot was being looked after was only five minutes or so away. Time sure flew when you were kissing your partner. Or rather, ex-partner. "I think we need to talk."

"I agree, but not here or now. Later, over brunch."

He nodded and retreated to his side of the car. But her scent still seemed to surround him, filling his every breath, forcing him to fight desire. "So, tell me about this Mary. How did you find her in the first place?"

A ghost of a smile touched her lips. She was obviously well aware that he was trying to distract himself. "Joe gave me a pin with two figures on it—an abstract man and woman standing side by side, one dark, one light. He said that by seeking its image I'd find our murderer. He also said that I'd find the first stepping-stone to my past."

"So the pin led you to Mary Elliot?"

She nodded. "And to the truth about Rose Pierce."

"Which begs the question, how did he know?"

She sighed. "Maybe he *is* military. He walked like military, if that makes sense."

"So, in reality, he could be Blaine?"

"In reality, he's a changer, as I said. A crow."

"Crow feathers were found at the scene of Kathryn Douglass's murder." And he seriously doubted it was a coincidence. *Everything* about this case seemed—

one way or another—to be tying back to her, Hope-worth and this mysterious Joe. Or Joshua, as the case may be. He had no doubt the two were one and the same.

"But he can't be one of Hopeworth's products be-cause he has dark hair. Lloyd said all Hopeworth's creations have red hair, and that's certainly proven to be the case, even among the rejects."

All true. And yet, why did this Joe know so much? And how had he formed such an intimate connection with her? If he wasn't a Hopeworth product, he had to be at least a part of Hopeworth—and a part of the project that Sam had come from. A project that had been almost totally erased.

Besides, it wasn't as though a shifter capable of tak-ing on multiple forms couldn't easily change his hair color.

"Psychic connections such as the one you appear to have with Joe just don't happen between strangers. Despite the myths, such strong connections take time, and effort and—" He hesitated and then added softly, "intimacy."

"Joe and I have never been lovers."

"I never said that you were. But he could be some-one who was close to you in that place. Someone you leaned on for strength."

She shook her head. "There was only Joshua. In the dreams, it was always him and me against the rest."

Yet she had said that she didn't know if the dreams could be trusted as the truth. What if someone *had* altered them, perhaps not so much for content as for appearances? What if her twin wasn't who she thought he was?

That would certainly make the man who seemed to

know too much about her more of an option as the brother.

But why would he continue to keep his identity a secret if he was in mental contact with her now? What was he waiting for?

Since that was a question neither he nor Sam could answer, he switched topics.

"How trustworthy do you think the nurse's information is going to be when it comes to Hopeworth's habit of wiping out sections of their former employees' memories?"

Sam shrugged. "Mary's memories of the project *have* been restricted. I asked her the name of the project she worked on, and she said it hurts if she tries to remember."

"And yet she could talk freely about you and Joshua? You didn't think that odd?"

"No." Sam hesitated. "But Mary said we were all little more than numbers, so maybe that's why she could talk about us."

Gabriel frowned. "What?"

Sam grimaced. "Just something Mary mentioned the last time. She said she wished the military would give us names instead of numbers, because she couldn't keep up with all the different names we kept coming up with for ourselves."

"So the military might have restricted her from mentioning specific numbers, but because she knew you by particular names, she's been able to short-circuit the restrictions?"

"Possibly."

"Which means she might also know what other aliases your brother went by."

Sam's eyebrows rose. "I hadn't thought of asking that, but yeah, she might. It's worth a try, anyway."

It certainly was. Hell, *anything* that gave them *any* information about her so-called brother was a good thing, because he didn't trust her sudden revelation. Didn't like the fact that she'd been talking to someone for so many years and yet had no clue as to that person's real identity. Hell, how could they be sure it *wasn't* Sethanon? It wasn't beyond the realm of possibility, especially given Sethanon's interest in her over the years.

The car slid to a stop outside a large brick residence that had the air of a secure hospital rather than someplace homey and warm. Bars lined the front windows, and sturdy, locked gates guarded the pathways that led to the back of the building. There was a lot of landscaping evident beyond the gates, but it did little to blunt the initial impression of a prison-like environment.

"This it?" He glanced back at Sam.

She nodded. "Hopefully, Mary's doing a little better now than when I visited her the last time. Otherwise, we won't be talking to her for long."

"How ill is she?" Gabriel climbed out of the car. The early morning sunshine was bright despite the bitter wind, so he put on his sunglasses. And in the brief shift between brightness and shade, he thought he saw something move in the thick shrubbery beyond the gates.

He frowned, lowering the sunglasses a little and squinting against the sunlight as he studied the path along the right side of the building. Nothing more than bushes moving to the tune of the breeze.

And yet . . . something had moved. Something

other than plant life swaying back and forth. Something that had darted back into the shadows with inhuman speed, and yet had been human in shape.

Frown deepening, he walked around the car, waiting until his back was to the building before he said, "Can you feel anything out of place?"

She gave him a sharp glance and looked at the building. "No." She hesitated, frowning a little. "Yes. There's a faint feeling of evil coming from the right of the building."

The right of the building was where he'd seen the shadow move. "What do you mean by faint?"

"It's not a solid sensation. It's wispier, like I'm feeling something ghostlike rather than human." She shrugged and glanced at him. "Why? What did you see?"

"I'm not sure." He stared at the side of the building for a little longer but didn't see any further movement. And yet the sense that something was out of place remained. "I think something is about to go down. You want to get inside and talk to Mary Elliot? I'd like to check the outside of the building first."

She nodded and strode toward the front door. He headed sideways toward the suspect. But neither of them had taken more than a few steps when the screaming began.

He shared a brief glance with Sam, then ran like hell for the gates. One huge leap and he was over them, racing for the rear of the building.

He saw a shadow leap skyward on night-dark wings as he rounded the corner.

He shifted shape and gave chase.

* * *

SAM CRASHED THROUGH THE FRONT door, her badge raised in one hand and her weapon held low in the other. "SIU, folks. Stand back."

"Officer, please, there's no need—"

She ignored the woman at the reception desk and ran down the hall. How many times in the past had she been in a similar situation? Being so close to possible answers, only to have them snatched away by some force of evil? Whether that force was military or Sethanon's didn't matter right now. What mattered was getting to Mary's room and making sure yet another source of answers wasn't shut down.

Because the screams were definitely coming from Mary. Sam pounded down the hall, chased by footsteps and protests, her gaze on the main prize—the open door to Mary's room.

She slowed as she neared the room, took a deep breath, then stepped inside, weapon raised.

Only to discover the receptionist had been right. There was no need, and no threat. One of the four big windows that looked out onto the garden *was* open, but nothing more than a few inches. Maybe enough to let a bird in, but certainly not a human. The screen covering the window had tumbled to the ground, and the curtains flapped slightly in the breeze. Surely neither could be the reason behind the screams coming from the thin gray-haired woman standing in the middle of the room. The screen dropping *could* have frightened her, but not to this extent. Yet there was sheer terror in Mary's voice.

Two nurses stood on either side of her, talking to her in soft tones, obviously trying to calm her down. Sam had seen at least one of the women on her last visit here, so they probably weren't causing Mary's distress either.

She put her weapon away and stepped toward the trio. "Ladies, do you need any help?" She flashed her badge as one of the nurses looked around, then asked, "What happened?"

"Day terrors," the dark-haired nurse said grimly. "It sometimes happens when the mind regresses."

Sam walked into the older woman's line of sight, blocking the window and whatever it was Mary had seen. Or thought she'd seen.

"Mary?" she said softly.

The older woman blinked, then her gaze met Sam's and the right side of her face lit up in a smile.

"Josephine!" The word was slightly slurred, but understandable. Mary's stroke had robbed the left side of her face of mobility, but thankfully had left her capable of speech. "Oh, thank God you're here!"

She lurched forward, pulling out of the nurses' grip with surprising ease, and staggered toward Sam. Sam caught her, wrapping her arms around the frail body. She felt the shuddering of terror through the other woman's limbs, the steel of muscle underneath it.

Mary might be old and frail, but she had a surprising amount of strength left.

"It's all right, Mary. I'm here. No one will get you now."

The old woman shuddered. "I saw him, you know. I wasn't imagining it. I saw him."

"Shhhh. It's okay. You're safe." She stroked Mary's back with one hand and felt the terror begin to leave the older woman's body. "Who did you see?"

But Mary appeared not to hear her, caught up in

her distress. "He'll be back. Now that they know I'm here, he'll be back."

"No, he won't. My partner's out there right now, hunting him down." But who the hell had Mary seen? If only she could get an answer. "He'll catch him. That's what he does."

Mary pulled back a little. "I know. I was talking to him."

Sam frowned. "You were talking to Gabriel?"

Mary looked annoyed. "I don't know a Gabriel. I meant Joshua. Joshua will catch him. Where is he? I want to talk to him again." Her voice was petulant, like that of a child deprived of a toy. And in many ways Mary *was* a child. Much of her mind had gone, lost in memories of the past.

But did that mean she was lost now, or had she really seen Joshua? And if it wasn't Joshua who had scared her—as her words seemed to indicate—then who or what had?

"Maybe Joshua will come by later."

Even as she said it, Sam glanced up at the dark-haired nurse, who shook her head and said, "There were no visitors today."

So, it *was* all in Mary's imagination. But that didn't mean Sam couldn't get something useful, as long as she didn't push Mary too far. She motioned toward the sofa. "Mary, why don't you come sit down on the sofa with me?"

"Oh, all right. As long as they don't stick me again. They're always sticking me with things."

The second nurse came back into the room with a medical trolley at that precise moment, and Sam couldn't help smiling. "You don't want to be sick when Joshua visits again, do you?" She helped the elderly woman onto the sofa and knelt down in front of her. "How about you talk to me about his visit while the nurses make sure the other man didn't hurt you."

The old woman's smile broke loose at the mention of Joshua. "He was such a bonny child. You both were."

"When was he here, Mary?"

"Today, like I said. Just before that other man appeared." She shuddered. "I never did like the look of that one. He was nasty."

"Who was he, Mary?"

The woman frowned, as if trying to search for the memory was painful. "I . . . I can't remember his name, I'm afraid."

Clearly this was Hopeworth's blocks at work. Time for another tactic.

"So how did Joshua get here? He never checked in with the nurses."

The old woman snorted. "Well, he wouldn't, would he? He hates medical types. It's far easier for him to fly in through an open window and avoid all the fuss."

"So he came as a bird?"

"Yeah." Mary smiled. "You both had to be electronically chipped as kids so you didn't fly beyond the compound restrictions."

It sounded like Mary was getting her mixed up with someone else, because while she had changer genes, she certainly wasn't able to change. Though, admittedly, she'd never tried to, either.

A chill ran over Sam's skin and she rubbed her arms. Whoever had blocked her memories had been very thorough indeed if she could not remember something as basic as the fact that she could change shape.

Why block it in the first place, though? She could understand why Hopeworth and everything that had happened there might have been erased, but why the total erasure? Why take away something as harmless as the fact that she had a brother, or that she could shapechange?

And how was any of this connected to the mythical Sethanon?

"How many bird forms did he have?" she asked.

"Several. You always seemed to prefer being a small hawk, but he liked variety. A hawk, a crow, sometimes even a pigeon. None of those could fit through the window, though. So today he came as one of those annoying birds—minors, I think they call them."

Again Sam wondered if Mary's memories were true, or if she was getting imagination and reality mixed up. She glanced up as the nurse finished her exam.

"She's fine," the nurse said. "Just keep her calm."

Sam nodded, waiting until the two nurses had left the room before continuing her questions. "Did Joshua say why he was here, Mary?"

"He said it was all right to talk. He said they couldn't stop me anymore." Fear briefly crossed her half-frozen features. "Maybe that's why *he* came. He knew."

"He who? I really need to know which one of them, Mary, so we can stop him."

Mary frowned again, then eventually said, "The general. It was the general."

"Blaine? Or Lloyd?" It had to be one of them. Lloyd was an obstetrician, and apparently in charge of the Hopeworth breeding pens. Blaine had been the man behind the experiments and training, and maybe even the whole Penumbra project.

But if it was Blaine, which of the Blaines had been here? The one she'd met in Wetherton's car, or the one who'd been in Wetherton's office?

And did it actually matter? Just because she hadn't felt anything evil about the first Blaine didn't mean he wasn't.

"It was Blaine." Mary shuddered. "We used to call him the day shadow. Always creeping about, he was, and harder to spot than a ghost at dusk."

"Did he say anything?"

"Didn't get a chance, did he? He saw Joshua and scooted out of here as fast as he could."

"So he recognized Josh?"

Mary smiled. "You always used to call him that when you were angry with him. It was like you couldn't get his full name out fast enough."

Her dreams had never shown her angry at the man who was supposedly her brother. The only emotions in the dreams were fear and longing—fear of what the scientists were doing, and of what Joshua was going to do. And longing to be free, to have what she'd never had—a family, friends. Things she still didn't possess.

"Did we fight often?"

Mary shrugged. "You were as different as night and day, you two. You were always the fiery one, the one quick to judge. He was more . . . careful." She looked away for a minute, her gaze distant. "But for all that, I always thought he was the more dangerous of the two of you. He never seemed to have limits of any kind. And he did some nasty things."

"We both did," she said softly.

Mary's gaze met hers again, and she raised a slightly shaking hand to brush Sam's skin with dry fingertips. "In many ways, you were always the good one. What you did, you had to do."

Her words made Sam remember the pin Joe had given her. Had it been more of a clue than she realized? Had the abstract man and woman on its surface—one light, one dark—represented her and the man who was supposedly her twin?

Had Joe been trying to tell her that he knew not only who she was, but who her brother was? And did that mean he was a friend or foe? For sure, he'd warned her of trouble more than once, but that didn't mean she could trust him. Hell, for all she knew, Joe might be Blaine in disguise.

"Mary, was there anyone on the project who went by the name of Joe Black?"

Mary frowned. "Not that I remember. But then, I didn't know everyone on the project, because I was basically confined to the nursery and housing areas. Nor did I know all the secret names you two called yourselves. Only some."

"Can you remember some of the other names?"

"Not really. I only remembered Josephine and Joshua because those were the names you used most often."

"What about Sethanon? Is that one of them? Or maybe the name of someone who worked there?"

"Sethanon?" Her frown deepened. "I don't think

there was anyone on the project called that. It's such an odd name that surely I'd remember it. But Joshua was once caught reading a book by that name, I'm sure."

A chill went through her. "Sethanon is a book title?"

"Yeah. I caught him reading it well before they did, and I warned him. But he took no notice."

"So we weren't allowed to read fiction?"

"No, only what they gave you. On technologies, weapons, stuff like that." Mary shrugged. "No one ever knew how he got that book. When they took it off him, he got mad." She looked away again. "Joshua would never have hurt me, I knew that, but that day I was afraid. And not just of him, but of both of you."

Sam raised her eyebrows. "Why both of us?"

Mary's gaze came back to Sam's. "Because separately you were powerful, but together—I swear, heaven and earth trembled in fear of your wrath that day."

Sam swallowed heavily but didn't ask what had happened. Right now, she really didn't want to know. It was enough to know that she was not what she'd presumed—and that the past she'd spent most of her life trying to uncover was one better left shuttered. And yet, now that she'd started down the path of remembering, there was no turning back. The military and their rising level of interest ensured that, if nothing else.

Besides, the dreams were becoming relentless. Remembering was being forced on her, whether she wanted it or not.

"If we were so powerful, Mary, how did they ever restrain us?"

Her smile was grim. "Simply by placing special pellets under your skins, and threatening the death of one if the other did anything out of place."

She remembered the dream in which she and Joshua had been running up a slope on a moonless night. Remembered the promise he'd made as fire danced across his fingertips that soon they would have their revenge and be free.

He'd obviously found a way to remove the pellets and fulfill that promise.

"How did you escape the fire that destroyed the project, Mary?"

"I don't know." She frowned. "There was an explosion, and heat—horrible heat—and the next thing I remember I was outside on this grassy slope." She rubbed her arms. "I think an angel saved me that day. I should have died with the rest of them. The nursery was the second place the fire hit."

"And the first?"

"The arena where they used to train you both."

Something in the way she said that scratched at Sam's instincts. "Both of us? What about the others?"

"There were no others. Not in . . ." Mary hesitated and rubbed her forehead. "It still hurts if I try to say the name. Joshua told me it wouldn't."

Sam lightly squeezed the older woman's free hand. "You don't need to say the name, Mary. I know the project." She hesitated. "So, Joshua and I were the only ones in Penumbra?"

Mary nodded. "There were others created. Lots of others. But none of them survived past toddlerhood.

No one knew why, but I reckon it was because you were twins. You had each other, and you took care of each other. The other little ones had no one but themselves."

Karl had said that walkers came as a pair. That they had to, or they could become lost in the very power they were destined to control. Was that the reason she and Joshua had survived when the others hadn't? Because they were twins? Yet if Joshua was her base, why did she appear to have a connection with Gabriel?

And if Hopeworth had studied walkers, and were intermixing walker genes with those of other races, how could they not know that walkers had to come as a pair to survive?

"So we were the only twins they bred?"

"They didn't breed you as twins. It just happened in utero. One whole became two."

A chill went through Sam. *Two halves of a whole.* Joe had said that, too. Another clue she hadn't taken note of.

God, who *was* he?

And was he friend or foe? Or something else altogether?

"So once the project was destroyed, you left?"

Mary nodded. "I went on to work for several adoption agencies."

"And the military hasn't tried to contact you before now?"

Mary shook her head. "Not until now."

So what was different about now? But even as the question went through her mind, Sam remembered Blaine's reaction as he'd come out of Wetherton's office. Remembered his certainty that they'd met before, that she knew just who he was and what he did in the military.

She was the reason he'd come to see Mary.

He'd wanted to confirm his suspicions, and Mary was the one person left alive who seemed able to connect her with that red-haired child bred and raised in Hopeworth.

This meant Mary couldn't stay here. Blaine would be back—and if there was one thing Sam was certain of, it was that she didn't want Blaine anywhere near either her or Mary. And while Mary might be living in a fantasy world most of the time, what she did remember of the past was enough to confirm any suspicions Blaine might have. And once that happened, they would come after Sam in force. She'd been bred to be a weapon. It didn't matter if her abilities were buried along with her memories. They'd want her back regardless.

Maybe that was why Joshua had come here, to give Mary permission to tell all. Maybe he was trying to speed up Sam's memory so that she could escape Hopeworth's clutches once again.

She glanced around as Gabriel walked into the room. "Any success?"

He shook his head. "I saw a crow fly away from the window, but by the time I shifted shape and flew after it, its lead was too great."

Joshua in crow form? Or Joe? And if it *had* been Joe, what did he want with Mary? "I wouldn't have thought a crow would be faster than a hawk."

"Neither would I." He stopped beside the sofa and gave Mary a smile. "Are you all right?"

"I don't know you," Mary said, somewhat crossly. She glanced at Sam. "Do I know him?"

"This is my new partner, Mary. His name is Gabriel, and he's going to arrange a nice place for you to stay while we track down Blaine."

Gabriel raised his eyebrows, but he didn't refute the statement. "Somewhere nice and safe."

The mobile half of Mary's face lit up. "A holiday would be nice. Gets boring, this place does."

Sam patted the older woman's knee and rose. "We'll just go talk to the nurses and arrange it, then."

"And lock the damn window," Mary said. "I don't want that bastard coming back to visit me while you're gone."

Sam obeyed, locking the window and closing the curtains for good measure. When they were out in the hall, Gabriel asked, "What was that all about?"

"Mary was screaming because she saw Blaine." Sam glanced back at the room to ensure Mary wasn't moving around, then looked back at him. "And if Blaine *was* visiting her, it's because he wanted to confirm his suspicions about me."

Gabriel frowned. "But the nurses said she had no visitors."

"No visitors that checked in with them. That doesn't mean there weren't any."

"Or that Mary wasn't imagining it."

Sam nodded, conceding the point even if she didn't believe that was the case. "What, exactly, did you see when you climbed out of the car?"

"I thought I saw something move—something that was human in shape and yet held no substance."

"And later, when you gave chase?"

"A crow, as I said."

She blew out a breath. "A crow is one of Joshua's shapes, apparently." But it was also one of Joe's. And one of them, more than likely, was Kathryn Douglass's murderer.

If they were two separate beings, that was. It was more than possible Joe and Joshua were one and the same.

"So this Joshua of yours is Blaine?"

The sudden edge in his voice surprised her, though, as usual, there was little emotion to be seen in his expression. She shook her head. "Not unless he can be in two places at the same time. Mary was talking to Joshua when Blaine appeared. Blaine apparently recognized Josh and ran. Joshua gave chase."

"So if it was Joshua I was chasing, what happened to Blaine?"

"Who knows? But Mary called him a day shadow—apparently he could creep around without being seen."

His eyebrows rose. "Meaning he could still be here? Can you feel him?"

Sam extended her senses, searching, but there was no sense of the shadowy evil she'd felt earlier. Blaine—if it was indeed Blaine she'd sensed—had gone. She shook her head.

"So, the question is," Gabriel said, "why were both men here today?"

"If you believe her—and I do—then Joshua was here to tell Mary that it was okay to tell me everything. He apparently told her the military could no longer stop her."

He studied her, his face unreadable. "And Blaine?"

"As I said, I think he was here to confirm his suspicions. Mary worked in the nursery. She's probably the only one left alive who has any true knowledge about me and Joshua."

"Did you ask her about Sethanon?"

Sam nodded. "She didn't know anyone by that name, but said that Joshua was punished once for reading a book with that title."

"A book? He named himself after a book?"

"Well, if Sethanon is actually Joshua, then yes. But it's a bit of a long shot, isn't it?"

Gabriel shrugged. "We've never been able to find a birth record for someone with that name, so it has to be an alias. And there's no rule stating an alias can't come from a book title."

"But if Joshua *is* this Sethanon of yours, then how has he managed to remain unknown so long?"

"I think the only people who might be able to answer our questions are Blaine and Lloyd," Gabriel said. "Both of them were involved in the Penumbra project."

"And neither of them will be inclined to be forthcoming."

"I agree." Gabriel hesitated. "Look, let's get Mary moved; then we can talk some more."

Sam studied him for a moment, again noting the sudden edge in his voice. "About what, exactly?"

"About crows. The one seen here, and the people you know who are crows."

"Why do I get the sudden feeling I'm not going to like the direction of this conversation?"

"Probably because you won't." His expression was suddenly grim. "Remember when I mentioned Kathryn Douglass being murdered, and a crow feather being found at the murder scene?" When she nodded, he said, "There was something else, too—a warning about not reviving Penumbra written in blood on the wall. I don't think it's a coincidence. I think that either your brother or the man you've been in psychic contact with is a murderer."

ELEVEN

"BUT WHY WOULD EITHER OF them want to murder Douglass when she had nothing to do with the Penumbra project?" There was no surprise in her voice, no anger. No emotion at all, really, except perhaps a tiny hint of weary resignation. As if this was just another shock in a day that had already provided several.

Gabriel shrugged. In truth, he had no answer to that question, and certainly no proof yet that the feather they'd found in Douglass's apartment was linked to either the man from Sam's past or the man in her telepathic journeys. All he had was suspicion and a feeling that his guess was the correct one.

"She was in contact with both Blaine and Lloyd on an operational level. I suspect they had actually begun work on a project similar to Penumbra, and your brother or psi buddy discovered it. Hence the warning on the wall."

She studied him for a moment, then said, "Why would Pegasus be employed to revive a project like

Penumbra? Wouldn't the military want that sort of project under its own control?"

"Pegasus worked in conjunction with the military on a number of projects. Given the warning also said that Douglass was told not to proceed with the project, it suggests that maybe she was the reason behind its revival. We'll never know for sure now, given that she's dead."

"And it's not like the military will tell us," Sam said. "But the thing is, Penumbra was totally destroyed. It wasn't just the buildings, but most of the personnel and all the research materials, so neither Pegasus nor the military should have been able to revive it."

"Unless Douglass somehow came across research material relating to shadow walkers. If Karl has documents on it, there'll be other stuff out there as well. Maybe she started research, and then went to the military."

"But even then—"

"It might not have amounted to anything," he finished for her. "Except for the fact that they'd discovered the possibility that one of their test subjects had survived the destruction."

And that, he realized suddenly, was what the explosion at the Pegasus Foundation had been about. Those in control of Penumbra had been under the impression that fire was Sam's element to control. They'd intended to use her reaction to the firestorm at Pegasus to test whether or not she was who they thought—and then the med check afterward would have confirmed it. But then, why had they gone ahead with the test when he and Illie had shown up instead?

Had Douglass been confused as to the identity or

sex of the test subject? Or was there, as Illie had suggested, a deeper reason for him and Illie being given the test anyway?

And what would they have done if the two of them had died that day?

It was probably something they would never know, since Douglass was now dead. And Blaine and Lloyd were not likely to be fonts of information.

He just wished he knew what they thought about that message on the wall. Neither man had given much away, and though he believed Lloyd's comment that he had no idea why that particular message had been left with Douglass's body, Blaine had made no such comment. And Gabriel had a feeling that Blaine not only knew the reason behind it, but supported it. Which was an odd thing to think when Blaine was supposedly the man who'd been in charge of the project.

But he could admit to none of this aloud. Not to Sam, anyway. She had enough to worry about already.

"What I think," he said eventually, "is that someone is still trying to protect you. Whether that person is this unseen brother of yours, or whether it's the man you're psychically connected to, is something only you can answer."

"Why would my brother—the man you've suggested could be Sethanon—want to stop Penumbra when that very project could give him the army he needs to win his war?"

"I don't know. But I don't think it's a coincidence that the feather was found in Douglass's apartment." He hesitated, then added, "But I do think it's time you started asking some hard questions."

Anger flashed in her eyes, reminding him briefly of a burst of lightning. "You think I haven't been?"

"I think you've been delaying certain issues because you're afraid to uncover the truth."

That streak of lightning seemed brighter in her eyes, and this time it was accompanied by a stirring in the air that was vaguely reminiscent of the crackle of energy that raced just before a thunderstorm.

But before he could comment on it, his wristcom rang. He tapped it and said impatiently, "Assistant Director Stern."

"Hey, partner, got some news you might not want to hear."

"Spit it out, Illie. I don't have time for games right now."

"We found another body in Kathryn Douglass's apartment. It was cut into pieces and shoved into an upright freezer."

"How did the State boys manage to miss that?"

"Well, the body parts were covered by standard-issue meat trays and weren't immediately recognizable."

"I would have thought a severed human head would be immediately recognizable."

"A human head?" Sam asked, eyebrow raised in query. Gabriel noted with interest that the electricity in the air seemed to fade away once her attention was diverted.

"Well, *that* was at the bottom of the freezer, and it was only after undoing the black plastic around the body parts that we realized what we had."

"So why did you think to look in the freezer in the first place?"

"Well, rules say we have to do a thorough search of

the premises, but it was primarily curiosity that had me looking deeper into the freezer. Douglass was apparently a vegetarian, so what was she doing with a freezer full of meat?"

"Have you sent the remains to the labs for analysis?"

"Yeah, Finley's checking it out as we speak. I thought you might want to be there for his initial report."

Gabriel frowned. "And why would I want to do that?"

"Because if the head was anything to go by, the dead woman is an exact replica of Douglass herself, only a little younger."

Surprise rippled through him. "Did she have a sister?"

"No immediate living family. There are two cousins and an aunt now living in the United States, but that's about it."

"I'll head over to headquarters now. Anything else?"

"Not offhand. I'm still digging into her past."

"What about Blaine?"

"That's a big, fat zero. The military has not been forthcoming with information, either."

No surprise there. "Well, then, continue both investigations and let me know if you find anything." He hit the end button and met Sam's curious gaze. "They found another body at Douglass's apartment. One that looks identical to the murdered woman."

"A twin? Or a clone?"

"According to the records, Douglass had no immediate family."

"Well, if both Douglasses are dead, then it can't be

a shapeshifter at work. Those revert to their natural forms when they die, so at least one of them has to be a clone. Right?"

"Perhaps. But nothing in this whole mess is what it seems, so maybe we've also found a shapeshifter who does not revert." He rubbed his head, then pulled his car keys from his pocket and handed them to her. "Go back to the hotel and get some sleep. I'll make arrangements to get Mary transferred to a safe house and then go talk to Finley."

She took the keys from him, her fingers touching his only briefly, yet they sent an electric charge through his entire body. A charge reflected briefly in her eyes.

"What about our discussion?" she said softly. "And my brunch?"

"I'll meet you at the hotel around four this afternoon and drive you to Wetherton's. We can talk on the way. We'll have to do that rain check on the apology lunch after all."

Sam nodded and glanced into the room, as if to reassure herself Mary was okay, then walked away. He watched her for a few seconds, then started making arrangements to secure Mary.

"HOW'S THE EXAMINATION COMING ALONG, Finley?" Gabriel asked as he strode into the lab.

Finley cleared his throat and slid his thick glasses up the bridge of his nose with a gloved finger. "Well, this is certainly an interesting situation. Two identical bodies, both chopped into pieces, one a younger version of the other."

Gabriel stopped at the end of one of the tables and

examined the two sets of remains. The two women would definitely have been physically identical if not for the deeper age lines around the face of their original victim. "The cuts on the younger version appear to be from a sharp instrument."

"They are. It appears she was strangled before she was sliced apart."

"You've done DNA testing?"

"Yes. The younger one is the clone. It would seem Kathryn Douglass was planning to skip the whole 'age gracefully' idea."

No real surprise, given Douglass's name *had* been on Kazdan's list. "She wouldn't be the first woman in the world to resort to surgery to do that."

"This is a little more extreme than plastic surgery."

"Yes, but it's not exactly the first time we've seen this. There's Wetherton, for a start." Although Wetherton's reasons for transplanting into a clone seemed to be more about avoiding disease than gaining a younger body. "Any idea where the clone was murdered?"

"Not yet. Though there's no evidence at Douglass's that the clone was murdered there."

"No." And no reason for Douglass to want her clone dead, either. Not if she'd paid the sort of money Wetherton had to get a new body.

Gabriel studied the table containing the torn-apart remnants of humanity, then added, "There aren't many shifters who would have the strength to tear apart someone like that."

Finley sniffed. "Most cats could, but what we're dealing with here is a bear shifter. And it's one big bear, I can tell you."

Gabriel raised an eyebrow, amused by the comment. "Most bear shifters are big."

"Think brown bear, and add half the size again."

That *was* one big *mother* of a bear. "How can you be sure?"

"I measured the distance between the claw slashes left on the woman's back." Finley hesitated, then added, "It looks like he shifted while they were . . . um . . . making love. Nasty stuff."

Especially for Kathryn Douglass, Gabriel imagined. The differences between the anatomy of a human male and that of a bear would in itself have caused a lot of pain and damage. Probably even have torn her up fairly badly. "Anything else?"

Finley shook his head. "We've collected semen samples, of course. I'll do a search of both our database and the government's to see if there's a match."

Gabriel nodded. Most criminals these days had DNA samples taken as a matter of course, but it had taken a lot of years to implement the procedure thanks to the civil rights activists. Which meant, of course, that the database was not only constantly being updated, but also only reliable when it came to criminals caught in the last ten years.

And he very much doubted that the person behind these murders could be tracked down so easily.

"Let me know if you find anything."

Finley nodded absently and Gabriel left the lab, heading up to his office. He grabbed a cup of coffee from the autocook and sat down at his desk.

"Computer, update."

"Please state name and rank for voice verification."

He did so. The screen flicked to life and began listing all the reports and activities going on in the SIU.

With Byrne having taken official leave to cover
Stephan's need to be at their parents' compound with
Lyssa and his new son, control of the SIU was nomi-
nally in the hands of Harry Krane, Byrne's second in
command. However, neither Stephan nor he was
about to let an outsider take full control of the SIU,
so all reports and decisions were covertly siphoned
through to him. He then channeled all the appropriate information on, and held back the more clandestine reports for when Stephan resumed his position.

He found nothing of real interest until he read the
report from the bug Sam had placed in Wetherton's
office. And though it revealed little more than the
name behind one of Wetherton's many phone conversations, it sparked a whole lot of questions.

That name was *Les Mohern*.

Why would a petty criminal like Les Mohern suddenly come out of hiding to contact a government
minister like Wetherton? For that matter, why would
he even visit someone like Kathryn Douglass? Was
there a connection between the two that no one knew
about?

Maybe so. After all, Les's brother had worked for
Kazdan. He doubted that it was a coincidence that,
after his brother's death, Les had gone to ground.
Maybe he'd done so for a reason—such as fearing for
his life.

But if that were the case, why would he now surface to contact two high-profile people like Douglass
and Wetherton? Surely he had to know that both
would be under some sort of surveillance, given their
positions. Why would he risk discovery to contact either of them?

He clicked on Mohern's name and studied the

background report. *Bingo*—an address. He finished the remainder of his coffee in one gulp and stood.

He'd discovered long ago that when instinct scratched *this* hard, it was better not to ignore it. This Les Mohern was a key. But to what, he now had to discover.

SAM SLEPT.

And, as usual, she dreamed.

But this was not a dream she'd had before. This one was new. And terrifying.

The night was filled with smoke and fire and fear. The very air burned so hot the metal walls around her were beginning to bubble and melt. And yet the heat and the flames never touched her, skittering around her as she ran through the madness. Seeking safety, seeking freedom.

Lights flickered ahead, scattering brief patches of luminescence through the smoke-filled darkness and highlighting the figure ahead. For an instant that figure seemed huge and hairy, with fearsome claws that rent and tore at those stupid enough to try to stop him. Then the lights went out again, and it was just Joshua running ahead, telling her to hurry, that this was their chance. Their only hope.

And she obeyed, running after him hard, ignoring the many screams, even rejoicing in them.

Until she heard that one scream.

Mary.

She stopped abruptly. Ahead, Joshua had also stopped, his actions reminding her briefly of a puppet jerked to stillness by its master.

He swung around. "There's no time for this, Samantha."

"She cared for us, Josh. I can't let her die for that."

"She was *paid* to care for us. It was her job, her duty. She is no better than the rest of them."

"She sang us nursery rhymes and told us stories that made us laugh. She gave us dreams of a life beyond this place. And she left the window open for us at night, giving us what freedom she could. I will not let her die."

"It's too late. I can't let you—"

"You can't stop me."

Before he could react, she thrust out her hand. Power flowed through her, surging from the floor— from the earth itself—up through her body and out her fingertips, leaping the distance between them and hitting him hard. It flung him backward, into the thickness of the fire and out of sight.

He wasn't hurt. The fire could never hurt him. It *was* him—a part of his soul, a part of his being.

But it was *his* protection that was keeping her safe from the flames, and as that protection briefly flickered, then went out, the full force of the firestorm hit. Heat flowed over her, scalding her skin, her lungs.

She closed her eyes and called to the sky and the power of the storms. Wind swept in, buffeting the flames away, bringing with it the coolness of the night, giving her air to breathe that wouldn't scorch her insides.

With the wind swirling around her, providing a buffer from the flames and the heat, she backtracked, running through the halls to the nursery area.

To discover hell itself.

Fire was a wall that ran on for as far as the eye

could see—a seething, writhing mass of red, gold and white fury that crawled up the nursery walls and across the ceilings. It was hot and hungry and very, very deadly. Surely no one could survive in the fiery doom that the nursery had become.

And yet Mary's scream rent the air, her voice high-pitched and filled with pain and terror.

A trap? Maybe. Probably.

But something inside wouldn't let her walk away until she discovered the truth. The older woman had made the darkness of this place survivable in so many small ways. They owed her her life, at the very least.

A hand grabbed her arm, its touch cold and violent as it yanked her back. She knew without even looking that it wasn't Josh.

That it was Lloyd.

Fear leapt, and her heart began to race. It was instinctive, that fear, bred into her from birth itself. And yet there were monsters far worse than Lloyd walking these halls. But neither those monsters nor Lloyd himself were going to stop her tonight. Not when the havoc Josh had created had finally given them the hope of freedom.

Energy crackled across her fingertips as she swung around, but she kept her fists low, out of sight. Lloyd wore a fire suit and breathing apparatus, and though the mask distorted much of his features, his fury was still evident in the glow of his eyes.

"Stop it, you little bitch." He shook her violently enough to rattle her teeth. "Stop it now, or I'll kill your brother."

She reached into the pocket of her overalls and pulled out the small electronic device that would have injected the lethal poison into Josh's skin. Josh had hers safely tucked away in his pocket. She had no idea why he wanted to keep them, but she obeyed his wishes, as she usually did.

"You mean with this?" She raised the device so that he could see it.

He swore and raised his hand, as if to hit her. But she gathered the energy that danced all around them and froze his blow in mid-motion. Surprise, then fear, flickered through his eyes. It felt good. So very good.

Never underestimate your enemy was a lesson drilled into them from babyhood, yet it was a lesson their controllers had never fully understood.

Or perhaps it was more a case of never fully understanding what they had created.

Either way, it had finally culminated in this moment, where she and Josh held the power.

"No more," she said softly. She glanced down to where his fingers gripped her arm and telekinetically pulled them away one by one, snapping bone each time.

Sweat broke out across Lloyd's forehead, but he didn't utter a sound. And she wanted him to say something. Wanted him to scream, as she had screamed so many times.

She stepped back from him, keeping him still and in place as she raised her hand. Lightning arced between her fingertips, small flashes of fury that lit the smoky orange air with a pure white light. "Fire is not my element. It was never my element, but you people would never see that."

He opened his mouth, but no sound came out. Probably just as well, as she had no doubt what he was trying to deliver was just more abuse or yet an-

other threat. She smiled coldly and unleashed the
lightning. It arced around him, playing with him like
a cat with a mouse, touching, leaping away, then
touching again. When it finally settled, he screamed.

She closed her eyes, breathing deep the sound. Again,
it felt wonderful. But after a second or two, she picked
him up telekinetically and threw him against the
melting, bubbling metal wall. It melted his suit, his
skin, and his screams reached a fever pitch before
shutting off abruptly. He was dead before he hit the
ground.

She studied his body for a second, feeling little—
not even the pleasure she'd thought she'd feel. *Damn
it,* she'd been dreaming of this moment for as long as
she'd been able to form conscious thought, and yet
now that it was here, there was nothing. But now was
not the time to worry about such things. She spun to
face the nursery.

The firestorm had grown, but Mary still screamed.
Where the hell was she? There were few places
that would provide shelter from such fury, not for
this length of time, anyway. She bit her lip and half
reached for the full power of the storms, then
stopped. She couldn't afford to douse the flames, not
if she wanted to escape this place, and calling to the
storms would do that. She might be able to call them,
might be able to channel some of their power and
some of their elements, but she wasn't strong enough
to control their full force, because control was something she was still teaching herself. The scientists
thought she was earth and sun and that Josh was
wind and water. They had it half right. She was earth
and wind, and Josh was sun and water. She could
call storms and quakes, Josh fire and floods. In the

long, barren years of their childhood, she'd always sat in on Josh's lessons, and him on hers, each learning what they could while continuing the lie, then practicing when they were alone and beyond the watchful eyes of the scientists. Though, to some extent, their abilities *did* overlap. If she called in the storms, he could control the water, and he would do so now because he wanted everyone dead. But she was also earth, and earth was the ruler of the other elements. She could stop him, but not without bringing the entire complex down and therefore destroying the one person she was trying to save.

She blew out a breath and directed some of the cold wind that swirled around her at the flames, forcing the heat and the fire away enough to form a corridor. Then she ran through.

The heat battered her, despite the swirling air. Sweat dribbled down her spine, her forehead. The smoke was fierce, a wall of darkness threatening to overwhelm her narrow corridor. She ran as fast as she could, following the screams and praying for a miracle.

And after praying for such an occurrence all her life, it seemed someone was finally listening.

Mary was in the shower room with all the water taps turned on, so that she was surrounded by a ring of water. The heat was still enough to scald her skin and clothes, yet she was alive and awake and conscious. A miracle in itself, since the outside walls of this room were a maelstrom of destruction.

Mary's expression was an odd mix of fear and hope as she spun around. "Josephine? What is happening? What have you done?"

"We're doing what we promised we'd do. Escaping." She hesitated and held out her hand. "Come with me. I'll keep you safe."

Mary studied her for a heartbeat, then her gaze went to the flames. "The heat alone will kill us."

"No, it won't," said a voice from behind.

She turned and met her brother's gaze. Saw both the fury and the understanding. "Don't try to stop me, Josh. I have to do this."

"Even at the risk of recapture?"

"Even at." She hesitated. "But Lloyd is dead."

"Lloyd will never be dead." He smiled and touched a hand to her cheek. His fingertips were tinder hot, and yet inexplicably tender. "It seems you are not the weapon that either they or I might hope you to be. Not yet, anyway." He glanced past her. "Mary, we don't have much time. Move it."

Though he was barely a teenager, Josh's voice held a depth of command not even their trainers had achieved. Mary obeyed.

He caught Mary's hand and said, "I have to do this for your own safety, so sorry in advance." And before Mary or she realized what he was doing, he'd knocked the older woman unconscious. But he didn't let her fall, catching her kinetically before glancing at Sam. "She'd have slowed us down, otherwise. You lead. I'll keep the flames at bay."

He did, but it was still close. He might be flame, but flames often gained a life of their own once given the freedom to run, and these flames had grown beyond the life—though maybe not the intent—of their creator.

They ran from the maelstrom into the dark, cold night. But it was a far-from-silent night—shouts, confusion and fear came from the many people who milled nearby. Some manned fire trucks, some hoses and some whatever came to hand—such as tractors scooping earth into the flames. But no one in the crowd saw the three of them leave. Night was their ally, their only friend, and even when lit by fire, it protected them from sight.

They ran up the hill and collapsed at the top, at the place where she and Joshua had spent so many nights staring at the stars and dreaming of this moment.

And, like when she'd confronted Lloyd, now that the moment was here, it didn't feel as great as it was supposed to feel.

She listened to the sounds filling the night, to the screams of people and the groan of a building ready to collapse—sounds that were interspersed with the harshness of their own breathing. It was Josh who broke the silence.

"You must finish it."

She closed her eyes, knowing that for those who still remained alive inside it was better to end it quickly, and yet not wanting to be the one who took their lives. "There are some who deserve death who are not in those buildings."

He nodded. "Blaine, for one."

"Yes."

"I have plans for him—never fear." His voice held the deadness that always chilled her. This was not her brother, but rather the weapon the military had bred but could never fully control.

"And those plans do not include death? After all he has done?"

His smile was bitter, and yet so cold. So very cold. "No. Not as yet."

A shiver ran down her spine. "If I do this, I want out. Totally out. I don't even want to remember it."

He glanced at her, his smoky blue eyes suddenly seeming blacker than the night itself. "Neither of us can escape what we are."

"Maybe not, but I want the chance to live a normal life, Josh. Even if it's just for a while."

His gaze left hers. For several minutes he didn't say anything, simply studied the confusion below them. Then he sighed. "It will be hard for both of us. We are two halves of one soul, Sammy."

She smiled at his use of her nickname. It was the only one no one knew about, just as his secret name was one only she knew about, though it was one she rarely used. "I don't share your desires. I want a life. I want to be normal."

He glanced at her, his smile almost bitter. "We will never be normal."

"Maybe. But I want to try." She hesitated. "There's something else out there for me, Josh. Something, or someone, I need to find. And I need you to give me the time to do that."

He studied her a few seconds longer, then nodded. "Okay. Destroy that place, and we'll leave."

"And Mary?"

"She'll be safe here on the hill until they find her. She won't remember seeing us. I'll wipe out her memory of being rescued." He hesitated. "We'll find somewhere safe for you to go, and then I'll wipe out yours. Completely. But it might cost you your powers . . ."

"I don't care. I don't want them."

"Are you sure?"

"Yes. More than sure." She touched his arm lightly. "Thank you."

His smile was grim. "You know it won't work, Sammy. Not entirely. It's human nature to seek the unknown, and in your case, that will be the past."

"But in seeking, I will also be living a different life. I need that, at least for a while."

"And what if the powers come back?"

"Do you think they will?"

"They might, once you hit puberty. I don't know for sure, but it seems likely."

"Then I'll cross that bridge when I come to it," she told him firmly.

He grimaced and waved a hand toward the boundary fence. "Then let's get away from this place."

She glanced at the burning buildings and called to the earth underneath it. Power filled her, stretched her, with a rawness that felt at once so right and yet so alien. She waited, letting it run through every pore, every cell, until it felt as if skin and bone and being had melted away and she was nothing more than that rawness. Then she finally released it. A shudder ran through the ground beneath them, gathering speed and strength. With a rolling, groaning sound, the earth below the hill split asunder and whole buildings began to disappear. When everything had been swallowed, she let the earth rest again. Another shudder ran through the ground, one that echoed through her soul. She rubbed her arms and glanced at her brother.

"Let's hope we never come back to this place."

"Let's hope *you* never come back. Me, I have every intention of returning. There's still too much to be done here."

"Josh—"

"You have your dreams, and I have mine. Leave it at that, Sammy."

He rose and held out his hand, and she clasped it and let him lead her to freedom.

THE DREAM CAME TO AN abrupt halt and Sam woke with a start. For several seconds she did nothing more than lie on her bed, staring up at the ceiling as her heart galloped and sweat rolled down her cheek.

Or maybe it was tears.

As her heart began to slow to a more normal rate, she let her thoughts return to the dream in an attempt to grasp all the implications.

Because, as usual, the dream had answered some questions and raised many more. For a start, how had they escaped Hopeworth itself? Sure, their section might have been destroyed by flame and earth, but that quake had been very centralized and wouldn't have destroyed—and indeed, didn't destroy—the rest of the base. Plus, there was the fact that she'd had a tracker in her side—a tracker that had been inserted at birth and had been discovered by the SIU when she was being investigated for Jack's death. Surely that would have been activated as a matter of course, even if they weren't sure who had and hadn't perished in the fires and subsequent quake.

A quake *she'd* brought to life.

God, how scary was that?

She thrust a hand through her sweaty hair and wondered if she still had that power now. If she did, then it was still locked behind the walls of forgetfulness Josh had raised. She hoped it remained there forever. No one should have a power like that.

No one.

And if it started to appear, the way the storm powers were beginning to appear?

She shuddered and sat upright, hugging her knees to her chest. *Worry about one thing at a time,* she told herself fiercely. These were dreams, nothing more, no matter how much they felt like truths. And until she found the boy—the man—she knew as Josh, until she talked to him, there was no proof that anything she dreamed had happened.

And even then, this could all be part of a larger game, one in which she was a major, if unknowing, player. And the dreams might be nothing more than a subterfuge someone desperately wanted her to believe.

Though she didn't think so.

She rubbed her arms and glanced at the clock. It was close to four. Gabriel would be here soon, so she had better start getting ready. And anything was better than contemplating the monster she might have been.

She climbed out of bed and walked across the room to the bathroom. A long shower made her feel better in body if not in soul, and by the time she'd dried her hair and dressed, it was nearly five.

With no sign of Gabriel.

She glanced at her watch to be sure the clock was right, then picked up the phone and dialed his cell phone number.

No answer.

She swore softly. Either he'd been sidetracked or he'd forgotten. Or both.

She left a message, then disconnected, grabbed the keys and headed out the door. If he wanted his car back, he could damn well come and get it.

The traffic was hell, as usual, and it seemed to take forever to get from the hotel to Wetherton's. She drove into the parking lot under Wetherton's building, using her SIU identification to get through the security system. Then she parked near the elevator before catching it to Wetherton's floor.

Jenna Morwood answered on the second knock, lines of exhaustion around her dark eyes. Her expression could only be described as relieved.

"Pleasant day, huh?" Sam said with a grin.

"You could say that," Jenna said. "Our dear minister is lucky he still has teeth left. Touchy-feely little bastard."

"Thankfully, I don't appear to be his type. Anything untoward happen today?"

Jenna frowned. "Not really. I thought we were being followed several times, but I couldn't spot a tail, nor could I read any thoughts of ill intent."

"Did Wetherton do anything unusual? Meet with anyone unusual?"

"Nope. All that happened today was boring politician stuff. I'm hoping like hell this mission doesn't go on for more than a few days."

So was Sam—especially now that her dreams were becoming more detailed. More graphic. She couldn't keep doing her job with any sort of efficiency if she wasn't sleeping. "Unfortunately, the boss seems to think it'll continue for months."

"Then here's hoping he's wrong." Jenna smiled wryly. "Though he generally isn't."

"No." Sam glanced past Jenna as a bump came

from Wetherton's bedroom. "The minister took a nap at this hour?"

"Yeah, the poor man was so exhausted doing all that ministerial sitting about on his ass that he had to come home for a nap at four. He left via the vent at four fifteen."

Sam raised an eyebrow. "Did you manage to get the tracker on him?"

"With all his attempts to feel the merchandise? Oh yeah. He flew to an abandoned apartment complex on Rathdowne Street, stayed there for half an hour, and then went to a low-profile men's club on Spencer Street. He actually returned about ten minutes ago."

"Did we manage to get observers at either place?"

"Not the first one, but definitely at the second."

"Who'd he meet?"

Jenna gave an unladylike snort. "The minister enjoyed several lap dances, and then disappeared into the members-only section. Where, we discovered, a more exotic range of services is offered."

"So basically, the minister had himself a hooker this afternoon?"

"Better her than me," Jenna said, amusement in her voice. "I'll do my lot for kin and country, but I have my limits. And fucking a man like Wetherton is definitely one of them."

"That's not just limits, that's called having taste."

"That, too." Jenna smiled as she leaned sideways and snagged her coat off the hook behind the door. "Luckily, the lecher is yours to deal with for the next twelve hours."

"Joy."

"Indeed." Jenna waved goodbye and retreated

quickly to the elevator. Sam closed the door and turned around to find Wetherton watching her from the bedroom doorway.

She raised an eyebrow and tried to ignore the heat of embarrassment touching her cheeks. She and Jenna had been speaking softly, so there was very little likelihood of Wetherton overhearing their comments. And yet the annoyance in his eyes suggested otherwise.

"Anything I can do for you, Minister?" Sam asked politely.

"Where's Jenna going?"

"Shift change, Minister. You have my delightful company once again this evening."

He looked her up and down. "We're going out again tonight. You could have worn something more appropriate."

"I'm your bodyguard, not your date. I'm dressed very appropriately, believe me."

He grunted—whether in agreement or not, she had no idea—then turned around and walked back into the bedroom. She waited until he came back out and asked, "Where are we going tonight, Minister?"

She actually knew, because she'd read his schedule, but it never hurt to check.

"The opera. I'm meeting a friend there."

Just as well she *had* checked. The opera certainly hadn't been listed on the schedule. "Minister, until we uncover who might be after you, maybe it would be better to skip some of your social engagements."

"No. I refuse to let the actions of an idiot unhappy with the current government curtail what I want to do. That's only giving other idiots incentive to do the same."

"I think the men behind these attempts are more than just idiots with a bone to pick."

"You'd be surprised, Agent Ryan. These days the government attracts a high caliber of idiot." He shoved his arms into his jacket. "Let's go. I can't be late."

She opened the door, checked the corridor, then ushered him through. "Am I permitted to ask who you might be meeting tonight?"

"Just a friend." He glanced at her as he pressed the elevator button. "A male friend."

Uh-huh. He'd heard them all right. "A trusted male friend, or merely an acquaintance?"

Wetherton hesitated. "An acquaintance, but I trust him."

"That doesn't mean I have to. Name, please?"

"That's unnecess—"

"It is when your life has been threatened twice," she cut in. "Name, Minister?"

"The other girl is much pleasanter," he muttered, then added, "Les Mohern."

Les Mohern? Why did that name ring alarm bells in the back of her mind? Was it simply because it wasn't on the list of known associates and friends Stephan had given her, or was it something else? She repeated the name into her wristcom and ordered a search. With any luck, something would come up before the long night was over.

Now all she had to do was hope it was a long, *unexciting* night.

But even as the thought crossed her mind, instinct suggested it was going to be anything but.

TWELVE

GABRIEL GRIPPED THE BRANCH WITH his claws, keeping his wings spread until he'd gained his balance. Once he had, he settled his wings against his sides and looked around. Dusk was settling in and, with it, a storm. Wind shook the branches, making the leaves all around him shiver and dance, and the growing darkness held a strong scent of rain. It was a clean, fresh fragrance that did little to erase the stench of the house below.

Les Mohern hadn't lived at the address the SIU had on file for a good two years. It appeared that even before his brother's disappearance, Les had lived the life of a gypsy, never staying too long in one place. His subsequent trail had taken some uncovering, but the SIU's computer system was one of the best, and eventually, it had picked up a small trail of receipts that had led Gabriel here.

Mohern's latest stopover was a dump. Literally.

Whoever it was that Mohern was scared of, it had to be pretty damn bad for him to be squatting in a place like this. The stink was almost overwhelming—

the sort of odor that could get under your skin and linger. The small house that Mohern was using as a refuge was situated on the corner of the refuse center, and it had to be crawling with all sorts of bugs, mice and rats. Even Gabriel, with the soul of a hawk, shuddered at the thought of staying there. Sharing his bed with cockroaches and rats was not his idea of a good time.

He studied the nearest windows carefully but could spot no movement. And though darkness was closing in, there was no light from within. He walked along the tree branch, looking into other windows, but the result was the same—no immediate signs of life.

He spread his wings and took to the air again. With dusk fading into night, his brown and gold coloring was unlikely to be spotted. Though in truth, a hawk soaring over a refuse station was a good camouflage. Places like this were a haven for hunters of all varieties— winged or not.

He drifted on a current, studying the mounds of rubbish, seeing smaller spurts of movement that spoke of rats and other vermin, but little else of interest.

Until he reached the far edge of the dump and saw two men forcing a third onto his knees. A fourth man watched these proceedings, a gun held at the ready by his left side.

It was, Gabriel thought, oddly silent. Though the man he presumed was Mohern struggled, he wasn't screaming. Maybe he figured there was no point. Out here, only the rats would hear.

As the fourth man raised his weapon and the captive's struggling became more violent, Gabriel swooped downward, spreading his talons and screaming as he did so. The harsh call echoed loudly across the wind-swept silence.

The stranger with the gun glanced up. His eyes widened and reflected fear a second before Gabriel slashed him across his face and neck.

Blood spurted, spraying his feathers, its sweet aroma taunting his hawk senses. The stranger dropped the weapon, his hands going to the stream pulsing from his neck. Gabriel wheeled around and saw one of the men holding Mohern dive for the dropped gun. Gabriel dove and slashed with a talon, but the man ducked, grabbing the weapon and firing off a shot in one smooth movement. Gabriel flung himself sideways and felt the burn of the bullet's passage past his tail feathers. He squawked as if hit and dropped behind a mound of rubbish. There he shifted shape and, in human form, freed his weapon and carefully edged to the far end of the stinking mound. The man with the gun hadn't moved, his weapon held at the ready as he eyed the mound behind which Gabriel hid. The other man stood behind the still kneeling Mohern. There was no gun in evidence, though Gabriel had no doubt he had one somewhere. Thugs like these rarely went anywhere unarmed. He fired off two quick shots that took both men out, then waited for several seconds, trying to ignore the stinking reek of rubbish as he listened to the night, seeking any sound that might mean these three men had not been alone.

But the only sounds to be heard were the pleas for help from the man whose throat he'd slashed and Mohern's rapid breathing as he struggled to free his hands from their restraints. Not an easy thing when the restraints were wire and his hands were behind his back.

Gabriel stood up and got out his vid-phone to call in a cleanup team as he walked across to the injured man. He did a quick search for ID and other weapons, and found and secured both. Then he administered what medical help he could, using strips torn from his shirt to bandage the wound. After that, he cuffed the man. Even a man in danger of bleeding to death could be dangerous, and the look in *this* man's eyes suggested that if he were able to finish what he'd been sent here to do, he would. Gabriel then checked the other two men to ensure they were both dead, collecting their weapons in the process, then walked over to Mohern and stripped off the tape covering his mouth.

Relief was evident on Mohern's gaunt features, but his blue eyes were wary, distrustful. "Whoever you are, thanks."

"You may retract that once you see this."

Gabriel showed him his badge, and Mohern grimaced. "Typical of my luck lately. Still, being caught by a cop is better than being dead."

Gabriel put his badge away, but not the gun. He didn't trust Mohern any more than he trusted the men who'd intended to kill him. "Why were they going to execute you?"

"Because I know too much." Mohern looked past Gabriel for a second. "Because the man they work for knows what we . . . I . . . saw."

Gabriel undid the wire restraining Mohern's hands, motioned him to rise, then quickly patted him down. No weapons, no ID—not that the latter was surprising since he was about to be executed. "Tell me what you saw, and I might be able to protect you."

Mohern snorted. "Yeah, I've heard that song before. It wasn't true back then and I doubt it's true now."

"Is that because your brother told Jack Kazdan, and died as a result?"

Mohern's eyes narrowed. "Now why would you say something like that?"

"Because Kazdan was a cop, and your brother was supposedly his source."

"Even if that was true, why would you suspect one of your own of killing my brother? Don't you all stick together, regardless of the crime?"

"I'm not one of Jack's lot. I'm SIU. Big difference. And Jack might have had a badge, but he was still a criminal. I know that, and you know that. So tell me what cost Frank his life."

Mohern studied him for several seconds longer, then said, "I want a new ID."

"That will very much depend on what it was you saw."

"I saw a murder. And I saw the murderer."

"A murder isn't big enough news to warrant a new ID."

"What if the person murdered was someone who had serious military connections? And what if the murderer wore one face coming in, and another going out?" He paused, then added, "What if one of those faces was the face of the man who paid us to kidnap Wetherton?"

Fuck. Was Mohern saying what he thought he was saying? Gabriel hoped so—if only because it was about time they had some damn luck. "Is that why you contacted Douglass last week? Why you called Wetherton and asked for a meet this evening?"

Mohern's gaze widened. "How did you know that?"

"Because part of the SIU's duties is to randomly monitor government officials." Which was the truth, as far as it went.

Mohern grimaced. "Well, shit. My luck has really run out this week, hasn't it?"

"Not really. If we hadn't been monitoring things, you'd now be a feast for the rats and stray dogs." He studied the man for a moment, letting the words sink in before adding, "So why contact either of them?"

"In Wetherton's case, I thought he might help me get a new ID in exchange for my continued silence. As you can see, it was becoming harder and harder to hide out."

"And Douglass?"

He shrugged. "I was paid to deliver a message."

"What sort of message?"

"I don't know. It was in an envelope and I didn't think it wise to open it."

"And the man who asked you to deliver the envelope?" Gabriel had no doubt who it would be, but it never hurt to have it confirmed.

"Was the same man who asked me to kidnap Wetherton."

Hence the bloody message on Douglass's wall. "Why would you think Wetherton would be willing to help someone like you?"

Mohern sniffed. "Well, Wetherton's not the real deal, and he can't afford to have that sort of information revealed, can he?"

"How do you know he's not the real thing?"

"Because the real Wetherton was killed and replaced months ago, wasn't he?"

This was getting better and better. "So who placed the clone? Jack?"

Mohern shook his head. "He gave us the job, though. Said he knew someone who was looking for a couple of hands for a snatch-and-ransom job. Said it paid well." He shrugged. "He gave us a number, and we called it and got our instructions. Of course, it turned out the ransom part was a lie."

So why would someone like Sethanon—and they were almost ninety-nine percent sure it was the elusive Sethanon behind Wetherton's replacement—be using two off-the-street thugs for a job as important as snatching a government minister? Unless, of course, he wanted no traceable connection if the job went sour. "Can you remember the phone number?"

"Won't do you any good if I could. It was a public phone box. I checked at the time."

Damn—not that he expected anything less. Sethanon was too canny to be caught by something as careless as a traceable phone number. "So you kidnapped Wetherton, as directed. Were you also involved in the murder?"

"No. But Frank saw the copy standing over the real version after we delivered him."

"Did anyone know Frank saw this?"

"No. And we were being well paid, so silence comes as part of the package."

"This delivery . . . Was it to an abandoned apartment building on Rathdowne Street?"

It was a loaded question in many respects, and Mohern answered it blithely. "Yeah. How'd you find him?"

"We know because we've been tracking the minister's whereabouts for some time. I guess you didn't find the tracer when you tried to dump the body, did you?" Which was a lie. Gabriel had never had time to place a tracer, and the only reason *he'd* been saved was the twin bond he'd spent so long trying to block—although the tracer Karl had placed on *him* had also helped.

"So that's how you were able to escape." Mohern stopped, as if suddenly realizing what he was admitting, and then shrugged. "Jack was really pissed off about you getting away that day."

"Why?"

"Because he got his ass kicked by the big man."

So it was Sethanon who'd wanted him that day. *Interesting.* As was the fact that they'd been heading up to the Dandenongs. Surely that would mean their enemy had a compound up in those mountains somewhere, yet the many searches since had turned up nothing. "How'd you get paid for that job?"

"Cash."

"Who were the other two men?"

Mohern shrugged again. "They were there to deliver the cash and collect the body. When you appeared on the scene, we were asked to help stop you."

"Who asked? The two men, or someone else?"

"The voice on the phone. He said it would take more than two to stop you." He paused. "You broke Frank's nose, you know."

"Frank was lucky I didn't break his damn neck." Not that it would have mattered. Frank died not long after, probably killed by the man they'd both trusted.

"So, if you didn't see this man at either event, why are you so sure that he's behind both Wetherton's kidnapping and Douglass's murder?"

"Because I've got ears. The voice of the man who

gave us the job was the same voice in the murdered chick's apartment."

No wonder Sethanon wanted this man dead—Mohern could identify him by voice, and had seen at least two of his identities. As the sound of a footstep carried on the wind, he glanced around and saw Agent Briggs and three other SIU officers—one of them a medic—making their way through the muck. He pointed to his still-living captive, and then returned his attention to Mohern. "Are you sure about all this?"

Mohern nodded. "I was in the apartment when she was killed."

"So you didn't actually see her murder?"

"Didn't have to. I heard the screams, and saw what was left of her after." He sniffed. "She was a pretty thing."

A pretty thing who'd ignored Sethanon's warnings, and had paid the price. "So how were you able to get into a secure building, and how come you weren't caught?"

He grinned. "A mate of mine was working the night watch. He gave me the codes for a share of the profits. I only took little things, things that were valuable but weren't likely to be immediately missed. It's quite a profitable scam in a building like that." He stopped, as if suddenly remembering he was talking to a man who was basically a cop. He cleared his throat and shrugged. "As to how I escaped detection, I think it was pure dumb luck. My mate called me when Douglass entered the building, so I had time to hide. No one expected me to be there, so no one bothered checking for intruders."

"So how did you see the murderer moving about?"

"I was hiding in the guest bathroom. I saw him through the crack between the door and the frame."

"Give me a description."

Mohern did. Gabriel wasn't surprised to discover that the identity he used to gain entrance to the apartment matched the description of one General Blaine. But it was nasty to discover that the second identity was that of a scruffy man with brown hair so thick and scraggly that his face couldn't be seen, giving him the appearance of someone more bear than human. Only he was a bear who walked with military precision.

That was almost the exact description Sam had given of the man she knew as Joe. So the man she seemed to place so much trust in, the man who seemed to hold so many answers about her past, was not only a murderer, but he might very well be the man they'd been hunting for so many years. The man who had vowed to subjugate or destroy the human race.

Sethanon.

SAM CROSSED HER ARMS AND leaned back against the wall. The flocked wallpaper scratched at her back even through her sweater. Impossible, she knew, given the thickness of her sweater, and yet still her skin itched. Maybe it was just uneasiness, the growing sensation that something was very, very wrong.

She frowned and scanned the theater's foyer for the umpteenth time. The only ones out here were the usher, the pacing Wetherton and herself. Everyone else had gone inside to watch the opera. And the usher didn't appear threatening—he was just a gray-haired old guy wearing a crisp blue suit and a bored expression.

There wasn't even a tingle along the psychic lines—no crawling knowledge that something was here that shouldn't be here.

And yet something was.

Or rather, some*one* was.

She could smell him. His scent was sharp, almost acidic, and though she couldn't immediately put a name or a face to the scent, recognition hummed through her.

And then it hit her.

Duncan King. The redheaded, green-eyed man who'd accompanied General Lloyd to their meeting at Han's restaurant a few months ago.

At the time, she'd thought him nothing more than a psychic drain, a leech who tried to suck all that he could from her mind via a seemingly harmless handshake.

But he was obviously a whole lot more. He could be invisible, for a start.

His scent was coming from the right—the same area where the bored usher stood, but more toward the corridor that led to the men's room.

There was no one actually standing there, of course. And even her psychic senses weren't coming to the party, which was odd.

Or maybe it wasn't.

When she and King had shaken hands in the restaurant, she'd not only felt the leeching sensation, but a power that was similar to, and yet different from, the kind of energy that she felt in storms—one that was a little more earthy in feel, and yet not the same as the energy she'd drawn from the earth during her dream. So who was to say that he hadn't been trying to use that energy to make himself invisible to all her senses? Maybe she wasn't even supposed to remember King's presence, let alone see him.

So why was he skulking around this foyer? Who was he here for?

Wetherton? Her? Or someone else altogether? Whatever his purpose, her best option seemed to be a cautious retreat. Better safe than sorry when confronted by someone more than human—someone who didn't *need* a weapon but was one. Her dreams, and her experiences with Hopeworth of late, had taught her that much, at least.

She pushed away from the wall and approached Wetherton. "Minister, I think your date has stood you up."

He scowled and glanced at his watch. "It's a business meeting, not a date. And I have no doubt he'll be here. The matter is important."

"He's over half an hour—" Her phone rang, stopping her mid-sentence. She grimaced and drew it from her pocket, stepping away from Wetherton but making sure she kept within viable protecting distance just in case the scent that was King moved or attacked.

"Agent Ryan speaking."

"Sam? Gabriel."

Like she wouldn't recognize his voice? The man obviously had no idea just how attracted she was to him, despite their little encounter in the car. "Would this be the Gabriel who was supposed to meet me at five to pick up his car?"

He paused. "Yeah. Sorry about that."

"Say that with a little more sincerity and I might

actually believe you." She decided it was better *not* to be a bitch—as much as she might want to—and said, "What came up?"

"Les Mohern."

As he said the name, the memory kicked into place. "Mohern? Wasn't he one of the names in Jack's book?"

Wetherton swung around at the mention of Mohern's name, his scowl deepening. "What do you know of Mohern?"

His voice was sharp, almost angry, and yet something in the set of his shoulders and the way he stood spoke of fear. She held up a hand to silence him, which didn't go down well, if the clenching and unclenching of his fists was anything to go by.

Not that she thought he intended to hit her. Wetherton didn't have *that* much courage.

"Frank Mohern was on Jack's list," Gabriel said. "Les is his brother. He apparently had a meeting with Wetherton tonight."

"A meeting he's late for."

"That's because he almost got himself killed. I saved his butt, and he's been singing his little heart out in an effort to get a deal."

"Any particular song I need to know about?"

There was another pause, then, "Most definitely. The Moherns were involved in the original Wetherton's snatch and replacement, and Les happened to witness the murder of Kathryn Douglass."

"So he can identify the murderer in both cases?"

"Yes."

Something in the way he said that made her stomach clench. And she knew, without him saying a word, just who Mohern had probably seen. She forced her voice to remain light, casual, as she said, "Anyone I know?"

Again he paused. "It sounds an awful lot like the description you gave of the man you know as Joe."

She briefly closed her eyes. Joe. The man who had saved her life. The man who answered her many questions without ever hinting at the whole picture.

The man who might well be the enemy of human-kind.

Damn.

As she opened her eyes, air shimmered. She frowned, studying the area to the right of the usher. The shimmer happened again, reminding her briefly of smoke coiling away from a small breeze. Only it wasn't smoke, wasn't just air, but a signal that King was on the move.

"Gabriel, I've gotta go. Meet me later and we'll talk."

"Sam, wait—"

She didn't, cutting him off and putting the phone back into her pocket. With King on the move, the sensation of wrongness had sharpened. And she had a bad feeling that she and Wetherton really should get the hell away from the theater and that man.

"Minister, I'm afraid your date has had a slight accident and has been taken to the hospital. If you'd like, I can take you there."

She gripped his arm as she spoke, intending to forcibly move him, but he wrenched himself free.

"Don't be ridiculous. I have tickets for this opera and I fully intend to use them!"

"I wouldn't advise—"

Before she could get the rest of the sentence out, the

shimmer that was King found form. And he had a gun pointed directly at Wetherton.

"Minister, look out!" Even as she gave the warning, she freed her weapon and whipped off two quick shots. The laser's soft hiss seemed to reverberate across the silence but it connected with nothing more than air—at least until it burned through the garish flocked wallpaper and then the wall behind it.

King reappeared several feet away from his original spot and fired. Sam threw herself sideways, hitting Wetherton and knocking him out of the way. Then she hit the carpeted floor with a grunt, the bright heat of King's laser skimming her side, burning through her jacket and scalding her hip. She swore, but rolled onto her stomach and fired another shot. Again, the bullet tore through air, not flesh.

For God's sake, how was she supposed to protect Wetherton from someone who could become as insubstantial as the wind?

She obviously couldn't. Retreat was the only option they had left. All she could hope for was that King wasn't as fast as he was invisible.

She twisted around to warn Wetherton, only to find him lying unmoving on the floor. His face was slack, his expression frozen in a mix of surprise and horror. A sharp but neat hole had been burned into the middle of his forehead. She half-imagined she could see brain matter through that hole, even though she knew logically that was impossible given the distance, the position of his body and the fact that lasers cauterized the wounds even as they created them.

This wouldn't look good on her record. First she'd killed her partner when she was in the State Police, then she'd allowed the man she was supposed to be guarding to be assassinated. If Stephan didn't haul her ass back to the broom closet, she'd be surprised. Still, it wasn't as if anyone else could have prevented this. Truth be told, no one else would have even *seen* King.

At least one of her earlier questions had been answered—King was here for Wetherton. But why would the military want him dead? Even if they knew Wetherton was a clone, he surely wouldn't have any knowledge about Hopeworth that could be dangerous to them.

And yet Blaine had visited him. Had been in Wetherton's office for hours. Testing him, reading him, perhaps? If that *was* the case, what had they discovered that now warranted his death?

The only person who might know the answer to that question was King. And he was on the move—not toward her but rather the door. She hit the alarm button on her wristcom, scrambled to her feet and caught sight of the usher cowering behind one of the ornate columns near the staircase. She grabbed her badge from her pocket to show him.

"Call the SIU. Tell them Agent Sam Ryan has a priority-one situation. Tell them I need a med team and backup straight away." The wristcom's alarm *should* evoke an immediate response, but she wasn't going to take a chance. Not this time.

The usher nodded, and Sam ran out the door and into the chilled night. King hadn't found form, but for some reason, the shimmer of air that surrounded and hid his form was more noticeable in the darkness. "SIU, King. Stop or I'll shoot."

Passersby glanced at her, their expressions becoming alarmed when they saw the weapon in her hand. Some hurried on and others retreated. She didn't really care either way, as long as they kept out of her line of fire. She kept her gaze on King and her finger on the trigger.

He didn't answer, didn't turn around, didn't stop.

She lowered the laser and ran after him. There were too many people out on the street to risk firing the weapon, and King was more than likely aware of that fact.

The heels of her boots hit the concrete noisily as she ran—a quick tattoo that spoke of speed and urgency, and one that at least had people scrambling to get out of her way. But however free her path was, however fast *she* was, King was faster. The farther away he got, the harder it was to see or smell him.

And then he disappeared altogether.

She swore softly as she slowed, then finally stopped. With her gun raised, she scanned the immediate area. They'd run far enough from the theater district that foot traffic was sparse. This end of Victoria Street was close to Market and Elizabeth streets, so there were still plenty of cars passing by. Their lights skimmed the sidewalks and nearby buildings, briefly illuminating the shadows. No one hid there, not even a shimmer. Sam continued to turn slowly. Movement caught her eye in nearby Leicester Street. It was nothing more than a flare of orange that died as quickly as it gained life, and yet the sight of it had her up-until-recently-dead psychic senses coming to life.

The enemy waited in the deeper shadows haunting that side road. And it wasn't King.

She pressed the locator button on her wristcom again, then slowly, carefully, eased toward the road.

The closer she got, the more her skin crawled. Then the familiar wash of heat hit, bringing with it the certainty that the enemy who waited was a shifter—a shifter whose very essence felt malevolent.

And it was a malevolence she knew.

Her steps faltered, and her hands suddenly felt clammy against the grip of the laser. Not so much because of the thick sensation of evil, not even because she'd felt this particular baseness before.

But because Blaine—the enemy that waited in the shadows—was not alone.

He was here.

The man who had saved her life at least twice.

Joe.

And she wasn't entirely sure whether he meant her good or ill. There was something almost . . . gloating in his aura. As if he'd waited for this moment for a very long time.

She took a shuddering breath and released it slowly. Her best option now was retreat. She'd be stupid to confront Blaine alone. There were two men ahead and the invisible King still floated about somewhere nearby. However much she wanted answers, however much she might want to grab King for shooting Wetherton, she wasn't a fool. She was one against three, and while she might be an enhanced human, just like them, she was the only one who *didn't* have full knowledge of her powers.

She retreated a step, but she stopped when something cold and hard pressed against her spine.

"I can't allow you to do that." King's voice was so

soft that she doubted the men ahead would even hear. "Move into the side street, please. No sudden moves."

For all of a second she thought about spinning and knocking the weapon from his hand. Or maybe even twisting sharply to shoot him dead. But the latter had already proven impossible, and she had a sneaking suspicion he'd react faster than she ever could.

So she walked on, her arms by her side and the laser still secure in one hand. She doubted he'd forgotten its presence, and the fact that he let her keep it meant either that he had no fear of it or that she'd be dead long before she could ever press the trigger.

Neither thought was a pleasant one, so she concentrated instead on the road ahead, trying to pinpoint the men who still hid in the shadows.

Blaine moved out of them once she'd entered the street, stopping in the middle of the road, his expression pleased, almost amused.

"This is the last place I expected to find you, General," Sam said, stopping several feet away from him. King didn't object, and a covert glance over her shoulder uncovered why. He was no longer behind her. She scanned the immediate area but couldn't spot him. Nor could she smell him. But then, the soft breeze could have been blowing his scent away from her. She was sure he hadn't gone far.

Still, it was odd that he was here with Blaine. She'd been under the impression that he was Lloyd's assistant, not Blaine's.

"Maybe so," Blaine said, voice all oily satisfaction, "but I must say it is extremely pleasing to see you, number 849."

The number rang distant bells, and she had a sudden

memory of a room filled with clear plastic cribs, each one not only possessing a wriggling, crying baby but a black card clipped to the front that carried a number and visual details. Hundreds of babies born to the cold sterility of a lab, many of whom were destined to die long before conscious thought or fear formed.

An odd mix of anger and apprehension shot through her, but she raised an eyebrow, trying for a calm she didn't feel inside. "849? Sorry, General, but I have a name, not a number."

He raised an eyebrow, his expression still one of condescending amusement. "Maybe now, but not when you were in Hopeworth, my dear."

She knew it was useless to argue. He was too certain about her. Maybe he'd uncovered hidden files in Hopeworth. Maybe that brief moment between them in Wetherton's office had given him information that he'd been able to use. Either way, it didn't matter. She was never going to admit the truth. Not to him, anyway. "I'm afraid you're barking up the wrong tree. I've never been near Hopeworth."

"Forgetfulness is not surprising, given the horrible events of that night, but you are military in birth and in design and we both know it. And I have every intention of returning you to your birthplace *and* birthright." He paused, then said, "Tonight."

So he thought Penumbra's destruction was an accident? That she'd escaped by chance rather than design? How could he? How could anyone in the military be breeding what they were breeding and have no true idea just what their creations were really capable of?

She took a step back, and this time King didn't stop

her. "Sorry, General, but I'm not who you think I am, and there is no way in hell I'm going anywhere with you." She raised the laser, letting him see it for the first time. "Move and I'll shoot."

His sudden laugh sent a chill skittering over her skin. There was nothing sane in that cold sound. "You could never hit me with the laser, child. I am faster than the wind, and lighter than shadow. You can't kill a shadow—don't you know that? Didn't your precious nanny teach you anything?"

She blew out a breath. What was the point of going on with the pretense that she didn't know what he was talking about? All he had to do was get her back to Hopeworth and the truth would be revealed. She *wasn't* a creature of natural selection, so what she should concentrate on now was escaping both this man *and* Hopeworth.

"My nanny taught me lots about humanity, General, and for that I owe her more than I can ever repay." Sam paused. "Why did you want Mary Elliot dead?"

"I wanted her knowledge, but the mere fact that you came to see her was enough to satisfy my uncertainties." He gave her a cold smile. "And in the end, you walked into my trap much more easily than I ever dreamed possible. King, get the laser from her."

She tensed, waiting for some sound, some sensation, some feeling that King was obeying his master's orders.

But King didn't answer. Blaine frowned. "King? Did you hear me?"

"I heard." The answer came about half a dozen steps away from Blaine's left shoulder. If she squinted, she could just make out the slight shimmer of his position. But with Blaine so close, she didn't dare squint for long.

"I gave you an order, son. Obey it."

"King is not yours to command, General."

The voice came from behind Blaine, but it wasn't King's.

It was Joe's.

THIRTEEN

GABRIEL GRIPPED MOHERN'S ARM TIGHTLY as he rushed him through the sterile halls of the SIU. Technically he wasn't a prisoner, so he wasn't cuffed, but Gabriel had a feeling the petty thief had begun to have more than a few second thoughts about "singing like a bird" during the car ride here.

And though it was unlikely he'd get very far away in the monitored and tightly secured halls—not to mention Briggs keeping a close eye on him from behind—Mohern had escaped Sethanon's clutches for many months and therefore had to have more native cunning than what he was currently showing.

They reached one of the interview rooms and Gabriel punched in a code. Then he pressed his hand against the print pad. The machine hummed to life, a blue light sweeping his prints before the door clicked open. He waved Mohern inside, then turned to Briggs as she stopped beside him. "Give him coffee and a meal, and then take his statement."

"What about my new ID?" Mohern said from the center of the sparsely furnished room.

"That'll be under discussion after you sign the statement." Gabriel looked back at Briggs. "If he doesn't sign it, keep him here until he does."

"Hey, you can't do that. It's against the law."

Briggs grinned. "We're SIU. A law unto ourselves."

"Great," Mohern muttered, as he sat down.

Gabriel kept his amusement to himself. "Get him to do a photo ID of all the men present at both Wetherton's murder and Kathryn Douglass's."

Briggs nodded. Gabriel turned and headed for the elevator. His phone rang before he got there. "Assistant Director Stern," he said, as he punched the elevator's call button impatiently.

"Mitchell from Monitoring, sir. Agent Ryan just pressed her wristcom's alarm button, and we've also received a priority call from an usher at Her Majesty's Theatre. Apparently he called on Agent Ryan's orders."

Gabriel's gut clenched. He should have known something had happened when she'd hung up so abruptly. And yet she had to be all right, because he would have sensed anything else. "What did the usher say?"

"That she has a priority-one situation and wants a med team and backup. The man she was with has been shot. She's gone after the suspect."

Which under normal circumstances she undoubtedly could have handled. But given just who Wetherton might have been involved with, as well as who might have wanted him dead, it was better not to take chances.

"Send two teams immediately." Gabriel hesitated. "Has she hit the locator?"

"Yes, sir." Mitchell paused. "Victoria Street, near Leicester."

"Tell the teams to take control of the situation at Her Majesty's. I'll back up Agent Ryan."

"Yes, sir."

The elevator door opened. Gabriel stepped inside and punched the button for the rooftop. The fastest way to get there was by flight.

And he had a growing feeling that he had better get there *damn* fast indeed.

THERE WAS NO SENSE OF movement. One minute, the night behind Blaine was empty, and the next Joe was standing there. It was almost as if he could wear the night like a veil, shucking it off or using it as cover where necessary. Very much like she could do herself, though she had a lot less control over the ability.

He hadn't changed that much since she'd last seen him, sitting in the chair of a sidewalk café and sipping coffee while avoiding direct answers to her questions. His appearance was still that of a street bum, his thick, overly long hair and beard disheveled and apparently unwashed. But his brown eyes were intense and somewhat sad, and he held himself like a soldier—purposeful, balanced, powerful.

A man ready to move, to fight, at a second's notice.

Blaine swung around so that he was able to see both of them. "Who the hell are you? And how the hell did you get through the cordon of my men?"

"Who am I?" Joe repeated the question, his voice apparently amused. But she knew him through her dreams, and she could almost taste the fury he wasn't showing. "I am many people, General. Joe Black and

Chip Braggart are the most common of my nonmilitary aliases, but they are not the ones I use most."

No wonder she'd sensed an odd sort of familiarity whenever she'd been near Braggart—it had been Joe, in another form.

"A shifter." Blaine's voice was disdainful. "I gather you were here beforehand, because there is no other way you could have gotten past my men."

"You think so?" A smile touched Joe's lips, though she couldn't say how she knew this when the forest of his beard covered his mouth. "There are a number of ways anyone with skill could have. But perhaps it is better if I show you. King, watch him."

"Yes, General." King stepped out of the shadows. In his hand was the biggest damn gun Sam had ever seen. It was similar in size to a rifle, but wider, with an oddly shaped flat end.

Blaine's eyes widened, the arrogant confidence seeming to falter. "Where the hell did you get that? You don't have the authority—"

"No, but you do, General." The voice was Joe's, but his hirsute countenance had gone, replaced by a replica of Blaine himself.

And suddenly one large piece of the puzzle fell into place.

"It was you," Sam said. "I pulled *you* out of Wetherton's car that night, not the real Blaine." Which was why she kept getting different reactions in his presence. Her senses *knew* Joe—and obviously they saw him as no threat, no matter what form he took.

The real Blaine was a totally different story.

And right now, Blaine's eyes were narrowed and dangerous looking. She shifted, her finger tightening just a little around the laser's trigger. He might be confident that she couldn't hit him with it, but if he moved in *any* way, she'd damn well try.

But she had a horrible feeling he was working up to something bigger than a laser could handle.

Tension ran through her, and her finger tightened on the laser's trigger reflexively. A soft hum ran across the momentary silence, and Blaine gave her a quick look. There was no fear, no concern. Just amusement.

"Yes, it was me," Joe answered. "Unfortunately, that was the night the military began to realize they might have a problem."

"Those newspaper images of me carrying an unconscious Wetherton were something of a revelation, given I wasn't even there." Blaine paused and studied his double for a moment. "Who are you?"

"Guess, General. Let's see how clever you really are." Joe's glance ran past Blaine and met Sam's. Something trembled deep inside. She knew that gaze, knew the fierce hardness behind it, even if the eyes were currently the wrong color. "The general thinks he's calling in the troops. He doesn't realize he's already let them go."

Blaine snorted. "My men would not be fooled so easily."

"Your men have been fooled for years, General. And to continue the ruse, you must die. King?"

"No!" Sam said.

She raised the laser and fired, without even thinking about it. She had no real desire to protect Blaine, especially since he intended to take her back to Hopeworth. But the cop in her just couldn't stand here and let a murder happen.

King fired at Blaine at the same time she fired at

King. This time her laser found its target, burning a hole through King's hand and into the weapon he held. It made a sizzling, popping sort of sound, and smoke began to rise. King swore and threw it away.

The weapon exploded before it hit the road, sending shards of metal and energy skimming through the night.

Deadly, but not as deadly as the beam that had hit Blaine.

His mouth was open, as if he were screaming, but no sound came out. His body was shimmering, moving, bubbling, as if water boiled under his skin. He didn't move, just stood there, statue-like, as his skin gradually began to darken and then peel and drift away on the gentle wind, like paper held too close to a fire. And then the boiling water began to bubble out, running down his body and splashing across the roadside. Only it wasn't just water, but blood and flesh and God knows what else.

Her stomach rose and she spun away, heading for the nearest curb. By the time she'd finished heaving the little bit of food she'd eaten that day, the splashing had stopped. The only sound to be heard on the whispering wind was the distant beat of traffic.

King was gone again. She couldn't say why she was so sure of that, especially when she had a hard time getting any real sense of his presence.

But Joe was here. Watching. Waiting.

She wiped a hand across her mouth, took a deep, shuddering breath and turned around. He still wore Blaine's form.

"You killed him to take his place?"

"I've been taking his place for years. It was useful, while it lasted."

She remembered a teenager saying, in that same sort of dead voice, *I have plans for him, never fear.*

The same teenager who said he had every intention of going back to that place once he'd taken care of her, because there was still too much to be done at Hopeworth.

A chill that was soul deep ran through her. Yet she kept her thoughts to herself, saying only, "Why did you kill Kathryn Douglass?"

His smile was gentle, amused. "Douglass had contacted the military about reviving the Penumbra project. I have no idea where she found the notes, but I couldn't let that happen. I *did* give her fair warning. We are unique, Sammy, and I intend to keep it that way."

"Why go back as Blaine afterward? To gloat?"

"Partially. I also wanted to see how Lloyd took the warning." His sudden grin was fierce. "Neither he nor the military took it well."

"But that Lloyd is not the real Lloyd." She hesitated. "I killed him the night Penumbra was destroyed."

"If you remember that, then you should remember that *that* Lloyd was yet another replica. The real general donated his body for scientific purposes on his death years before, and his replication became the military's first real success."

But not their last. "And what were we, Josh? Their fourth? Tenth? Fiftieth?"

"We were never considered a successful creation," Josh said. "More of a frustrating one. They never could control us—not totally."

He smiled, and this time it was a smile she remembered. A smile that echoed all the way through her, bringing tears to her eyes.

He began to change, to shift, his body seeming to fade into the night for several heartbeats before it regained form. Became an older version of the boy who'd haunted her dreams for so long.

Part of her was fiercely glad to see him again.

Part of her feared him, because she suddenly remembered the conversation she'd had with Gabriel in the car. Her comment that Sethanon was waiting for Hopeworth to breed him an army. His comment that Sethanon was someone she knew in Hopeworth, someone who had been involved in the project.

No, no, no, she thought. *Not Josh. Not my brother.* She closed her eyes for a moment, then said softly, "Are you Sethanon?"

"Yes."

She stared at him, uncertain whether she was more angry or scared. "So why tell me Sethanon was not a name you'd ever called yourself?"

"Because it isn't. But I never denied others might have called me that."

"Who? Not the SIU, from what I can gather."

"No." He half shrugged. "It started with the scientists. The day they took that book off me—"

"The day you scared the hell out of Mary?"

"Yes." He smiled again, but it was a cold thing that sent chills down her spine. "Some of the scientists took to calling me Mad Seth under their breath. I simply ran with the name when it became beneficial to do so."

"Like when you were attacking the SIU?"

"A strong SIU is a hindrance to my plans, so attacking them as Sethanon not only decimated their numbers, but had the side benefit of them chasing someone who doesn't exist."

"But they know you exist now, Josh, and they now know what you are. You've all but played into their hands."

"I've done nothing but confirm their suspicions. I have no problems with that."

He studied her for a moment, and the sadness she'd often noted in her dreams of him was back in his eyes. Only it was deeper this time. Much deeper. Then he looked up, and his expression changed, became hard.

"I can feel you up there, Assistant Director. Please come down and join the discussion."

There was a flutter of wings and a soft thump, then footsteps. Gabriel stopped beside Sam, close enough that his warmth washed over her, yet not so close that he was touching her. His gaze met hers. "You okay?"

Sam nodded. "Josh won't hurt me."

Gabriel's gaze moved to her brother. "I wouldn't be so sure of that."

"You would be if you knew anything at all about the two of us." Josh's gaze was every bit as cold and hard as Gabriel's. "And you'd certainly not consider firing the laser you have in your hand."

Even as he said the words, Gabriel revealed the weapon. It was a laser, all right, and a lot bigger than the one Sam held. "I'm not firing it, just using it to place you under arrest. You willingly admitted you murdered General Blaine and Kathryn Douglass, and you more than likely destroyed her clone, as well."

Josh raised an eyebrow. "You were floating about up there for longer than I thought."

"I guess I was. Raise your hands or I *will* shoot."

Josh flexed his fingers. And suddenly the stirring wind seemed to be a whole lot hotter. Fear raced through Sam.

"Josh, no!"

The words were barely out of her mouth when a bright blue beam of light lit the darkness. Her heart seemed to lodge somewhere in her throat, and her fear intensified until it seemed her entire body shook under the force of it. It wasn't just fear for Josh, but for her own safety as well.

Why, why, why?

The question rolled through her mind as the normally swift and deadly blue beam arced across the night in seemingly slow motion. Josh watched it, eyes narrowed, moving only when it seemed too late. The laser sliced through his forearm, skimming through his jacket and shirt before burning a trail along his skin.

She knew, because she felt it. Pain ripped through her, and she staggered backward, gasping in shock and dropping her laser to the ground. Sweat broke out across her forehead, but she clamped down on the scream that bubbled up her throat, so that it came out more like a hiss. She grabbed her arm with her free hand, supporting it carefully.

"What the hell?" Gabriel's voice was soft, but it hinted at pain. He, too, had felt the burn of the laser, but indirectly through her. "Sam, are you okay?"

"Yes." She stared at her brother as the final pieces began to fall into place.

"Two halves of a whole," he said softly.

She closed her eyes. Took a deep breath. The pain was fading, but not the deeper pain that came with realization. She might not remember everything, but she knew enough.

"That's why you saved me," she said. "You cannot exist without me."

"Sam, you want to explain what's happening?" Gabriel said.

She glanced at him. The laser was still held straight and steady. He might not know what had happened, but he was still intent on capturing Josh.

Not realizing—or maybe not caring—that Josh would never, ever, allow himself to become someone's prisoner again.

Not knowing that in trying to maim or kill Josh, he'd be doing the exact same thing to her.

"You felt what I felt," she told him.

"I know that. But why the hell were you feeling what he was feeling?"

She wrapped her fingers around his arm. If he tried to fire the laser, she'd feel the movement of his muscles. Would try to stop him.

"Josh and I are twins. Two parts of a whole."

He frowned and glanced at her quickly. "Fraternal twins. So?"

"You forget that we are military creations, born in a lab." She hesitated, then licked her lips. "Our life forces are connected and combined. If he dies, I die."

His shock was evident in the way his muscles tensed. "That's not—"

"Just as it's not possible for you to feel when she is hurt?" Josh commented. "We are linked, the three of us, more than any of us could want."

She glanced sharply at Josh. "You once said that you would let Gabriel rot in hell except for the fact that I would come and rescue him. But that was a lie, wasn't it? You knew, even then, that hurting him would hurt me."

He smiled. "It wasn't a lie. Just not the entire truth."

"Many things you say aren't the entire truth, Josh."

"Would someone care to fill me in on this conversation?" Gabriel's voice was filled with frustrated anger.

And that was dangerous, given the situation.

She squeezed his arm and wished he'd lower the weapon. "Josh is Joe. They are one and the same man."

"And who is Joe?" His voice was hard. Cold. He'd heard their conversation; he just needed confirmation.

Josh glanced at her. "Tell him."

She closed her eyes and took a deep breath. "Seth-anon."

Gabriel's muscles moved. She threw her weight against him, knocking him sideways. The deadly blue beam shot skyward, briefly illuminating the rooftop of a nearby warehouse before disappearing from sight.

She hit the ground with a grunt, but rolled swiftly to her feet. Josh was gone, cloaked by night and moving swiftly away.

You've finally found what you began searching for so long ago. You found, in Gabriel, that piece of yourself you always felt was missing, no matter how close our connection. You have chosen your path, and it is not mine. His words rolled through her mind, at once soft and sorrowful and yet somehow determined. *I have given you time, as you asked that night, but I shall wait no more. It begins, Sammy. Do not try to stop me.*

I have to, Josh. This time, I have to.

Then we shall truly discover who is the stronger power.

I guess we will.

He disappeared from her mind and her senses, just as Gabriel grabbed her arm and swung her around roughly.

"Why the hell did you do that?"

"Because you would have killed him."

"And rid the world of a monster!" He spat the words, his fury so great it was almost smothering her, making it difficult to breathe.

"And in killing him, you would have killed me!" She raised her eyes to his. "Or was that a price you were willing to pay?"

For a long time, he didn't answer. She began to think he wouldn't when he released her arm and pushed her away from him, almost violently.

"He shot Andrea. That was the face of the man who shot her."

Oh God. She closed her eyes and battled the sting of tears.

"I didn't know—"

"Would you have cared?" he asked, savagely. "She was just one of the hundreds of agents Sethanon has killed across the country, yet you protected him here tonight."

"Because—"

"Because you believe a lie," he spat. He thrust a hand through his hair. Then he made what sounded like an anguished growl and walked away without a word.

She took a deep breath and released it slowly.

The war Jack had warned her about was about to begin.

And she was stuck in the middle between a brother she couldn't support and a man who would do whatever it took to avenge the death of the woman he had once loved.

A death that had been caused by her brother.

It was laughable to think that she'd once believed that when she discovered who she really was, all would become right in her world.

But nothing was right. It had all just gone straight to hell. And it had taken whatever hopes she might have had of a relationship with Gabriel with it. With everything that had happened tonight, with all that she'd remembered and discovered, it was *that* that probably hurt the most.

She blew out a breath and turned around. To discover Gabriel waiting for her at the end of the alley.

Hope ran through her.

He didn't say anything as she approached him, his expression neutral and the green-flecked hazel depths of his eyes giving little away.

She stopped in front of him. Her heart was beating a mile a minute, dread and hope combining to make her stomach churn. But she somehow kept her voice calm as she said, "I cannot help my past. I cannot change what I am. And I certainly can't let you kill him." She hesitated, then added softly, "I don't want to die, Gabriel."

He studied her for a moment longer and said, "But will you help me stop him?"

"Yes." Because she didn't want this war any more than he did. She wanted peace. All she'd *ever* wanted was peace.

And somewhere to call home.

"That's all I can ask for, then." He held out his hand.

She placed her fingers in his, felt the strength of them wrap around hers, and for the second time in her life, she suddenly felt as if she actually belonged somewhere.

It was such a powerful feeling that tears stung her eyes again.

She'd left the ruins of the Penumbra project believing there was something out there for her. Something, or someone, she needed to find.

Against all the odds, it seemed she'd found that someone.

All she had to do now was hold on to him.

EPILOGUE

SAM WATCHED THE FOAMY FINGERS of ocean creep across the damp black rocks of the cliff not far below them. The power of the waves shivered through her, setting her soul on fire. More than ever, she felt at home here. Felt *right* here.

"I can see why you bought this place." Gabriel stopped beside her, his hands shoved into his jacket pockets and his breath condensing on the cool evening breeze. "It's wild and untamed and somehow perfect."

She glanced at him, a smile teasing her lips. "You almost sound envious."

"I think I am." His gaze met hers, and there was something in his eyes that warmed her even more thoroughly than the energy of this place. "Are you sure you want to try this?"

She nodded. "Mary said I could shapechange. That Josh and I did it often. If I could do it then, I should be able to do it now. It's just a matter of remembering."

Gabriel nodded in agreement. "I'll guide you

through the process as best I can. Just remember, if you *do* change shape, don't stay in it for too long. Your muscles won't be used to the stresses of your alternate shape, and I don't want to see you tumbling off the damn cliff."

"The sea won't hurt me," she said.

"No, but smashing down on the rocks certainly will. So please, just this once, do as I ask."

A smile teased her lips. "Afraid of getting Illie back as a partner if anything happens to me, huh?"

"Well, you are *far* more kissable than he is."

She raised her eyebrows. "Meaning you've attempted to kiss Illie? I didn't know you were inclined that way, Gabriel Stern."

"There's a whole lot that you don't yet know about me," he said, amusement creasing the corners of his eyes. "That, however, is not one of them."

Yet. That one word warmed more than anything else he'd said so far. "And thank goodness. I'd hate to think I'd have to keep an eye out for men as well as women competing for your attention. Hell, it took me long enough to even *get* your attention."

"You had it from the very beginning," he said mildly. "Now, are we going to attempt this? Because that storm is getting closer and I'd really rather be sitting beside the fire in that ramshackle, run-down house of yours when it hits."

So would she. But not yet. Not just yet. Her gaze went to the black clouds sweeping toward them. Their energy tingled through her, as fierce as the sea itself. It was the perfect night for flight. The perfect night to find a part of herself she'd lost long ago.

She took a deep breath, then said, "Right. What do I do?"

"First off, relax. Breathe deep and release the anger, the fear and the tension."

"I'm not afraid."

"But you *are* tense. I can feel it," he said. "So breathe in deep and, when you exhale, imagine each time you're casting away a little bit more of that tension."

She did as he bade and, after a few minutes, a sense of calm fell around her.

"Now," he said. "Imagine there's a well deep down in your soul. Imagine it filled with warm and eager light. Feel its welcoming caress surround your fingers, your hands, your arms, as you reach for it. Feel it flush through your entire body."

Even as he spoke, energy began to pulse through her body. It tingled through her, around her, a force that was both familiar and foreign. As sharp as the storm and the sea, and yet very different in its feel.

"Imagine that light surrounding you, embracing you. Feel it in every fiber, every muscle. Let it become you, and you it."

The energy surged, encasing her in a pulsating mesh. She felt as if she were teetering on the edge of a precipice, about to step into the unknown. Except it wasn't unknown, because she'd been here before, and the memories were beginning to surface. In her mind's eye, she began to see the hawk she was about to become.

"Now," Gabriel said, voice soft, "imagine the hawk. Welcome her into being."

She didn't have to imagine. The hawk was with her, in her. It always had been; all she'd needed to do was remember her. And she *did* remember. The magic surged through her body, its touch fierce, joyful, as it unmade one shape so that she could become the other.

And then she was soaring up into the dusk, into the electric air, into freedom. And oh, it was glorious. She laughed in sheer delight, the sound the harsh cry of the hawk. Gabriel soon joined her, following her as she wheeled around on the updrafts, his gold and brown plumage glowing in the fading light of day.

It didn't last long. As he'd warned, her muscles quickly began to tire. Reluctantly, she arrowed down, calling to the shifting energy as she neared the ground, hitting it in human form but a little too fast. She stumbled several steps before she caught her balance.

"So how was your first flight?" Gabriel said.

She spun to face him, her grin so wide it felt like her face would split from the force of it. "Amazing. Magical. I want to do it again, and again and again."

He laughed and caught her hand, tugging her toward him. "Tomorrow," he said softly. "*If* your arms aren't leaden from this evening's efforts."

"You, Gabriel Stern, are a party pooper." She wrapped her arms loosely around his neck. "But even so, I do have this insane desire to kiss you senseless right now."

"Then by all means, do so," he said, but his smile gave way to seriousness. "There is, however, one thing you should know before you do."

She raised an eyebrow, and oddly felt that once again she was standing on the edge of that precipice. This time, however, she was stepping into the unknown—but it was an unknown she didn't fear. "And that is?"

"Hawks mate for life," he said softly.

Something more than joy, something that was delirium and elation and euphoria all wrapped up in one explosive package, rushed through her, making her want to sing and dance and cry all at the same time. "Meaning you could never get rid of me now, even if you wanted to?"

"Not even if I wanted to," he said, his gaze fierce in the fading light of the evening. "Not that I want to. Not anymore. You're everything I thought I'd once lost, Sam. It might have taken me damnably long to realize it, and I might have been a bastard along the way, but I want you in my life, come what may—and no matter what your brother might throw at us—both now and in the future."

She laughed then, and for the first time in a long time, that laughter was as free and as happy as she felt. Because for the first time in a long time, she had not only a past, but a future, and someone to share it with. And she didn't have to worry about holding on to him. He was hers, now and forever.

As if to prove the thought, he kissed her. It was slow, sensuous, and, most of all, it was an affirmation of belonging.

"Why don't we take this inside?" he said after a while. "Maybe we can explore, in greater detail, that desire of yours to kiss me senseless."

She smiled. The explorations wouldn't stop with just kisses, and they both knew it. "It sounds like a perfect idea." A perfect beginning.

And it was.